DON COYOTE

A TAMPA BAY TROPICS THRILLER

GEORGE L. FLEMING

ST. PETERSBURG PRESS

Published by St. Petersburg Press

St. Petersburg, FL

www.stpetersburgpress.com

Design and composition by St. Petersburg Press

Cover design by St. Petersburg Press and Pablo Guidi

Paperback ISBN: 978-1-940300-17-7

eBook ISBN: 978-1-940300-18-4

First Edition

DON COYOTE

For Linda, the love of my life for over forty years, the most extraordinary person I have ever met, and, of course, the inspiration for Ms. Reed O'Hara.

Je t'aime, mon beau guerrier.

PROLOGUE

NOGALES, ARIZONA 2001

"Hey, what did Jesus say to the Mexicans when He was up on the old wooden cross?" Sergio Garcia asked his partner, Jake Dupree.

The two men, dressed in dirty tee shirts, jeans, and cowboy boots, had been sitting in a dilapidated blue pick-up truck for over five hours.

Dupree understood Garcia was trying to break up the monotony, so he played along.

"I don't know, *pendejo*, what'd Jesus say to *Los Mexicanos?*" Dupree said.

Garcia grinned broadly, showing off his perfect white teeth.

"Don't do anything 'til I get back."

The two men laughed, though Dupree felt rather guilty.

"Really, Serg, pulling out that old chestnut about lazy Mexicans," Dupree said. "Have to admit though, it's kinda funny."

Dupree gave Garcia a fist bump.

It was March in the Sonoran Desert. Though the sun was setting, the temperature remained an aggressive one hundred and four degrees.

Dupree and Garcia had parked their pick-up in a gathering of mesquite trees, creosote bushes, and saguaro cacti. The two men relished the paltry shade.

They were situated about fifteen miles east of Nogales, Arizona or, depending on one's perspective, Nogales, Mexico, as the two towns buttressed one another on the U.S. southern border.

There wasn't a person or structure or paved road for as far as the eye could see.

Mierda, no back-up on this mission, Dupree thought.

But that was how Dupree preferred to operate. His mission probably would require deadly force, and he didn't want any witnesses. His form of deterrence left no room for detainment, only clean up and body extraction, sometimes just simple makeshift graves.

The Mexican narco cartels used the expression "*plata o plomo*" to persuade law enforcement to cooperate with their illegal drug activity. Silver or lead. Bribes or bullets. Choice was obvious for virtually all Mexican police officers, whether municipal, state, or federal: accept the bribes or die.

Dupree employed his own mantra: *plomo o plomo*. Lead or lead. Bullets or bullets. And when it came to the bad guys, Dupree always shot to kill — some of his critics might say *over*kill.

Dupree and Garcia were on loan to the Drug Enforcement Agency from the Central Intelligence Agency. They had DEA badges and IDs, but they were black op CIA through and through.

Between them, they had thirty-five sanctioned kills from all over the world and within the United States. Using handguns, automatic rifles, knives, sniper rifles, fragmentation grenades, and PETN explosives, Dupree and Garcia had killed men, women, teenagers, and the occasional livestock. And they never regretted a single kill; their targets were extremely bad people out to harm the United States in a variety of ugly ways.

You can try to dance with us, Dupree believed, but you won't get off the dance floor alive.

This particular mission, though, had a fascinating wrinkle: for the first time, Dupree and Garcia were going to take out a mother and son duo.

Patrona and Don Coyote formed an effective mother and son team, specializing in human trafficking and illegal drug export to the United States. Their headquarters was in Nogales, Mexico. They trafficked people and drugs along the border between Arizona and Mexico.

Their favorite port of entry was east of Nogales, where they had painted "*La Frontera*" on a section of the U.S. border fence.

Typically, Patrona and Don Coyote accompanied around forty fellow Mexicans as they entered the United States illegally. The vast majority of these illegal immigrants simply sought more opportunity in the U.S.

Over the course of ten years, and after trafficking over twenty-thousand Mexicans into the United States, Patrona and Don Coyote had made several million dollars plying their trade.

And what was the secret of their success?

Simple, really.

Simply ingenious.

The Mexican pilgrims paid mother and son handsomely for safe passage into the American Dreamscape. But the *coup de grace* was that these individuals agreed to haul across the border sixty-pound back-packs filled with cocaine and heroin. It was multi-tasking gone gonzo.

And the DEA had had enough of Patrona and Don Coyote. But the DEA lacked manpower and resources to close down this operation that became known as *La Frontera*. So in the spirit of fostering inter-agency rapport with the DEA, the CIA sent their best team of *sicarios*, or assassins, to dispatch mother and son on behalf of the DEA.

And that is how Dupree and Garcia came to be sitting in a steel oven disguised as a pick-up truck.

Intel indicated that Patrona and Don Coyote would cross the U.S. border today. They would come bearing gifts of Mexican illegals and narcotics.

Dupree used Razor HD field binoculars to keep an eye on the section of border fence where these coyotes and their human cargo probably would cross.

Dupree was only twenty-two years old and already a stone-cold killer. There were no red flags in his biography that suggested he would become an assassin. He was born in upstate New York to French-American parents. In high school, he excelled in the classroom, played piano for the school orchestra, and lettered all three years on the hockey team. Whether using a compound bow or a bolt-action long range rifle, Dupree was a superb deer hunter. When he graduated from high school, he wanted to travel the world while defending his country, so he skipped college and joined the U.S. Army. Not long after Jake became a U.S. Army Ranger, the Central Intelligence Agency identified him as a superb sniper and persuaded him to join The Company. Jake was an excellent field operative trainee at The Farm in Virginia. Before long, he became a prized black asset at the CIA.

Garcia, who was growing more bored by the minute as he sat in the tortuously hot pick-up, had followed a more circuitous path to the CIA. Born in Guatemala, Garcia grew up an orphan in the tough streets of Guatemala City. At age thirteen, he was a *sicario* for the MS-13 gang. His specialty was riding on the back of a motorcycle and firing on the poor soul who happened to be his target. Garcia never once killed or wounded innocent bystanders. Over a five-year span, he executed twenty-two MS-13 rivals, malcontents, and informers. He earned the nickname, *El Bebe que Mata* — The Baby Who Kills. The CIA station in Guatemala City took notice of Garcia and brought him into the fold, plying him with thousands in cash and U.S. citizenship. At his new employer's direction, Garcia assassinated numerous U.S. enemies in Central America, Mexico, and the United States.

Garcia and Dupree shared a modest adobe house hidden in the Rincon Mountains outside of Tucson. The two men comprised one of the CIA's most lethal hit teams.

Today was going to be business as usual for Dupree and Garcia: at the behest of the DEA, and with the blessing of the CIA, they were to eliminate Patrona and Don Coyote, once and for all.

"You have to be kidding me," Dupree exclaimed while looking through his field binoculars.

Garcia became alert.

"What . . . what's going on?" he said.

"Look for yourself, Serg."

Dupree handed the binoculars to Garcia, who scanned the section of border fence that the smugglers were expected to use.

"Well smack my ass and call me an *hijo de puta*," Garcia said. "That fence section is raising like a garage door."

Indeed, the fence section rose *exactly* like a garage door, and out came two heavily armed *soldados*, along with Patrona and Don Coyote and about thirty Mexican illegals. Mother and son appeared unarmed, but the *soldados* sported AK-47s. The illegals wore large backpacks and carried plastic jugs of water.

"The *cajones* on that woman," Garcia said. "I guess this answers the question as to why Mexicans never cross the border in groups of three."

"All right, Serg, I'll bite," Dupree said as he checked his AR-15 rifle. "Please tell me why Mexicans don't cross the border in groups of three."

Garcia produced a toothy grin and said, "*Porque, borracho*, there's no *tres*-passing allowed."

Dupree shook his head in mock disgust.

"Serg, that's your all-time worst joke."

"*No es una broma, es la verdad.*"

"Truth or not, enough screwing around," Dupree said. "Time for a hostile takeover."

Both men got out of the pick-up truck. Dupree held his AR-15. Garcia employed an Excalibur assault rifle, a standard issue rifle of the Indian Army. They put on bulletproof Kevlar vests over their sweat-soaked tee shirts. Dupree wore Oakley sunglasses; Garcia preferred Ray Bans, since he felt they made him look cool and sophisticated.

Time to close the deal, Dupree thought.

Patrona and Don Coyote were caught completely by surprise. After all, they had made this trip hundreds of times, and not once had they met resistance from the U.S. Border Patrol or the DEA. They considered it just one more stroll through a giant sandbox.

Only this stroll had been interrupted by two men pointing automatic rifles at them.

"DEA, *cabrones, ponte en el suelo, ahora!*" Garcia yelled.

"*Si, si, por supuesto*," Patrona said. She appeared to be in her early fifties, and was an attractive woman with long black hair in a ponytail and a fit figure. She wore a green safari hat, sunglasses, a beige tee shirt, brown cargo pants, and expensive looking hiking boots. But not a single piece of jewelry.

Patrona slowly dropped to one knee. She raised both arms.

In deference to the boss, everyone else, including Don Coyote, dropped to their knees and raised their arms.

Except for the two *soldados*.

Taking his focus away from Patrona, Garcia yelled to the two body-guards, "*Mira, ponte en el suelo tambien!*"

The bodyguards remained standing.

His AR-15 still raised, Dupree stepped forward.

"Serg, let's take out these assholes."

Garcia nodded.

He and Dupree fired their automatic rifles, delivering multiple rounds into the two *soldados*, who never had a chance to return fire.

Still clutching their AK-47s, the bodyguards *whumped!* onto the sandy ground.

Patrona purposefully sacrificed her *soldados* to draw attention away from her.

Still on one knee, she swiftly reached behind her back and pulled a Glock semi-automatic pistol from the waistband of her cargo pants.

Without hesitation, Patrona aimed her pistol at Garcia and shot him twice, hitting him in his throat and dead center in his forehead.

Sergio Garcia, CIA black operative and ersatz DEA agent, fell dead to the ground.

Much of his brain blew out of the back of his head — the bloody chunks of brain on the desert floor resembled grisly clusters of peyote buttons.

Dupree and Patrona fired upon each other simultaneously.

Dupree took a shot to his Kevlar-protected abdomen, which made him stagger backwards, though he remained on his feet.

Patrona fared much worse: Dupree shot her twice in the chest. And she had no Kevlar vest. She spun like a dreidel and fell dead face-down onto a silver cholla cactus.

All of this deadly drama took less than a minute to play out.

The Mexican illegals remained on their knees, too fearful to make the slightest movement. They dutifully kept their arms up and their hands behind their heads. Clearly, it wasn't their first rodeo — they knew the drill.

Don Coyote, though, had disappeared. During the shootout, he scampered like a roadrunner behind a large berm about fifty feet from his mother's body.

In a minute or two, he intended to crawl even farther away. As he had no firearms — he actually hated guns — his only option was to retreat and live to smuggle another day.

His first thoughts centered on self-preservation, then he thought of his dear dead mother.

Ay mi madre, lo siento, mi gran Patrona, he thought.

Don Coyote quickly devised a two-part plan. He'd get the hell out of this bloody shit storm by walking the fifteen miles to Nogales — wouldn't be easy, but he was strong enough to pull it off. Then he'd take the helm of the family smuggling business and promptly reimburse the Sinaloa cartel for its lost drug cargo.

The second part of Don Coyote's plan was personal. Deeply personal. He'd track down this DEA *pendejo* who murdered his mother, introduce him to Nogales hospitality by letting Gila monsters feast on him, then hang 'im high on a saguaro cactus.

Algun dia, sicario, algun dia, Don Coyote thought. *Tan verdadero, tan verdadero.*

He crawled away with the stealthiness of a Western coral snake.

Meanwhile, Dupree approached the group of Mexican illegals, who resembled a weathered gray garden of kneeling statutes.

Dupree first wanted to make certain the risk of further gunfire exchange had passed, then he'd tend to his fallen partner, who remained motionless on the ground.

The tiniest spark of humanity left in Dupree prevented his simply executing the Mexicans. That, and he wasn't sure if he had enough ammunition.

Pointing his automatic rifle at the group, he said to them in Spanish, "Get up and get out of here — leave the backpacks, but take the water."

The Mexicans didn't have to be told twice. All of them jumped up and tossed the drug-laden backpacks into a haphazard pile. They then ran en masse north to Tucson.

Dupree didn't care if they ran north or south.

"*Gracias, el jefe,*" one Mexican said to Dupree.

"Fuck you," Dupree said.

The Mexicans headed north by northwest into the Sonoran sunset.

Dupree was frustrated Don Coyote had escaped. But there wasn't time to search for him. He needed to call in back-up and stay at the side of his dead partner.

"Someday, Don Coyote, some day," he said. "So true, so very true."

Dupree held Garcia's limp hand. For the first time in his life, he wept uncontrollably.

1

Don Coyote was mesmerized by Goliath, his beloved Chihuahua, floating above him in the living room of his leased mansion in South Tampa.

If only the South Tampa tooties could see this, he thought.

To celebrate his fiftieth birthday, Don Coyote tied together fifty helium-filled balloons, placed the tiny Chihuahua in a black velvet bag affixed to the balloons, and let Goliath gently float away.

Goliath had done this circus act before, so he appeared quite content gliding five feet in the air across the expansive room.

In fact, Goliath already was falling asleep.

Don Coyote became lost in his thoughts.

He sat back in a large La-Z-Boy recliner. Smiling at Goliath, he ran his hand through his long graying hair. Even at fifty, he remained a dashingly handsome man — in the right light.

Don Coyote no longer thought of himself as a human trafficker. Rather, he considered himself a matchmaker.

I mean really, a trafficker of human beings, of God's creations, he thought. How absurd and coarse and distasteful. Yes, I've come a long way from wrangling drug mules through the Sonoran Desert. Today, I'm a beacon of light. No, that's not it. I'm a lighthouse of love. Yes, much better. I bring people together who otherwise might not have found each other. I offer bright optimism for grand possibilities in a dark, pessimistic world.

Having gone from a human trafficker and drug smuggler to a matchmaker, Don Coyote still adhered to the formula of means, motive, and opportunity: Don Coyote's clients were people of considerable means who were highly motivated to pay lavishly for an opportunity to own other human beings.

It was the twenty-first century slave trade, *el estilo Mexicano*.

And Don Coyote was passionate about answering his clients' insatiable needs.

Of course, he enjoyed the millions in filthy lucre he earned from his horrific enterprise.

However, he truly relished moving about so freely in *sol y sombra*, sun and shade.

Hardly anyone paid him attention in Florida, whether it was Miami, Orlando, or now Tampa. Dressed in his Mexican *guayabera* shirts and sporting unlit Cohiba cigars, he seemed a perfectly harmless *viejo*, or older man.

In Mexico, he was *el jefe*, a boss man of considerable respect and admiration, especially in Nogales. He was *el patron*, or the master, of his highly specialized field, and he was both loved and feared.

Besides, he thought, NAFTA made drug smuggling in the United States so easy, my dear Mother Maria was nearly obsolete not long after she started *La Frontera*. Just gotta keep innovating, is all.

Don Coyote considered his innovative enterprise as an art form. His matchmaking entailed painstakingly aligning the right masters with the right slaves. Love dovetails, he called them.

Especially challenging for him was that the slave had to be a free person willingly, even gladly, entering permanent servitude — once Don Coyote applied his seductive verbal and pharmacological persuasions.

It rarely surprised him at how happily Americans left the bright light of freedom to join the pitch blackness of slavery.

Probably too much sugar in their diets, Don Coyote thought. Affects their thinking clearly.

Yes, he ruminated, what an ideal metaphor. Sun and shade. Day and night. Good and evil. Two beautiful worlds living in peaceful co-existence. Really, can't have one without the other.

Don Coyote was reminded of the noble bullfighting arena. *Sol y sombra* dictates the cost of seats at the Mexico City bullfighting arena that seats sixty-thousand people. The least expensive — but least attractive — seats are in the punishing sunlight. The much more expensive seats are in the cool, refreshing shade.

In the bullfighting arena, as in life itself, everything costs more in the comforting darkness.

Don Coyote, in fact, thought of himself as a brave matador imbued with cunning and *machismo*. He always entered his ring, his arena, intent on dancing with, then dominating, his prey.

He conceded there was an important distinction to be made regarding his bullfighting metaphor. Traditionally, the meat from the fallen bull was given free to the very poor. Don Coyote's captured prey went for an outrageous price to the very rich.

More specifically, the very, very rich in Mexico.

Genius, really, Don Coyote thought. Export from *Los Estados Unidos* American flesh, usually young *gringas*, to discerning, high-end Mexican customers.

It was Montezuma's Revenge, re-tooled.

Perhaps I might put it in less prosaic terms, he thought. It's not like I'm running a Chicago stockyard from the days of yore. Let's see, how about if I'm more *scientific*. Got it, what I do is romantic perverse reverse osmosis. Damn, I'm impressed. Should put that in a brochure.

Don Coyote continued to watch Goliath float above him.

He chuckled softly, as today was going to be special beyond its being his birthday.

He was closing in on dual prey. Twin sisters to be exact. Identical twins from a wealthy South Tampa family. Mannerly. Polite. Educated in private schools. Stunningly beautiful. Only eighteen. Virgins. The pride and joy of their parents. Perfection twice over.

And with their family being among the Tampa Bay elite, there was a fabulous quality of cruel justice to this deal.

Mexicans aren't so lazy and stupid, are we, you *gringo* fuckers, he thought.

Just at that moment, the twin sisters walked side by side into the living room. They sat down on a leather sofa next to Don Coyote's recliner. Simultaneously, they crossed their ankles and turned their legs to the right.

They wore matching yellow dresses with white peep-toe heeled sandals. Their youthful beauty made make-up almost unnecessary, though their nail polish was a striking coral red. Their long blonde hair flowed down their backs.

The twins' posture was exquisite as they sat on the edge of the sofa. They kept their hands folded in their laps.

If they had plebian nicknames, which they certainly did not, they would be "Prim" and "Proper".

You know, I don't really think of myself as these girls' enslaver, Don Coyote thought. No, I'm conducting an intervention on behalf of Morgan and Cecilia. They're so miserable having grown up with these insufferable bores for parents. In time, the girls will discover their true purpose in life and, therefore, will be much happier. Naturally, it'll help keeping them properly medicated. Love through science, my dears.

"Young ladies, time for your vitamins," Don Coyote said to the twins, who were mesmerized by the aerial Goliath.

Well, not really vitamins, he thought.

Truthfully, the twins' "vitamins" was cyclobenzaprine, twenty milligrams to each twin, three times a day, and taken with demitasse cups of angel's trumpet tea.

Don Coyote knew from experience that that much powerful muscle relaxant is risky business. However, he factored in the twins' youth and excellent physical fitness — they were former soccer and lacrosse players. He determined that these dosages of cyclobenzaprine kept the sisters relaxed, pliable, and slightly intoxicated.

The angel's trumpet tea, though, was far trickier. Normally, he imported the white and pink pendulous blooms from Chile, Venezuela, and Brazil. Yet he lucked out in Tampa: he found a local plant nursery that sold angel's trumpet shrubs, which he planted in the backyard of his South Tampa mansion. The six shrubs provided more than ample blooms for his mad chemistry.

Angel's trumpet, or *brugmansia*, is rich in tropane alkaloids, which induce euphoria and sometimes hallucinations. Those who drink angel's trumpet tea usually end up in a zombie-like state. And the side effects often include memory loss, convulsions, paralysis, even death.

Through trial and error — including a person dying — Don Coyote perfected the correct number of angel's trumpet blooms to steep with boiling water. He masked the tea's bitterness with raw Manuka honey.

"Oh goody, Father, I've been looking forward to my vitamins," one twin said.

"Me, too, Father," the other twin said.

Now which twin is which, Don Coyote thought.

"You first, Morgan," he said, looking at both twins.

Morgan reached for the muscle relaxant tablets and a cup of angel's trumpet tea.

Yes, that's it, Don Coyote thought. Morgan has a tiny mole on her neck below her left ear lobe. Gotta remember that.

He handed Morgan the tablets and tea.

She swallowed the muscle relaxant with dainty sips of the tea.

"My turn, Father, my turn," Cecelia said eagerly.

"Yes, my child, you're next," Don Coyote said. "My, I must trumpet aloud how you're both such angels. And you're not far off from journeying south to heaven, for a lifetime of blissful servitude."

Don Coyote handed the tablets and demitasse cup of tea to Cecelia, who happily took her "vitamins" with the tea.

In less than thirty minutes, the twins would board the express train to nirvana.

Don Coyote had to move quickly, as he didn't want the sisters to fall asleep again during the video interview.

Recently, the twins thoroughly embarrassed Don Coyote. Heavily sedated with cyclobenzaprine and tropane alkaloids, the sisters fell asleep on this same sofa during a preliminary interview. The prospective Mexican buyers, a shockingly wealthy couple from Puerto Vallarta, were put off by the twins' slovenliness. They could find doped-up

American runaways anywhere. And they wanted their slaves to be zombie *like*, not actual zombies.

What this couple desired was more difficult to obtain — well off, intelligent, educated, virginal, and fairly alert American twin sisters.

Well, that *faux pas* of the twins zonking out won't happen again, Don Coyote thought. I'll get this deal moving before my girls become somnolent.

"Ready for the next interview, my cherished ones?"

"Yup," the twins said in unison. After all, they were eager to make up for the last disastrous interview.

"'Yup', 'yup'?" Don Coyote exclaimed loudly, startling the floating Chihuahua. "How dare you use common vernacular in my presence. Shall I paddle you both again?"

"No, no, please no, Father," the twins said.

Morgan, the obvious alpha, then said, "Please, Father, forgive us for our crass language. We shall endeavor not to disappoint you again."

"Yes, well, *humph*," Don Coyote stuttered, clearly impressed that the psychotropic fog hadn't yet enveloped Morgan. "See that you don't disappointment me again, Morgan *and* Cecelia."

"Yes, Father," the twins said.

Fifteen minutes passed since the twins' dosages. The sisters appeared a bit loopy, which would make them malleable during the interview. And they would remain in this state for at least an hour.

More than enough time to make that couple come around, Don Coyote thought. 'Course, lost a million to persuade them to come back to the table. Still in all, four million dollars — pretty sweet.

"Morgan and Cecelia, I need to contact your potential sponsors in Mexico. I'll first speak with these lovely people in private, then we'll have a group chat. I'm confident your new home will exceed your expectations, and you will achieve all that has been preordained."

Good God, what unmitigated bullshit, he thought.

"Oh yes, Father, we believe good things are about to happen for us," Cecelia said. "Morgan and I trust you. We believe in you. We know you are a great man who transacts all time and space."

"'Transcends', Sister, you meant 'transcends', not 'transacts'," Morgan said, as she gently patted her sister's knee.

"Thank you ever so much, Sister," Cecelia said. "Father, you *transcend* all time and space. You are beyond physics."

"*Tan verdadero*, so true," Don Coyote said, trying to recall when he last had heard such gibberish. "My philosophy is that complete servitude will set you free and will enrich everyone around you. And you two are my finest acolytes, my golden-haired cherubs."

Morgan absolutely beamed with pride.

"If we are cherubs, does that make you our celestial father?"

Morgan's eyelids drooped slightly over her hazel eyes. Cecelia, who had the same color of eyes, wasn't far behind her sister in drowsiness.

Time to move, Don Coyote thought, or I'm going to lose these two again.

"Yes, I am your celestial father, whose birthday happens to be today," he said, hoping to perk up the twins.

"Happy birthday, Father," the twins said loudly, which caused Goliath to yip from above.

"Thank you, girls. In honor of my birthday, I am going to sing a short song that I composed myself."

"Let's hear it, let's hear it," Morgan said, her eyes sparkling like amber crystals.

"Very well, my dear, here we go," Don Coyote said.

He cleared his throat, then sang in a rich baritone voice.

Es la verdad
Que yo soy un viejo,
Pero por lo menos
No soy un pendejo,
Tan verdadero,
Tan verdadero,
Tan verdadero.

MORGAN AND CECELIA APPLAUDED WILDLY. GOLIATH JOINED IN BY barking from his skybox.

"Father, please translate for us," Morgan said.

"Very well," he said, obviously smitten with his performance. 'I sang, "It is true that I am an old man, but at least I am not an ass. So true, so true, so true.' "

"So *very* true . . . and so *very* naughty," Cecelia said, as she raised her eyebrows and smiled at Don Coyote.

"Hmm, I think it's time for you two to get changed while I speak with your prospective masters," he said.

Morgan and Cecelia rose from the sofa and stood at attention, albeit unsteadily.

"What shall we wear, Father?" Morgan asked.

"Sun dresses, white sun dresses," Don Coyote said. "Of course, no bra or panties."

"Of course," Cecelia said in a coquettish tone. "*Feliz cumpleanos, El Padre.*"

Morgan chimed in, "Yes, yes, Father, *feliz cumpleanos*, and you are such a beautiful singer."

And you are such a precocious liar, Don Coyote thought.

He was fascinated with how twins competed for a parent's undivided attention, as if each twin wanted to be an only child.

Divide and conquer the little brats, he thought. Pit 'em against each other, they'll never come at me as a unified force. Good enough for the Romans, good enough for me.

"*Gracias*, *gracias*, now off you go," he said.

He had grown impatient, since he was aware it would take a while for him to set up Skype on his laptop.

The twins gracefully left the living room and walked down the hallway to their bedroom.

Goliath remained peacefully suspended in the air, hovering near his master.

Finally alone, Don Coyote, an analog man struggling in a digital world, began tapping with a single index finger on his laptop.

2

———————

Tampa attorney Reed O'Hara was getting frustrated. She tapped her Mont Blanc pen on a notepad as she sat at her large desk in her office, which was atop the tallest commercial building in downtown Tampa. She was working on an innovative project that had plenty of moving parts. And she was getting little cooperation from the two men sitting across from her.

Reed had listened to these two men long enough.

She leaned forward in her high-back leather chair and waved her right hand across the desk that was covered with stacks of legal documents.

Her wave was a signal — an order, actually — for the men to be silent.

The two men immediately stopped talking.

"I don't care how long it takes, how much it costs, or however many roadblocks we face," Reed said. "We're going to have a professional basketball league in Tampa Bay featuring teams comprised of male *and* female players."

Anyone who knew Reed O'Hara wouldn't be surprised at her taking on this project. While she was all about the advancement of women in a male-dominated culture, she emphasized integration and cooperation over separatism and confrontation.

In fact, the advancement of women was a theme that permeated every venture in her life.

At only thirty-six years old, Reed was among the most respected attorneys in Tampa Bay. She worked hard, adhered to her professional ethics, networked constantly, and cared little for status and celebrity.

Graduating with high honors from the University of Florida College of Law, she ventured to Tampa Bay, which she thought was a tropical paradise. Recognizing her brilliance and sold work ethic, the silk-stocking law firms zealously pursued her.

Reed began her law career with a large and prestigious Tampa law firm that defended Big Tobacco. After only five years, she grew disenchanted with the oftentimes cruel delay tactics in defending Big Tobacco.

But she played it smart. She avoided the trap of buying a large South Tampa home and owning a luxury sports car, thereby resulting in a massive debt that would've obliged her to stay with the law firm.

Instead, Reed lived modestly and saved her money during those five years.

Having accrued substantial funds and legal experience, Reed struck out on her own, creating the O'Hara Law Group.

And it was a smart decision.

Knowing full well how its defense counsel maneuvered, Reed successfully brought several large class-action lawsuits against Big Tobacco, resulting in her amassing a personal fortune of over three hundred million dollars.

With her solo practice on such secure financial footing, she came to focus almost exclusively on helping women involved with acrimonious divorces, spousal abuse, medical malpractice, and work-place sexual harassment.

But Reed didn't let her law practice consume all of her energies. She constantly looked for new endeavors and challenges. For instance, she earned a black belt in *tae kwon do* and became an expert shooter in both handguns and rifles.

Reed first learned to snow ski in the Colorado Rockies, and she occasionally traveled to Grindelwald to ski the Swiss Alps.

She reveled in flying a trapeze in Runaway Bay, Jamaica, and flying aloft the Roatan Island tree canopy on zip lines. And she couldn't be happier galloping on a Paso Fino horse across the windward beaches of Aruba.

However, Reed O'Hara was so much more than a thrill seeker.

She co-owned with her husband, Jake Dupree, the Namaste cabaret club in Tampa.

Namaste was not a trashy strip club, which sadly were so common in Tampa. Rather, Namaste hired performers, most of whom were beaten down and nearing their end days, to dance on stage in a tasteful, sensual manner along the lines of the Moulin Rouge cabaret in Paris. The overwhelming majority of these women suffered from drug, alcohol, and physical abuse. With Jake as Namaste's manager, and Reed keeping a lower profile, the couple was able, with Namaste, to turn around the lives of dozens of women.

But Reed wasn't content with practicing the law and operating a cabaret.

Knowing full well that Florida was a sunny place for shady people, Reed became a private investigator after completing a Class CC private investigator internship and acquiring a P.I. license.

When time permitted, she delved into intriguingly seamy investigative matters, and her specialty became finding missing women.

She always included Jake in these investigations — he, too, was a licensed private investigator.

They formed a very capable team that didn't ballyhoo their successes.

For instance, Reed and Jake never received public recognition for solving the case of the Catholic priest murders. Privately though, local law enforcement knew that the case would not have been closed without Reed and Jake's involvement. That was satisfaction enough for the couple.

But as for creating a co-ed basketball league in Tampa Bay, not everyone was on board.

"Reed, have you thought through this new basketball league idea?" Harold Balzac said.

Balzac sat in a chair across from Reed's desk.

He was an elderly man who owned several car dealerships in Tampa Bay. He also headed up the Tampa Sports Authority.

"I mean, how in the heck are you going to organize this new league?" Balzac said.

Reed held up a thick garnet notebook, on whose cover was printed in gold letters, "The Tampa Bay Basketball League: A Blueprint for Progress."

"All the details are here, Harry," Reed said. "But I'll be glad to give you the highlights."

Balzac nodded his approval.

Every time Reed met with Balzac, she was repelled by the unpleasant combination of his body odor and Old Spice cologne.

Does that man *ever* bathe, she thought.

By contrast, Clive Cutler, who was sitting next to Balzac, always was impeccable in his personal hygiene — today, he smelled of Giorgio Armani's Aqua di Gio, one of Reed's favorite men's colognes.

Normally, Cutler was a friendly and loquacious individual. After all, he was a successful real estate developer, so he was equal parts carney and blarney. Today, though, he was strangely silent as he slunk down in his chair.

"Here's how it's going to work, gentlemen," Reed said. "There will be ten teams, each with an equal number of male and female players. The teams will represent communities throughout Tampa Bay. We'll draft players who played high school or college ball from anywhere in Florida. Games will be played . . . . ."

"How about the coaches?" Balzac interjected.

Reed smiled wanly at Balzac.

"Harry, there will be five female coaches and five male coaches," she said. "Now, if I may go on, games will be played . . . ."

"Please continue, Reed," Balzac said. He behaved like a sports pope.

Cutler gently tapped Balzac's shoulder, then said to him in a low voice, "Cut it out, Harry, you're being a twit."

"No worries, Clive," Reed said. "After all, this is a fact-finding meeting. Questions are always welcome. Now . . . games will be played in college and high school gymnasiums during the summer. Admission will be modest, in an attempt to build a fan base. Food trucks will provide food and beverage concessions. Absolutely no alcohol served. The league will market jerseys, shorts, lids, and other gear, all produced by local sports apparel companies — again, prices will be kept low to grow that all-important fan base."

Balzac leaned forward in his chair. He took a sip from his bottle of Publix spring water that he'd brought with him.

"Reed, I admire your spunk, I really do," Balzac said. "As head of the Tampa Sports Authority, I just worry about what the NBA — and I guess the WNBA, for that matter — will think about this project."

That's right, Harry, put the WNBA in a secondary position to the NBA, Reed thought.

"I don't know, Harry, sounds like you're saying a little lady such as myself shouldn't take on a project that requires a pair of balls, a pair of really big balls," Reed said.

Balzac's face blushed — he wasn't accustomed to a woman speaking to him in such an unladylike manner.

"What . . . oh my . . . no, I mean . . ." Balzac sputtered.

"Relax, Harry, I'm just flaking your biscuits," Reed said. "But truly, I don't worry over what the WNBA — or the NBA, for that matter — thinks about this new league."

Cutler patted Balzac's hand. He was worried his old friend would suffer another coughing attack, as Harry Balzac was battling emphysema contracted from smoking too many Hav-A-Tampa cigars.

Though Balzac pouted over being dressed down by Reed, he didn't start coughing.

"C'mon, Harry, listen up," Cutler said. "I mean, your face is hung like a half moon. You shouldn't care two bits about what those basketball leagues think. Hell, they've been stiff arming us in Tampa Bay for years."

Balzac's complexion returned to its usual pasty white hue.

"You're probably right, Clive," Balzac said.

Cutler smiled broadly.

"Why, I *know* I'm right, old friend," Cutler said. "I see nothing wrong with Reed's innovative idea, know what I mean? O'Hara has the start-up capital, I'm sure an impressive network of potential investors — heck, I might buy a team — and she has superb organizational skills. Dadgum, Harry, Reed O'Hara has the *huevos rancheros* to pull this off."

Reed understood Cutler's angle: he was placing the viability of this new league squarely on her shoulders. If the league fails, then she gets all of the blame. But if it succeeds, then people like Harry Balzac will try to gobble up the glory like so much paella at the Columbia Restaurant.

Reed gave Cutler her signature Mona Lisa smile.

"Thanks for your heartfelt support, Clive," she said, trying mightily not to roll her topaz-blue eyes. "And Harry, can I count on your support from the Tampa Sports Authority?"

Still pouting, Balzac simply nodded his head affirmatively.

"Well good, that's a huge relief," Reed said. "Gentlemen, here are binders that provide all of the details, including timelines."

Balzac and Cutler each took a binder.

"Of course, I will own the league, but I will offer individual team franchises," Reed said. "Harry and Clive, you might consider owning a team."

Nothing but crickets from Balzac, though Cutler nodded approvingly.

I'll win *both* these guys over, Reed thought. Still can't figure out why Clive is here, I invited only Harry. And Clive isn't his usual expansive self today — something must be bothering him.

Though Cutler stayed seated, Balzac rose from his chair, shook hands with Cutler and Reed, then swanned his way out of the office.

Reed and Cutler sat in silence across from each other.

Well, this is awkward, Reed thought.

Luckily, the cavalry arrived: Roman Delaney, Reed's office manager, tapped on the open office door.

"Is there anything you need, Reed?" Roman asked.

Even with Reed's office door open, Roman wasn't comfortable leaving her alone in her office with a man. He hadn't forgotten the time the Russian mob attorney Jasper Conway was abusive toward Reed while Roman was out to lunch. Fortunately, Reed thoroughly handled Conway, even providing him an impressive demonstration of her *tae kwon do* skills when Conway threatened her.

"No, I'm fine, Roman, but thank you," Reed said. "I think Clive and I are going to have a private chat."

Having understood Reed's signal, Roman nodded, then left the office, closing the door behind him.

"That obvious, huh?" Clive said.

"Yuppers," Reed said.

"Well, thanks for speaking with me, Reed. I really need your help — that's why I came here today."

Clive began to weep.

"What's wrong, Clive? Are you in trouble?"

Clive pulled out a white handkerchief and wiped the tears from his eyes.

"No, I'm not in trouble, but I'm certain my twin daughters are. Morgan and Cecelia have been missing for ten days. I contacted the Tampa Police over a week ago. They still haven't found my girls. Police said if they've been kidnapped, I should wait for a ransom demand. But nothing's happened, no ransom demand, no word from my daughters, no *nothing*."

Reed leaned forward in her chair, folded her hands, and put her elbows on the desk.

"All right, Clive, I want you to give me all of the details that you can," Reed said. "But first, I need to reach out to two of my colleagues. They'll be a big help in finding your daughters."

A glimmer of hope sparkled in Clive's eyes.

Reed buzzed her office manager.

"Roman, tell Ravel and Chenoa to get here immediately. And bring us a large pot of fresh coffee."

3
___

"*Feliz cumpleanos*, Don Coyote," Lucia Da Rosa said.

"*Gracias, Senora Da Rosa*," Don Coyote said. "*Eres demasiado bueno.*"

"*De nada, El Patron*," Lucia said.

Don Coyote was still seated in his South Tampa living room. After some fits and starts, he was able to set up a Skype video conference with Lucia and Mateo Da Rosa, the Puerto Vallarta couple interested in purchasing the Cutler twins.

"I'm so happy we could talk again about this grand adventure with Morgan and Cecelia," Don Coyote said in Spanish to the couple.

The Da Rosas were in their mid-forties, married for twenty years, childless, and very wealthy. They were devout Catholics, generous supporters of charitable causes, and considered rising stars among the Puerto Vallarta upper class.

And the Da Rosas carefully groomed this bright, shiny image of a philanthropic power couple so involved with improving the community.

They spoke openly about the pain over not being able to have children — it was even money within their social circle as to whether it was Lucia's or Mateo's fault they couldn't conceive. And the couple made quite a show of volunteering for and donating large sums of cash to the local church orphanages.

But the Da Rosas shared a dark secret: they couldn't care less about having children. In fact, Lucia had had two abortions, each one performed very quietly in Houston. You see, little tykes running around their mansion would put a crimp in their shared perverted passion, that of owning other human beings.

It wasn't enough for the Da Rosas to have a cadre of personal assistants, housekeepers, gardeners, and bodyguards whom they overworked for paltry wages.

No, Lucia and Mateo Da Rosa wanted to buy Morgan and Cecelia Cutler to be their sex slaves. And they were willing to pay millions to own twin upper-class American virgin sisters.

"Is there anything more I can tell you about the twins?" Don Coyote asked.

Lucia and Mateo, an attractive and physically fit couple, smiled lasciviously on the laptop screen.

"Well, yes, we do have an important question," Mateo said.

The three Mexicans continued to speak in Spanish, so as to prevent Morgan and Cecelia from overhearing them.

"And what is your important question?" Don Coyote said.

"Have you verified that Morgan and Cecelia are indeed virgins?" Lucia said.

Again with her devilish smile, Don Coyote thought. These two give me the heebie jeebies. Ah, what I do for the almighty American dollar.

Don Coyote rolled a cigar between the thumb and index finger of his right hand.

Can't wait to fire up this beauty, he thought.

He let out a slow breath.

"Yes, Lucia — if I may address you by your Christian name — I had the girls examined by a gynecologist who confirmed they are indeed virgins."

Cost me ten thousand to keep *that* on the down low, he thought.

"So their hymens are intact," Mateo said eagerly.

Why is it the upper class can be more crass than an eighty-year-old Tijuana whore, Don Coyote thought.

"Yes, of course, Mateo, the twins' hymens are as intact as the Virgin Mary's."

Maybe that'll shame them a bit, he thought.

"Oh, goody, goody," Lucia exclaimed.

She clapped boisterously, then crossed herself.

Good God, what a *pendeja*, Don Coyote thought. I mean, I know I'm about to sell two girls into slavery, but the Da Rosas need to show a little restraint here.

"Anything else?" he asked.

The Da Rosas became very serious.

"Yes, there is," Mateo said.

"And that is . . . ." Don Coyote said.

Really, it's time to close this deal, he thought.

"You're absolutely certain the girls are willingly entering into this arrangement," Lucia said.

"Yes, my dear Lucia, Morgan and Cecelia are ready and willing to enter into eternal servitude. They will meet your every need, succumb to your every desire, answer your every demand. They have saved their virginity just for you."

Lucia and Mateo were visibly aroused over Don Coyote's assurances. They appeared to be squirming in their seats.

"We are satisfied, *El Patron*," Mateo said.

Her eyelids drooping, Lucia nodded in agreement with her husband.

Am I a closer or what, Don Coyote thought.

"All that remains, Don Coyote, is for us to be re-introduced to Morgan and Cecelia," Lucia said. "If all goes well, I'm confident we can bring this transaction to an end and pay you the four million dollars — in cash."

Hmm, who's closing whom now, Don Coyote thought.

He looked up at Goliath, who still was floating across the living room. The Chihuahua appeared to wink at his master.

That's right, handsome boy, the deal's almost done, Don Coyote thought.

He called out to the twins, who were waiting patiently in their bedroom.

"Morgan and Cecelia, come out and say hello to the Da Rosas."

The twins padded side by side down the hallway and into the living room. They were barefoot and wearing matching white sundresses.

They blew kisses to Goliath, who responded by barking at them.

"Goliath, please hush," Don Coyote said.

He looked at the cigar he still held in this right hand, then slipped the cigar into a front pocket of his red *guayabera* shirt.

"Hello, Mr. and Mrs. Da Rosa," the twins said. "It's wonderful to see you all again."

An angelic duo, Don Coyote thought. What I'd give to find triplets.

"Hello again, Morgan and Cecelia," Mateo said in English over Skype on the laptop. "You two are simply beautiful."

"Simply divine," Lucia said in English as well.

Lucia winked at Mateo, who smiled back at her.

"Well now, Morgan and Cecelia, what do you have to say to the Da Rosas regarding your uncouth behavior last time," Don Coyote said.

The twins responded, "We were wrong, we are sorry, we repent, we will do differently."

Picked up that mumbo jumbo from some redneck televangelist, Don Coyote thought. Fascinating how skillful these TV preachers are with mind control. And you know what, to be the best, you gotta learn from the best.

"We accept your apology, girls," Lucia said. "And don't you two look so fetching in your sundresses — you are the picture of purity."

Morgan and Cecelia beamed with pride.

"And now we would like to see you without your sundresses," Mateo said.

The twins smiled and nodded their heads.

Morgan lifted her white sundress over her head and gently tossed the dress on the sofa.

Cecelia followed suit.

As instructed by Don Coyote, neither twin wore a bra or panties, and they had covered their bodies with baby oil.

Don Coyote motioned for them to move their long blonde hair away from their breasts.

They complied.

"Perfect, absolutely perfect, and such nice tan lines," Lucia said in a throaty voice. "Turn around, please — and I mean right now."

Again, Morgan and Cecelia complied, though they swayed ever so slightly.

About time to end this show, Don Coyote thought. Won't be long before the drugs get the better of my girls.

"They're gorgeous," Mateo whispered. He began touching his crotch. Lucia saw this, and promptly slapped his knee. He stopped pleasuring himself.

No doubt who has the bigger *cajones* with this couple, Don Coyote thought. Lucia's going to eat up my twins. And I bet she's a lousy sharer.

"Thank you, Morgan and Cecelia, that will be all for now," he said. "Please pick up your dresses and return to your room."

Once more, the twins complied.

Goliath growled at the sisters as they walked underneath the floating Chihuahua.

"So, Mateo and Lucia, do we have a deal?" Don Coyote said.

"Yes, *El Patron*, but tell me, would you take two million in gold?" Mateo said.

Don Coyote paused for a few seconds before responding.

"No, Mateo, four million, and not a U.S. dollar less," he said. "Good God, those girls are rare and beautiful specimens."

"How about three million, and we'll cover all of your expenses?" Lucia said.

"No, no, no — four million is the final figure," Don Coyote said. "I've already reduced the original asking price by a million dollars."

"So you won't budge any further, *El Patron*?" Mateo said.

"Absolutely not."

Have to be firm with these cretins, he thought.

"Then I guess we'll proceed," Lucia said. "Of course, you'll advise us in our conveying the funds to Tampa?"

"Yes, I will, and upon receipt of the four million dollars, I will have Morgan and Cecelia transported to your home," Don Coyote said. "The entire process should take no more than eight to ten days."

"So we have a final deal?" Lucia said.

"Yes, we have a final deal," Don Coyote said. "Let's stay in touch, all right?"

"Let's do, *El Patron*," Lucia said.

The laptop screen clicked to its home screen saver, which was a photo of a matador in a Valencia, Spain bullring thrusting a sword into a defeated black bull.

Now it was only Don Coyote and Goliath in the living room.

Goliath had fallen back asleep. The dog's tiny head and front paws protruded from the black velvet bag.

Don Coyote pulled his cigar from the front pocket of his *guayabera*. He took off the wrapper and smelled the cigar, which was named the American. A box of twenty Americans had cost him over four hundred dollars.

A complete *yanqui-ophile*, Don Coyote loved the fact that the cigar was entirely American.

It was hand rolled at the J.C. Newman Company in Tampa's historic Ybor City, where hand-rolled cigars was a century-old tradition. Everything about the American was faithful to its name: the tobacco wrapper, the binder tobacco, the cigar molds, the boxes, and the labels, including the ink on the labels, all came from Florida, Connecticut, and Pennsylvania.

The American — what an appropriate name for a cigar born and raised here, Don Coyote thought. And it's so very sweet to light up an American cigar every time I sell *un yanqui o dos* to my fellow Mexicans.

"Goliath, those gringo pricks are getting a taste of their own medicine."

He spoke in a low voice, as he didn't want Morgan and Cecelia to overhear him.

But Goliath ignored his master, preferring simply to float dreamily across the living room.

Don Coyote cut off the cigar tip, then slowly rolled the cigar end in his lighter's tall flame.

He pulled on the lit cigar, tilted back his head, and languidly blew out the smoke.

"Not too bad, not too bad at all," he said aloud to no one in particular. "Really, as impressive as my Cohibas."

He pulled again on his twenty-dollar cigar, this time more heartily.

He sat enveloped in a cloud of aromatic blue-gray smoke.

"Pretty good day, my Goliath, our endeavors once again will pay off handsomely."

Goliath began to sneeze.

With each sneeze, the balloons dropped a foot or so, then Goliath slowly rose again.

"Never have gotten used to my cigars, have you. Oh well, it's just like Aunt Bee's pickles — learn to love it."

Don Coyote stretched out on his recliner and took another ambitious pull from his cigar.

Time to set in motion my plan for that *hijo de puta*, Jake Dupree, he thought. *Tan verdadero*, hate is a bigger motivator than love.

4

———

Reed O'Hara and Clive Cutler sat together in Reed's downtown Tampa law office. For about twenty minutes, they chatted about social events and local news, interrupted several times by comfortable silences — after all, they were acquaintances that over time became good friends.

On the surface, the pair resembled a father and his daughter getting reacquainted. Yet appearances often are wrong, and was no less wrong here: Clive was a spiky businessman who was powerful, wealthy, and intimately connected with the South Tampa elites; Reed was a revered and feared Tampa Bay attorney who was never intimidated and who demanded to be taken seriously.

Reed and Clive had clashed several times in the legal arena, usually centering on disputes over wages, contracts, and sexual harassment issues related to his real estate development empire.

Since the lawyer and the businessman were chiefly concerned with solving problems amicably, rarely resorting to a scorched earth approach, Reed and Clive came away respecting each other a little more each time they crossed swords.

And that was why Clive Cutler approached Reed O'Hara about his missing twin daughters: he knew her, he respected her, and he trusted her. Of course, it didn't hurt that Clive was aware of Reed's deep sensitivity toward women in peril. And Morgan and Cecelia certainly were in some kind of serious peril.

Roman had brought in a tray with a pot of Seattle's Best dark roast coffee, china cups and saucers, a large bottle of Evian water, and two Waterford crystal tumblers.

Reed and Clive quickly drank two cups of coffee each. The coffee helped to keep Reed focused and to perk up a previously morose Clive.

"Feeling a little better, Clive?" Reed said.

Clive refilled his coffee cup, then refilled Reed's. Their spoons tinged softly in the china cups as they blended cream and sugar in the coffee. Wisps of steam, like waifish ghosts, rose from their cups.

Clive sipped his coffee.

"Yes, Reed, I am a little better, because you have that Irish touch of making a person feel comfortable divulging very personal information, so personal it could leave him weakened and vulnerable."

"Two points right up front, Clive," Reed said. "One, stop referring to yourself in third person — it's annoying. Two, I'm not taking a deposition here. Be truthful as much as you can, but if you want to hedge a little bit, that's okay — I'll eventually figure it out."

Reed gave Clive her Mona Lisa smile.

What is she thinking when she smiles like that, Clive wondered.

Clive returned her smile; he seemed genuinely at ease, a feeling he hadn't experienced for ten long days.

He then said, "Well, I guess I should start at the beginning . . . ."

Roman knocked lightly on Reed's office door, and in walked two women who couldn't look more different from each other.

One woman pretended to creep up behind Roman and attack him; the second woman simply rolled her gorgeous green eyes at the other woman.

"Sorry to interrupt Reed, but I knew you wanted me to bring in Ravel and Chenoa as soon as they arrived," Roman said.

Standing at over six feet tall, Roman Delaney moonlighted as a mixed martial artist, traveling a few times a year to Thailand for *muay thai* boxing matches. A former crack-addicted gay prostitute who plied his trade in Tampa and St. Petersburg, Roman was one of several rescue projects for Reed. She met him one very late night on Florida Avenue in Seminole Heights. She persuaded him to enter a drug treatment center, where he overcame his crack addiction, and then attended Hillsborough Community College, taking courses to become a paralegal. Sadly, Roman was HIV-positive; consequently, he led a very healthy and regimented life, always maintaining a neat and professional appearance while working for Reed.

So Roman was none too happy when Ravel stood on her toes --- she was barely five feet tall --- and mussed up Roman's perfectly coiffed brown curly hair.

Roman spun like a Fiji mongoose and slapped away Ravel's hand. "Darn it, Ravel, you know I don't like you to touch me, especially my hair."

Obviously annoyed, he used his right hand as a makeshift comb to put his curls back in place, though they had hardly moved at all.

"Oh, suck it up, buttercup," Ravel said. "You're such a dandy, what with your pretty hair, Tom Ford polo shirt, Prada trousers, and Roos horsebit loafers."

Roman was aghast at Ravel's fashion sense.

"How on earth did you know all that?" he said.

Ravel gave him her Swiss version of the Mona Lisa smile.

"Hey, I read *Esquire*, digital version of course," Ravel said.

"I'm impressed, Ravel, I really am," Roman said. He finally was convinced his hair was back in place. "Just keep your Swiss Miss mittens away from my hair."

Roman knew his remark would set off Ravel.

And it did.

"Say it again, Nancy Boy, call me 'Swiss Miss' again," Ravel said angrily.

Being gay herself, Ravel rarely hesitated to use a gay slur against a homosexual or a lesbian. From her standpoint, it was the rainbow version of playing the dozens.

"All right, children, enough of this nonsense," said the other woman, whose name was Chenoa Jenks.

Chenoa struck quite a figure in Reed's office. She was nearly five-feet, ten-inches tall, and weighed all of one-hundred-twenty-five pounds. She wore shoulder-length black hair and had a Victorian porcelain hue to her skin — somehow, she avoided the omnipresent Florida sun.

Chenoa had just turned twenty-one. She was a former Catholic nun involved in the assassination of several retired Catholic priests living in the Tampa Bay area. Sister Chenoa was only nineteen years old when she joined two other nuns, both in their forties, in the systematic execution of these priests, all of whom were serial pedophiles never brought to justice. In their final assassination attempt, the two older nuns were shot and killed; Reed had captured Sister Chenoa, and decided to let her escape, since this sordid affair already had destroyed enough lives. Later on, after Sister Chenoa had forsaken her sacred vows as a nun, she approached Reed for a job. After much rumination, Reed took on Chenoa as her assistant in private investigations. As Reed once told her husband Jake, "Keep your friends close, and your crossbow-bearing former nuns even closer."

"Chenoa, don't give me any of your holier than thou *nun*sense," Ravel said. She had been feeling threatened by Chenoa, primarily in terms of vying for Reed's attention.

"Ravel, stop it right now," Reed said. "I will not tolerate such unprofessional behavior in front of Clive Cutler."

"Whatever," Ravel mumbled.

"What's that?" Reed said. She was about to rise out of her desk chair.

"I said I'm sorry for being unprofessional," Ravel said. "I hope I didn't offend the old guy."

Clive look up at Ravel and smiled benevolently at her.

"No worries, young lady," he said. "You remind me of my twin daughters."

"They the ones missing?" Ravel said. She pulled a chair right next to Clive and promptly plopped down in the chair.

Clive didn't seem at all taken aback at Ravel's behavior.

"Yes, sadly, Morgan and Cecelia, my golden-haired cherubs, have been missing for ten days," Clive said.

He put his balled right hand against his mouth and began to weep.

Chenoa sat down in the empty chair next to Clive. She gently took his hand from his mouth and held his hand.

"There, there, Mr. Cutler, it's going to be okay," Chenoa said.

Clive regained his composure.

He looked directly into Chenoa's bright emerald green eyes.

"Are you an angel?" he asked her.

"No, sir, I'm a former nun," Chenoa said. "Though I gave up my vows to the Holy Catholic Church, I still can't help soothing the troubled souls of good people."

"So you think I'm a good man?"

"Absolutely," Chenoa answered with confidence. She continued to hold Clive's hand.

"So kind and so young, it's a wonder," Clive said. "But if I'm a good man — and I like to think I've been a good father as well — why have my daughters been taken from me?"

"Because it's not your fault that Morgan and Cecelia have disappeared," Reed interjected. "Evil preys upon the innocent in darkness and in light. Whoever did this probably just had to work a little harder to wrest Morgan and Cecelia away from you."

Clive began weeping again.

"Oh, mother of God," Ravel said. She clearly had enough of what she considered a huge pity party. And from her standpoint, so influenced by Swiss reserve and rationality, Clive's self-pity only muddied what was most likely a dangerous situation for the Cutler twins.

Reed looked sharply at Ravel.

"What's your problem, Ravel?" Reed said.

Ravel rolled her eyes dramatically. She dearly wished she could smoke a cigarette or a joint, though she long ago gave up both habits at Reed's direction.

"My *problem*, Reed, is that we don't know for certain whether these twins have been abducted or merely took off on their own."

Ravel held her laptop computer on her lap — it was her electronic security blanket of sorts. She tapped her fingers on the cover of the laptop, as if she were riffing on a piano.

Despite Ravel wearing a wrinkled white tee shirt, black cargo pants, and scuffed black Doc Martens, Reed noticed that Ravel had beautifully manicured hands.

Looks like a gel manicure, and what an intoxicating red, Reed thought. Nice to see that I can still influence her.

Reed took a moment to study her own nails.

Physician, first heal thyself, she thought. Time for a manicure.

"A very good point, Ravel, we do need to slow down a bit and get more information before we develop a working hypothesis," Reed said.

"That's so cute, Reed, you're throwing me a bone," Ravel said, her round violet eyes alight with mischief.

Sprezzatura was how Reed described Ravel. Reed first came across *sprezzatura* in Baldassare Castiglione's *The Book of the Courtier*. *Sprezzatura*, according to the Italians, was a studied carelessness, a kind of nonchalance where you disguise your true art and desires and intentions behind a mask of reticence. *Sprezzatura* was defensive irony, and Ravel was a master of hiding compassion behind belligerence, of making her amazing skills with a computer seem so effortless. Her favorite response to a compliment was, "No big deal, *schlemiel*."

Reed was well aware that Ravel's fine-tuned *sprezzatura* was born of necessity. When the two women first met at the Namaste cabaret one early weekday evening, Ravel was a hot mess. She was abusing alcohol, tobacco, marijuana, cocaine, and methamphetamine. She was practically homeless, always hungry, and an illegal Swiss immigrant. In order to deal with the crooks, cons, pimps, thieves, and sexual degenerates that peopled her underworld, Ravel resorted to *sprezzatura* not as an artful pose, but as a life-saving Roman shield. Being barely five-feet tall, under a hundred pounds, and a single female, Ravel was an easy target wherever she went. So she presented herself as a lost wastrel and petulant lesbian, not good for anyone's nefarious or well-intentioned purposes.

That is, until she heard about Reed, who was letting the word out in Tampa Bay's grimy wet-sand-in-your-shorts underbelly that she wanted to help women in distress.

So Ravel made an unscheduled stop at Namaste in hopes of meeting the famous Reed O'Hara, or as Ravel described her, "Tampa Bay's Joan of Arc."

As luck would have it, Reed was making a rare appearance at Namaste.

Ravel scuttered into the nightclub well before the entrance fee of one hundred dollars kicked in. And there was Reed, sitting alone at a table and eating a salad.

For Ravel, it truly was love at first sight.

She marveled at Reed's naturally streaked blonde hair, her Caribbean blue eyes, her trim, athletic figure, and perfect little feet, tonight protected by brown leather sandals.

Oh my, Ravel thought, beautiful feet. I'd take the rest of tonight and all day tomorrow just licking and sucking those little cuties. Yum, yum.

Reed looked up from her meal and spotted Ravel staring at her. She recognized that look — she had gotten it from a multitude of men *and* women.

This little missy definitely needs some help, Reed thought. And the first item of business will be to teach her to not stare so boldly at people.

After a less than pleasant job interview of sorts, Ravel convinced Reed that her computer skills and "just goddamn overall brilliance" qualified her to be Jake's assistant office manager at Namaste. Reed had only one condition: Ravel first had to complete a drug treatment program at Tampa General Hospital. Ravel, in fact, completed the program, got clean and sober, and became a huge asset to both Jake and Reed.

Ravel was especially helpful with private investigations. She was the first to figure out who was murdering those pedophilic Catholic priests.

Which was why Ravel was sitting in Reed's office to discuss Clive Cutler's situation. And Reed was tolerating Ravel's insouciance because she recognized no one could quite do the voodoo that Ravel would do.

"Ravel, let's put our focus on Clive and his family," Reed said.

"Fine, all right," Ravel said. She opened her laptop, clicked a few keys, and appeared ready to work.

"Now, Clive, allow me to formally introduce my two indispensable colleagues, Ravel and Chenoa," Reed said. "They have unmatched computer skills, are plugged into Tampa Bay's darker networks, and are portraits of persistence."

Clive mumbled a greeting to both women, and shook Ravel's hand, then Chenoa's.

"I'm sorry for not being more animated, uh, ladies," Clive said. "I'm old, I'm fatigued with worry, and I'm beside myself with what might have happened to my girls."

"Okay, Clive, but don't start crying again," Ravel said.

Clive smiled at Ravel, and nodded in agreement.

Ravel first bumped with Clive.

Good, looks as if the old fart finally has his shit together, Ravel thought.

"Reed and Chenoa and Ravel, where do you want me to start?" Clive said.

Reed leaned back in her high-backed leather chair.

"Chaim Potok was right — beginnings are always the hardest", Reed said. "But we need to start there."

This time, Ravel didn't roll her eyes. Instead, she gave Reed a thumbs up.

"Got that right, Reed," she said. "Time for Clive Baby to give us the facts — and nothing but."

5

"For Ravel and Chenoa's sake, I'll start with some information about me and my family that's pretty much common knowledge in the Tampa community," Clive said.

Ravel fidgeted in her chair.

As I sit aging, she thought. I already have all this stuff. Guess I should let Old Man River get warmed up.

"Patience, Ravel, patience," Reed said. "Go on, Clive."

"Yes, well," Clive said, as he cleared his throat. "I am a rather successful real estate developer who specializes in state-of-the-art, environmentally sound, high rises, and the fifteen high rises I constructed, consisting of office space and condominiums, are one-hundred percent occupied."

"Jesus, Mary, and Joseph," Ravel quipped.

Clive smiled warmly at Ravel.

"Goodness, you are indeed just like Morgan and Cecelia," he said to Ravel. "I'm afraid that I'm forever in ABC mode."

"ABC mode?" Chenoa said.

"Yes — Always Be Closing," Clive said. "It's a sales technique."

"Thank you, Clive," Chenoa said in her soothing voice. "Now let's get back to you and your family."

Gently chastised by the young ex-nun, Clive continued.

"My work has been profitable, and my family has benefitted from my labors," he said. "I was forty years old when I married Elin Karlsson, a twenty-year-old Swedish immigrant who was a server at the Palma Ceia Golf and Country Club. Quite the beauty, really. So sweet, so friendly. Some of my fellow members weren't too pleased — they were jealous, truth be told — that I married Elin in a wedding ceremony at the very country club where she worked so hard for lousy tips."

"Please describe Elin when you married her," Ravel said, a bit too eagerly.

Reed frowned at Ravel.

"What's your damage, Reed?" Ravel said. "I'm only data gathering."

Clive smiled once again. He seemed to enjoy this filterless Swiss.

"No worries, Ravel, as they say in the islands," Clive said in a vain attempt to sound hip. "Elin is as beautiful today as she was when I married her twenty years ago. Her bright blue eyes and blonde hair captured me the moment she first served me a Manhattan at the country club."

"How . . . fucking . . . romantic," Ravel said, this time wisely under her breath.

Clive didn't miss the slight, though.

"Anyhow, Elin and I fell in love, got married, moved into a mansion on Bayshore Boulevard, and had twin daughters two years into our marriage," Clive said.

"Was Elin a stay-at-home mom?" Chenoa asked.

"Yes, of course, she was totally devoted to properly raising Morgan and Cecelia," Clive said. "She never complained about not waiting tables for a bunch of pampered jerks."

"And the twins, did they attend private schools?" Chenoa asked.

No, moron, they went to magnet schools in College Hill, Ravel thought.

"Yes, Academy of the Holy Names, from pre-K through their senior year of high school," Clive said with pride. "Cost me a small fortune."

"Is Elin a Roman Catholic?" Ravel said, knowing full well there was a sixty-three percent chance that Elin was raised in the Protestant Church of Sweden.

"No, Elin is a devout secularist, though she attended the Church of Sweden when she was a child," Clive replied.

She shoots, she scores, Ravel thought.

"So you're Catholic?" Chenoa said. She sat with her legs crossed, her hands in her lap; she stared down at her thousand-dollar Saint Laurent Opyum black sandals.

Forgive me, Holy Mother, but I do so love these bitchin' shoes, she thought.

"Yes I am, Chenoa," Clive said. "There was no question in our household that Morgan and Cecelia would matriculate at Academy of the Holy Names. You know, our entire family lives the Academy's motto, '*Esse quam videri*'."

"And that means in English . . ." Ravel said.

Reed and Chenoa spoke simultaneously, "To be, rather than to seem."

"Well, well, isn't that just so charming," Ravel said. "I'm getting all hot and bothered watching this Latin Tango."

"You're such an ass," Chenoa said to Ravel, who responded to Chenoa by making a V sign with her right index and middle finger, then darting her serpentine tongue through the V.

"Oh my," Clive exclaimed. His flushed face was the color of a watermelon Jolly Rancher.

"Enough, you two, that's enough right now," Reed said in a loud voice. "Don't make me turn this car around."

Everyone in the office burst out laughing. Reed was so pleased with her arch admonishment, she teared up a bit while she laughed.

"Okay, now back to Clive and his family," she said. "Did Morgan and Cecelia have any problems in school, Clive?"

"Not really, only the usual stuff — occasional hair pulling with bullies, falling in love and getting their hearts broken with boys, not studying as diligently as they should, dabbling a bit in alcohol and marijuana," Clive said.

"When the twins misbehaved, who punished them, you or Elin?" Reed said.

Clive again cleared his throat.

"Elin always punished them, took away their electronics, made them do volunteer work at Metropolitan Ministries."

"Hmm, why Metropolitan Ministries, and not Catholic Charities?" Chenoa said.

"Elin has never been enthusiastic about the Roman Catholic Church, so she thought the Protestant Metropolitan Ministries was more preferable," Clive said. "Since I ceded Morgan and Cecelia's punishment to Elin — you know, I simply couldn't be harsh with my angels — I didn't question Elin's edicts."

Ravel clicked away at her laptop, then paused and looked directly at Clive.

"So we have here the ideal petri dish culture for twin microbes morphing into girls gone wild," Ravel said to Clive.

She seemed quite pleased with herself.

"How so?" Clive said defensively.

"Are you kidding me?" Ravel said. "Identical rich little brats, an overbearing mother who was way too young to have twins and probably resented her daughters' high station in life just handed to them, and an indulgent father who spoiled the twins by giving them way too much in place of showing tough love and a unified front with his young wife."

You go, girl, Chenoa thought. Couldn't have said it better.

Clive sat in silence for thirty seconds, then said, "So you all think it's my fault that Morgan and Cecelia disappeared."

Wake up the house band, Ravel thought. The pity party's back on.

"Please pardon Ravel's bluntness, Clive," Reed said. "All she's doing, in her inimitable way, is trying to construct a plausible context for the twins to up and vanish."

Clive nodded in agreement with Reed, though he was starting to dislike Ravel's unvarnished abrasiveness.

"Yes, well, all right . . ." Clive said.

Chenoa cut him off.

"So Morgan and Cecelia have been missing for ten days?" she asked.

"Yes," Clive answered.

Keep it short and simple, so I don't get manhandled again, he thought.

"And you have no theory as to why they're gone?" Reed said.

"No, not one," Clive said.

"And you reported your daughters missing to the police?" Ravel said. She no longer was looking at her laptop screen.

"When did you speak with the police, Clive?" Chenoa said.

Before Clive could answer, Ravel said, "He filed dual missing person reports with the Tampa Police Department seven days ago."

Smug didn't begin to describe the expression on Ravel's face.

"How did you know that?" Clive said.

"Latte da, latte da, it's nothing really," Ravel said, channeling a sort of French Swiss Annie Hall.

Clive looked at Reed and raised his bushy eyebrows.

"This isn't an exaggeration, Clive," Reed said. "Ravel is among the best computer hackers in the world. Obviously, she hacked into the Tampa Police Department's mainframe."

"*Absolument, mon petit gingersnap,*" Ravel said to Reed.

"Whatever, Ravel," Reed said. "And I am not your little gingersnap."

6
____

At Reed's request, Roman brought in more bottles of Evian, along with additional crystal tumblers. He then took the liberty of filling the tumblers with the French Alpine water.

As Roman passed Ravel on his way out of Reed's office, he stuck his tongue out at Ravel, who smiled and blew him a kiss.

Like herding cats, it really is, Reed thought.

"Clive, I'll reach out to Pete Langdon, a Tampa police detective. He'll be happy to give us a status report on your missing daughters," Reed said.

Detective Langdon was involved in the capture of the priest killers. Though Langdon came off as a first-class ass when he first met Reed, he redeemed himself in Reed's eyes by cooperating with her search for the priest killers. Langdon's stock also rose when Reed learned he attended the University of Notre Dame with Judi Ploszek, Reed's good friend and personal counsel.

"Thank you, Reed," Clive said. "I haven't heard word one from the police."

Chenoa finished her water and carefully placed the crystal tumbler on a leather Tampa Bay Lightning coaster on Reed's desk.

"How did you learn that Morgan and Cecelia were missing, Clive?"

"It was a Monday morning, Chenoa. Elin called me at my office, she said the girls weren't in their bedroom when she went to awaken them at eight a.m."

"Bedroom? Singular? You guys live in a mansion, and your daughters share a bedroom?" Ravel said, all the while tapping away on her laptop keyboard.

Clive smiled benevolently at Ravel.

"It's the nature of twins, they don't like to be separated."

"And was there anything unusual about the young women that previous weekend?" Reed said.

"No, not really, Elin and I were home all that weekend," Clive said. "Morgan and Cecelia were enjoying their summer before college. They seemed not the tiniest bit bored. They spent most of their time in their bedroom, but occasionally came out and chatted with me — even swam in the pool a couple times with them."

"With you, not with their mother?" Ravel asked, still not bothering to look up from her laptop.

"Yes, the girls grew apart from their mother as they got older, and they wanted to hang out only with me," Clive said. "But of course, I'm a very busy man, and I haven't always been there as an attentive father.

"Let's explore that a bit, Clive," Ravel said, using a mock serious tone. "How does that make you feel, not being there for your girls? Don't be hesitant in describing your *feelings*."

Clive started to get upset, so Reed jumped into this briar patch.

"You all, let's stay on track here," Reed said. "So, Clive, there were no signs Morgan and Cecelia were going to take flight, voluntarily or otherwise?"

"None," he said.

Clive was pouting and had returned to his monosyllabic responses. For better or worse, Ravel had gotten on his nerves.

Ravel then tipped her cards.

"Clive, sorry if I annoy you, but there's a strategy at work here. People actually are more forthcoming when they're angry — they're super focused and simply moil and toil harder. I bet you have one little detail that you didn't think to give to the police, but in this testy environ, you wonder if it might be useful."

Clive paused for a full minute.

Get those synapses popping, old man, Ravel thought. I mean, Jesus, your daughters' lives may be on the line. *Think*.

"Well, Ravel, there is one odd little detail," Clive said.

Wonder if he's referring to Ravel, Chenoa thought.

"That's just wishful thinking on your part, Chenoa," Ravel said. She raised her eyebrows and made a puckered "o" with her lips.

Now how does this brilliant little badger do that, Chenoa wondered.

"Probably not important, but Elin told me she overhead the twins talking about Don Quixote, of all things," Clive said. "I don't recall Morgan and Cecelia being assigned Miguel de Cervantes' *Don Quixote de la Mancha* at the Academy. And I doubt they would take on such a hefty tomb on their own. Thought it might yield a clue or two, so I read the very long novel — took me five consecutive nights of staying up until three in the morning. Helped me from not going crazy with worry."

Reed filled her and Clive's tumblers with Evian water. She took a healthy sip.

I love this water, and I don't care that it's expensive, or that Evian spelled backwards is "naive", she thought.

"What did you take away from reading *Don Quixote*, Clive?" Reed asked.

He gulped down his water.

"Not one thing as it pertains to my girls. I mean, four hundred years old, and it's still a helluva read — Don Quixote isn't just a sweet, demented old man who thinks he's a chivalrous knight performing brave deeds with his knight errant Sancho Panza, he's actually a meddling, at times cruel, old crank who is especially good at disrupting the lives of younger people . . . ."

And there was the group epiphany.

Reed, Ravel, Chenoa, and Clive all looked knowingly at each other. They all experienced the lightning bolt realization that a wicked older man might have masterminded a scheme to seduce Morgan and Cecelia away from their parents.

"Pardon the language, but as we used to say in West Virginia, shit fire and fall back in it," Reed said.

Mmm, that woman really is almost heaven, Ravel thought.

"What do you think, Reed, have we got a working hypothesis?" Chenoa asked.

Before Reed could answer, Ravel interjected.

"A working hypothesis?" she said. "This is a fucking solid gold lead."

"You may be right, Ravel," Reed said.

"Spot on?" Ravel said.

"Absolutely spot on," Reed answered.

Clive sat forward in his chair.

"Does this mean you'll take me on as a client, Reed?"

Reed smiled warmly at him. She, too, was leaning forward in her chair. Reed was never more beautiful and alluring than when she was in complete control of a situation.

Madam Dominatrix, may I please be your Number One Sub, Ravel thought.

"Clive, you became our client when you confided that Morgan and Cecelia were in trouble," Reed said. "Shall we go over our rates and expenses?"

Clive, the worry-weary father, answered for Clive, the crafty real estate developer.

"Nope, no need," he said. "I'll pay you a half-million retainer, plus a hundred thousand in advance for any and all expenses. Bring my girls home safe and sound, I'll pay you an additional half-million. Sound fair?"

"More than fair, Clive, you have a deal," Reed said.

Clive shook hands with Reed, Ravel, and Chenoa.

Reed buzzed Roman, asking him to bring in a standard investigative services agreement.

"Yes, ma'am, right away," Roman said over the speaker phone.

Yes, ma'am, and how else can I kiss your sweet little ass, Ravel thought. God, he's such a suck-up.

"Okay, Clive, here's how we're going to start out," Reed said. "First, you take good care of Elin, whom I'm sure is completely stressed out. Try to oversee your business empire as best you can. Go easy on the alcohol, maybe try to exercise, and get some sleep. Same goes for Elin. I don't want Morgan and Cecelia coming home to Deadheads for parents, okay?"

Clive gave her a confident thumbs up.

"Ravel, check online and in person any of the hinky places in Tampa Bay where young people might mix with older men," Ravel said. "El Castillo and the Hub are prime hunting grounds for predators, right?"

Reed was in executive mode — with each pronouncement, she chopped her right hand into the palm of her left hand.

"Tippity tap, gingersnap," Ravel said. She pursed her lips at Reed, who just shook her head in mock disapproval.

There are times Ravel is *almost* irresistible, Reed thought. Stop it, get back on point. Right now.

"Chenoa, I'll need you to check out the Catholic churches in Tampa," Reed said. "Attend Masses, visit the charities, chat with your former colleagues. Basically, be on the lookout for an older man who seems a bit too friendly with young people, especially young women."

"All right, Reed, I'll start after this meeting," Chenoa said.

In fact, she immediately began texting some of her old Catholic Church contacts; luckily, she had stayed in touch with several of these individuals.

"Thank you, Chenoa," Reed said. "Now, Clive, I take it you and your daughters attend Sacred Heart Catholic Church in South Tampa."

"Yes, that's right," Clive said. "In fact, Morgan and Cecelia had just recently begun attending daily Mass at Sacred Heart."

"Two eighteen-year-olds voluntarily attending daily Mass?" Ravel said. "Little odd, isn't it?"

Clive sat in repose like Rodin's sculpture *The Thinker*.

"Yes, well, hmm, now that you mention it, I guess it was a little odd," Clive said. "Matter of fact, when I asked to join them for a daily Mass, they strongly discouraged me."

"Jesus H. Christ!" Ravel yelled.

"Ravel, calm down," Reed said. "Clive just provided us another solid lead, one that Chenoa will need to check out."

Chenoa nodded affirmatively.

"Whatever," Ravel said.

"Whatever back atcha," Reed replied. "Now, Clive, it's time to execute the investigative services agreement, and for you to cut us a check. We need to rock and roll on this."

Clive gave Reed another thumbs up, then pulled out his checkbook from his sport coat pocket.

"And don't worry, Reed, Clive Baby has more than enough funds in his account to cover that check," Ravel said, as she closed her laptop.

Clive filled out a check and handed it to Reed.

"And how on earth, Ravel, do you know how much money I have in my account?" Clive said.

"Simple really, I correctly guessed your password," Ravel said smugly. "Your password is '*tvillingar*,' it's Swedish for 'twins.' "

7

____

It was six o'clock on an already warm Thursday morning in downtown Tampa. Reed and her husband Jake were snuggling in their master suite's king size bed. They lived in a penthouse apartment atop one of the tallest buildings in the downtown skyline, affording them a magnificent view of Channelside, Harbour Island, Davis Islands, and Tampa Bay.

Using a remote control from her bed, Reed opened the bedroom's floor-to-ceiling drapes.

Dawn was approaching — a narrow pink ribbon of light separated the horizon from the black sky.

And as luck would have it for Jake, Reed found a new day's sunrise a kind of aphrodisiac.

Jake was sleeping in the nude, as usual, and Reed had pulled away the white eiderdown duvet, so that she might admire Jake's lean, muscular body.

She kissed Jake's lips, then began gently stroking him.

"Goodness, Reed, weekday morning sex?" Jake said, as he caressed her pert breasts. "Why, thank you very much."

"Why, thank _you_ very much for your proper manscaping," Reed said with a sexy giggle.

"*Mais bien sur ma belle irlandaise Rose*," Jake said. He was French American, an unapologetic Francophile, and sometimes spoke French more often than the Queen's English.

"Actually, *mo fhear ceile dathuil*, I am your *wild* Irish rose," Reed said.

Reed, an Irish American, was learning Gaelic. She had just described Jake as her handsome husband.

At least I think I did, she thought.

Reed pushed Jake on to his back, and fiercely straddled him. In one quick motion, she pulled off her Milwaukee Bucks tee shirt — it was one of her favorite NBA shirts, as it bore the silhouette of a twelve-point buck and the slogan, "Fear the Deer."

Jake held Reed's hips as she ground back and forth in a rapidly increasing pace.

In the span of only three or four minutes, Reed achieved a delightful orgasm, and Jake followed suit right behind her.

For several minutes, Reed laid on top of Jake, who held her while gently running his fingers up and down her back.

As the sun rose in the east, the couple was about to fall back asleep; all of a sudden, Reed raised her head and said, "All right, Jakester, enough lollygagging, time to shower, make some cappuccinos, and go work out."

"Yes, ma'am," Jake responded with feigned weariness. "Geez, why am I so sticky? Any chance I could get a moistened hand towel?"

Reed pivoted off Jake and on to her back.

"No way, Jose," she said. "What *you* can do is get a hand towel for each of us."

Which Jake dutifully did.

Reed and Jake put on workout attire and headed to their yoga room, which actually was a four-hundred square foot converted bedroom. They had placed a plyometric rubber cover on the wood floor, installed mirrors on one wall, put in recessed lighting, and topped it off with a state-of-the-art Bose sound system, which continually played meditative spa music as well as a variety of nature sounds — waterfalls cascading, birds chirping, waves crashing on a beach.

As soon as they entered their yoga room, Reed and Jake looked over to a corner of the room and admired their latest addition: an amber grass sponge atop a four-foot oak pedestal. The natural sponge resembled a Dali-esque abstract vase within a vase. A single recessed light shown down on the sponge.

"Nature is our finest artist, isn't it," Reed said. "Where again did you find it?"

"A place called Sponge Diver Supply over in Tarpon Springs," Jake said. "The store owners' family has been in the natural sponge business for over a century."

"And wasn't there a really pleasant person at the store, she helped you choose your sponge, right?" Reed said, as she began to stretch.

"Yeah, her name is Cloe — such a cool name," Jake said, as he began doing lunges. "She's all of eighteen years old. Works full time at the shop and is getting ready to go to college. Lives with her mom and two sisters and three dogs — oh yeah, and a black bunny named Nibbles."

Reed marveled at how easily Jake gleaned so much information from people in the course of short conversations. And without being creepy about it.

And the guy retains all of that information, she thought.

Reed continued to stretch.

"What did Cloe teach you about our sponge?" she said.

"Well, I'm glad you asked," Jake said with a smile.

Oh Lord, he has switched to pedantic mode, Reed thought. Guess I asked for it.

"Cloe said the sponge starts out as a porifera, you know, a multi-organism with pores that water circulates through," Jake said.

Reed stopped stretching.

"Don't you mean, the porifera has pores through which water circulates?" she said.

Jake stopped stretching as well.

"What does that mean" he said defensively.

"Allow me to illustrate with a joke," Reed said. She began bending down and touching her toes.

Oh boy, thus begins the lesson, Jake thought.

"A freshman at the University of Florida comes up to a senior and says, 'Excuse me, but can you tell me where the library's at?' " Reed said.

She waved her arms in a circular motion.

"The senior says, 'Don't you know it's bad form to end a sentence with a preposition?' The freshman responds, 'Allow me to re-phrase: can you tell me where the library's at, *asshole*'."

Jake laughed as he performed consecutive knee-highs.

"Point taken," he said. "Allow *me* to re-phrase — the porifera has pores that water passes through, *smartass*."

"*Touche*, my dear. Now let's continue with our unit on sponges."

Reed made a circular motion with each ankle.

"Yes, well, let's see," Jake said. "Okay, Cloe told me the porifera grow on limestone as much as sixty feet below the Gulf of Mexico, the divers use a knife to remove the porifera from the limestone, which actually helps to re-grow the porifera."

Reed was rotating her knees by putting a hand on each kneecap and swishing her perfectly round and muscular buttocks.

I really love this part, Jake thought.

"I know what you're thinking, Jake, and cut it out," Reed said, as she continued with the O'Hara twerk. "Go on with your sponge lesson."

"Yes, ma'am," Jake said.

He was slightly embarrassed over getting caught leering at Reed.

"Once the divers fill up a net, the porifera are brought aboard the sponge boat and cleaned with a peroxide solution to remove the jelly residue and to turn them yellow. And *viola*! You now have natural sponges."

"And will our sponge sculpture ever decay?" Reed asked.

"Nope, it'll outlast all of us," Jake said.

Reed and Jake finished stretching, and began practicing yoga.

In unison, they went into *balasana*, or child's pose, which was Jake's favorite because it was so relaxing. Then they practiced *biralasana*, or cat's pose, which enhanced spine flexibility. *Sukhasana*, a cross-legged forward fold, followed. Reed could drop her head all the way to the floor — Jake, not so much. They then went into *virabhadrasana II*, the warrior two pose, then the side angle stretch called *parsvakona sana*, and shifted to warrior one pose, *virabhadrasana I*, and then the mighty pose of *utkatasana*. The couple completed their yoga workout by returning to the child's pose.

As Reed and Jake headed into the master bath, Jake said, "Reed, you know how yoga gives me a zen boner, so why don't we take a nice hot shower together, if you know what I mean — and I think you do."

Reed took off her workout attire, wrapped herself in a fluffy white bath towel, and checked on the temperature of the master bath's sauna. She thought it prudent this time for her to use the sauna and for Jake to shower alone.

"Not happening, buddy," she said. "We're not having a repeat of last week when we ended up making love all day and could check off only one item from our to-do list."

"Reed, darling, we don't make love," Jake said mischievously.

Reed opened the sauna door and the scent of eucalyptus wafted out.

"Oh no? What do we do if we don't make love?" Reed said. She assumed the worst would come out of Jake's mouth.

"We don't make love, Beautiful, we make art," Jake said.

"Way to class-up your seduction, my sexy beast, but it still won't work," Reed said. "While I'm in the sauna, you shower, then I'll shower after you. You know what Offspring sings, 'You gotta keep 'em separated.' "

"Oh, all right," Jake said with genuine sullenness.

"One more item before I go in the sauna and get my body all wet and glistening," Reed said. "The use of 'boner' is *never* a turn-on for a woman."

And with that, Reed entered the sauna, pulled off her towel, and began soaking in dry heat.

8

———————

Reed sat at the kitchen island and watched Jake prepare their breakfast. She wore tan dress slacks, a white dress shirt, and brown Everlane loafers. She almost went with Maylis Espadrilles, but decided the colorful embroidered fabric was a bit too showy for her day at the office.

Jake already had prepared two large cappuccinos. He busied himself filling marbled blue and white ceramic bowls with a layer of vanilla yogurt topped with granola and tropical fruit. He set down the breakfast bowls on the kitchen island and joined Reed.

Since they wouldn't see each other again until very late at night, Reed and Jake always got caught up at breakfast. And there was a lot to discuss: Reed's law practice, Jake's management of their cabaret night club Namaste, their private investigation services, and which free agent acquisitions and trades will the thirty NBA teams pull off during the summer offseason.

Reed took an ambitious sip of her cappuccino, leaving her with the cutest foam mustache on her upper lip.

Jake used his right index finger to wipe off Reed's foam mustache. He popped the finger into this mouth.

"Hmm, tasty," he said. "So what's going on with your law practice?"

Reed had just finished a tablespoon of yogurt, granola, and mango.

"It's starting to heat up," Reed said. "I'm representing Lola Petti-bone in a dispute with her three adult children over the substantial estate her deceased husband Peter left her in his will."

Jake was working on a large slice of papaya.

"Let me guess, the kids aren't happy with their cut," Jake said, as he scooped up yogurt and granola.

"Bingo is your name-o," Reed said. "Except, the children are furious that they received nothing — Peter wrote them out of the will."

"What's their argument, that Peter was suffering from diminished capacity when he cut them out?" Jake said. "Peter was pretty much an old fart, right?"

Reed ate a small chunk of watermelon with an even smaller piece of cantaloupe.

"I believe the legal term is 'old geezer,' Jake, and yes, Peter was eighty-seven when he passed," Reed said. "He appeared sound and alert enough at the time to recognize that his grown children didn't love him and only wanted his money — kind of sad, really."

Just then, three black turkey buzzards floated by their living room windows.

Don't take it as a sign, Reed, *please* don't take it as a sign, Jake thought.

"Hmm, the vultures are circling," Reed said. "Looks like a bad omen to me."

She smiled mischievously at Jake.

"You're doing the Vulcan mind read thing again, aren't you," Jake said.

"Yuppers," Reed said. "Anyways, we have a hearing in three weeks, but I'm probably going to recommend Lola settles with her children."

Jake ate some honeydew melon.

"I don't get it, if Peter was of a sound mind when he cut out the children, and his will was a legally executed document, why can't you and Lola fight this in court?" Jake said.

Reed took a sip of her cappuccino.

"Oh, we could play hardball in court, and we'd probably win," she said. "But it would take years and be very expensive — makes sense to settle and move on. Lola will still end up with about seventy-five million dollars."

"I feel you, Reed, it does make a lot of sense to settle," Jake said. "So what else is happening at the O'Hara Law Group?"

"Well, I'm representing five women from The Spring. They want restraining orders on their violently abusive husbands and then file for divorce."

The Spring was a domestic violence center that provided a safe haven and support services primarily to women who were victims of domestic violence. Since 1977, The Spring helped over sixty-thousand adults and their children — and even their pets. The safe haven complex was located somewhere in East Hillsborough County, though its exact location was a well-kept secret.

"You're representing these women *pro bono*, of course," said Jake, who was a big supporter of The Spring.

In fact, he recently donated his beloved candy-apple red Range Rover to be auctioned off at The Spring gala fundraiser. The auctioned Range Rover yielded forty-thousand dollars, all of which went directly to The Spring's operational account.

"*Pro bono* it is," Reed said. "It's a yin and yang process for my law practice — the paying clients help me to represent other clients for free."

"Very zen, my love," Jake said.

Reed finished her cappuccino, then cracked open a chilled bottle of San Pellegrino fizzy mineral water.

"How is it at Namaste?" Reed asked

As manager of Namaste, Jake oversaw the twenty-five stage performers, worked with Chef Glenn in the smooth operation of Namaste's kitchen and restaurant, relied on Andre and his assistant Sierra, who also was a performer, to maintain tight security at the nightclub, and partnered with Ravel in keeping the books up to date and totally above board.

And just to make his job a bit more challenging, he often played original piano compositions while the performers were on stage.

Typically, Jake came in to Namaste at four p.m. and rarely made it back to the penthouse before four a.m. At least twice a week, though, he arrived at noon at Namaste to work on musical compositions at his piano.

"All's well at Namaste," Jake said. "Tatiana is in her third trimester and is about to go on maternity leave, so I hired Sehar. She's from New Delhi, India, and has fled from an insufferable arranged marriage that her parents tried to force on her."

"Did you have your contacts at the CIA check out her story?"

Jake flinched slightly at the mention of the Central Intelligence Agency. Though he rarely talked about his experiences at the CIA, Reed knew Jake had committed a multitude of violent and ugly acts all on behalf of God and Country. She also understood that he continued to be ravaged by PTGD — Post Traumatic Guilt Disorder. Aware that Jake stayed in touch with some of his former colleagues at the CIA, though, she sometimes asked Jake to have his buds vet Namaste's potential employees, as they often came from all over the world.

"Yes, my guys properly vetted her, and Sehar's story checks out," Jake said. "Plus, she tested negative for alcohol, illegal drugs, and nicotine. Fun fact, by the way, Sehar is all of four feet ten inches tall. Apparently, she's a helluva horse rider."

"Really? Has Ravel shown interest in Sehar?" Reed asked.

Ravel was adamant about avoiding sexual harassment, yet sometimes she had a hard time keeping her libido in check, particularly when a tiny attractive woman was involved.

"She did say to me that she'd like to put Sehar in her backpack and take her home," Jake said.

"Is that true, did Ravel really say that?" Reed said.

"Yes, but she was only kidding — all right, maybe half kidding," Jake said. "I told her to cut it out, and she mumbled and muttered that she'd behave."

"Do you believe her?" Reed asked.

"Yeah, sort of," Jake said.

"I guess that will have to do for now," Reed said. "And Tatiana, how's she?"

"*Very* pregnant, but what a stud — she wants to keep performing for one more week," Jake said.

Tatiana Smolenkov was a former ballerina from Kiev, Ukraine. Wasting away in Tampa, she abused marijuana and cocaine and alcohol, getting by with occasional stints at the city's ignoble strip bars. Through her employment at Namaste, Tatiana got clean and sober, and was making an excellent living as a performer. She and her daughter Katarina lived in a modest condominium in West Tampa. When Tatiana got pregnant with her somewhat steady boyfriend, she declined his marriage proposal, as she felt more empowered being single.

"I know what you're thinking, Jake," Reed said.

"Oh really, what am I thinking, my Gregori Rasputin wannabe," he said.

"With Tatiana, it's that Mother Earth turn-on of yours," Reed said. "When she's on stage and she takes off her top, you're mesmerized by her full breasts and big round belly."

Jake blushed.

"I have to admit Tatiana's performances tickle my ivories," he said. "Does that make me kind of a pig?"

Reed patted his hand.

"Not at all, my dear," she said. "There's nothing wrong with your admiring a woman's beauty. I admit your fascination with pregnant women is a bit eccentric, but even that's okay. I know for a fact that you'd never cross the line over to creepy male ooginess."

"No, no I wouldn't, Reed. I already have ample baggage to carry around."

Reed rose from her chair and carried both coffee mugs over to the espresso machine in the kitchen. She had no intention of making cappuccinos — it was her little ploy for getting Jake to prepare them.

"No, no, no, let me do it, Reed," Jake said. He moved into the kitchen with the agility of a Belizean black jaguar. "I will not allow you to wrest away a grand purpose in my life."

"As you wish, my dear Alphonse," Reed said.

Little surprise that her Mona Lisa smile appeared. Her sparkling blue eyes, which easily could start a war, were never more alluring than when she wanted Jake to do her bidding.

In five minutes, Jake had made two large cappuccinos. This week, he was using Lavazza Perfetto, a full-bodied Italian espresso roast. He had had his first cup of Lavazza coffee in a small restaurant in Nassau, Bahamas. He fell in love with the brew right then and there.

"There you go, *mon petit fromage*," Jake said. He set down the cappuccino in front of Reed at the kitchen table.

"Thanks, but call me your 'little cheese' again, and I won't teach you *sasankasana*," Reed said.

"The hare pose?" Jake said in a mock shock tone. "Say it ain't so."

"Oh, it's so," Reed answered.

"Well then, no more *mon petit fromage*, *mon petit lapin*," Jake said.

Both of them laughed heartily at Jake calling Reed his "little bunny."

"Now, any private investigations of which I should be made aware?" Jake asked.

Reed drank more of her cappuccino.

"Perfect sentence construction," she said. "And yes, a major case came in yesterday. I'm going to need your help, and we'll probably bring in Andre and Sierra as well. I already have Ravel and Chenoa doing spadework."

"Reed O'Hara, you have my complete attention."

"Yesterday afternoon, real estate developer Clive Cutler told me in my office that his twin daughters Morgan and Cecelia have been missing for ten days. After the first three days, he reported the eighteen-year-olds as missing to the Tampa Police Department. Nothing has turned up yet."

"And do we know whether the twins simply took off or have been kidnapped?"

"We don't know, but it may be a situation that's right in between," Reed said.

"Okay, sounds intriguing. No phone calls? No ransom demands?"

"Zip, zero, nada," Reed said. "Which makes it so puzzling. Clive doesn't think Morgan and Cecelia — I mean, good God, they're adults — upped and ran away. Granted, their passports are missing, but their bank accounts haven't been touched. And they left all of their belongings, including their dresses, their jeans, their shoes, their make-up, their jewelry."

"Maybe they took off, acting on an impulse," Jake offered. "Any boyfriends — or girlfriends — involved?"

"Nope, Morgan and Cecelia rarely had boyfriends, like so many other twins, they seemed to prefer each other's company," Reed said.

"Could the parents have driven them away?"

"Maybe. Clive hasn't been around very much, what with building his empire of dirt," Reed said. "Elin, the mother, doesn't seem particularly well connected with her daughters. She's secular now, but was raised as a protestant in the Church of Sweden. She wasn't enamored with the twins attending the Academy of Holy Names and going to Catholic Mass regularly. To be fair, this is according to Clive — I haven't yet spoken with Elin."

"Yeah, smart to hear from both sides. Has anything odd occurred recently?"

"Two seemingly disparate items," Reed said. "First, Morgan and Cecelia had been attending daily Mass every day, and they didn't want their father joining them. Second, and this is really peculiar, Elin overhead them talking about Don Quixote, you know, from the Spanish novel *Don Quixote de la Mancha*."

"What the hell, Reed," Jake said. Did you say 'Don Quixote'?"

"Yes, Don Quixote, why?"

"Don *Quixote*?"

"Yes, absolutely," Reed said. "Jake, what's going on?"

There's *no* fucking way, he thought.

"What? Oh, nothing," Jake said. "Sometimes I get nasty flashbacks at the most inopportune times."

"Are you all right?" Reed asked, showing genuine concern for her sunshine husband burdened with a dark past.

"I'm fine, really I am," Jake said. "The flashback already has passed. So what's your game plan, my love?"

"The plan is multi-pronged, like a mullet hook," Reed said. "Our working theory is that someone, maybe an older man acting as a father figure, has persuaded the twins to run off with him. I'm going to meet with Elin Cutler this afternoon. Ravel is checking out hangouts in Tampa, St. Petersburg, and Clearwater where older people meet younger ones. Ravel will coordinate with Sierra and Andre. The

Catholic Church is Chenoa's old stomping grounds, so she's reaching out to local nuns and priests, especially at Sacred Heart Catholic Church, where Morgan and Cecelia attended Mass."

Jake picked up the breakfast dishes and carried them into the kitchen. He started rinsing the dishes in the farmhouse sink, in preparation for putting them in the dishwasher.

"And how can I help?" he asked.

"Listen, you've got your hands full running Namaste, which will be demanding for you, what with Ravel, Sierra, and Andre sometimes not being there," Reed said.

"Yeah, you're right, of course," Jake said. He finished neatly placing the dishes into the dishwasher. "How about I check out the Don Quixote angle? I got a hunch that my old buds in the biz might be useful."

"That would be wonderful of you, my gorgeous Frenchman."

She walked back tentatively into the kitchen, as she was in unfamiliar territory. She gave Jake a passionate kiss.

"Wow," Jake said, as he began to nuzzle her long, elegant neck. "Care for a second round of making . . . art?"

Reed held Jake at arm's length.

"*Ni tharlaionn se,*" she said in Gaelic.

"Not happening, huh? Fine, fine, fine. I suppose we should get going, but first, how is your co-ed basketball league coming along?"

Reed busied herself putting paperwork into her gold leather briefcase that cost her a thousand euros at Galleries Lafayette in Paris.

"We're in the preliminary stages, which is okay since I don't expect opening tip-off until next summer," Reed said. "I'm getting movers and shakers like Clive Cutler and Harry Balzac to support the proposed league. Since I have this new case, I'll rely on Roman to continue reaching out to the local sports community."

"All sounds good, *mon amour,*" Jake said. "So, no time to talk about NBA trades and free agents?"

"Nope, we both need to get going," Reed said. "Tell you what, tomorrow morning, while I'm 'arting' your brains out, we'll talk about Kevin Durant and Kyrie Irving going to Brooklyn — I'll even wear my Nets tee shirt."

"Can't wait for tomorrow morning," Jake said.
With that, the couple set out to conquer the day.

9

———

The only way Chenoa could persuade Father Jack, a notorious cheapskate, to join her for lunch at the Columbia Restaurant in Ybor City was to offer to pick up the check.

"I can order anything I want and you'll get the check?" Father Jack said over the telephone.

"Yes, I'll pick up the tab, Jack," Chenoa said.

"I'll be at the Columbia at one p.m. sharp, and I'll bring a voracious appetite," Father Jack said.

He then clicked off.

"I'm sure you will," Chenoa muttered to herself.

While a nun, Chenoa had been a close confidant to Father Jack, who was appalled at so many of his fellow priests sexually preying on minors while the Roman Catholic Church hierarchy covered up their horrific acts.

Father Jack wasn't exactly a Boy Scout himself — rumors swirled about his having an affair with Sister Chenoa. However, he did his best to adhere to his priestly vows, and he always counseled Sister Chenoa wisely and lovingly whenever she had a problem.

Though he was aware of most of her weaknesses and fallacies, Father Jack never figured out that Sister Chenoa had a dark secret connected to the murder of pedophilic priests in Tampa Bay. When Sister Chenoa relinquished her vows, Father Jack was both puzzled and disheartened.

Since he hadn't seen Sister Chenoa for over a year, Father Jack was elated when she called to ask him out to lunch. Hailing from Canada, which endures a mostly deserved reputation for being a nation of penny pinchers, Father Jack was doubly elated that Sister Chenoa would pay for his lunch — at the Columbia, of all places.

Even on a weekday afternoon, parking was scarce on Ybor City's Seventh Avenue, where the Columbia has been situated since 1905. Luckily, Chenoa finally found a parking space not a hundred feet from the storied restaurant.

As she approached the Columbia, she admired the restaurant's arches and tile work, so reminiscent of the Moorish Alhambra Palace in Grenada, Spain.

Father Jack was waiting for Chenoa inside the cool, darkened waiting area of the restaurant. He was a handsome forty-year-old man who had jet black hair, deep brown eyes, a square jaw, and a deep tan, as he played a lot of golf and tennis in his off hours. He was physically fit and kept a narrow waistline.

As an outward sign of his dedication to Roman Catholic tradition, he was wearing on this sunny and humid afternoon in Tampa a full-length black cassock with a white Roman collar and black sash. His cassock's buttons, trim, and inside hem were black, not red or purple, for he had not yet risen to the upper levels of the Church's hierarchy.

His lone tell that he kept one foot — rather, two feet — in the secular world was his shoes: seven-hundred dollar black Thom Browne pebble-grain longwing brogues.

Father Jack immediately spotted Chenoa, so resplendent in an alluring bright yellow halter sundress and Christian Louboutin gladiator high-heeled sandals.

The priest gave the former nun a lingering hug, then smiled warmly at her.

"Sister Chenoa, I feel like Icarus around you and that dress," Father Jack said.

"Yeah, well, you probably should take your Holy Father's advice and not fly too close to the sun," Chenoa said.

"True that, Sister, true that," Father Jack said. He released his tentacle-like grasp of Chenoa.

"And, Jack, please don't address me as 'Sister'. The fact that I'm showing so much cleavage in this very expensive Zimmermann should say quite succinctly that I'm no longer a Bride of Christ."

Father Jack smiled endearingly.

"Fair enough, Chenoa," he said. "I guess it's a bad habit of mine to always see a person in only one way."

"Be careful, Jack, bad habits can be your ultimate downfall," Chenoa said.

This time, she smiled at him in an equally endearing manner.

This woman melts the wax on my wings, Father Jack thought.

The pair was seated at a table in the Columbia's bar, which had seen little change over several decades.

Chenoa admired the diamond pattern in the tile floor, the long oak bar with chair-backed stools, and the three sets of liquor shelves framed in arches. The old bar reminded her of a bacchanal altar.

Father Jack studied the lunch menu as if he were an archaeologist pouring over the Dead Sea Scrolls.

"Did you know, Sister, er, Chenoa, that the Columbia is Florida's oldest restaurant and is the largest Spanish restaurant in the world?" Father Jack said. "The Hernandez Gonzmart family opened the Columbia in 1905 as a corner café catering to the Ybor City cigar makers."

Chenoa smirked at Father Jack.

"Yes, I do know all that," Chenoa said. "It's on their website."

Well, so much for *my* going on the Columbia's website this morning, Father Jack thought.

He slumped in his cane chair and began sulking like Jackie Cooper, pouting lower lip and all.

"Jack, I'm sorry for being curt with you," Chenoa said.

She took a sip of a lychee juice and prickly pear nectar blend the attractive Hispanic bartender had prepared for her. She winked at the bartender, indicating her approval of the young man's mixology and of his devilishly good looks.

Not at all intimidated by Chenoa's flirtation, the bartender simply returned the wink and smiled at her.

Before I leave, I'm going to give that *guapo* my card, Chenoa thought.

"I accept your apology, Chenoa, but *really*, do you have to flirt with another man in front of me?" Father Jack said.

Chenoa set down her drink and looked directly at Father Jack.

"I'm no longer a nun, *Jack*, so I no longer give two hoots about the patrician Catholic Church trying to control every aspect of my life. I'm no longer being held down by The Man — at least not if I don't want him to."

"That's all fine and dandy, you know, but I thought we had a special relationship that entailed your demonstrating kindness and respect toward me."

"A special relationship! A special relationship!" Chenoa said loud enough for other patrons around her to take notice.

"Chenoa, please, let's not make a scene — you know how heated words ruin my appetite," Father Jack said.

He took a healthy sip of his appletini.

Crap, too much cider and not enough Belvedere, he thought.

"Ruin your appetite?" Chenoa said. "You couldn't ruin your appetite if we were having lunch in a slaughterhouse."

"That's uncalled for, Chenoa."

Chenoa finished her juice blend and held up her glass, signaling to *el guapo* that she wanted another. The eager bartender acknowledged her request, and immediately began fixing her drink.

"I'll tell you what's uncalled for, Jack, is your claiming that we have a special relationship," she said. "Just because we screwed a few times in the confessional booth doesn't mean that we have a special relationship."

A young blonde woman was having lunch with a much older man at the table next to Chenoa and Father Jack's. She overhead Chenoa and smiled knowingly at her.

Chenoa ignored the woman, as she was furious with Father Jack — her normally porcelain-hued complexion had turned coral pink.

The priest recognized that a flushed Chenoa was a dangerous Chenoa.

"You're absolutely right, and I'm sorry," he said. "What do you say we call a truce and order our lunch?"

"Truce it is," Chenoa said.

Father Jack ordered *empanadas de picadillo*, *croquetas de langosta*, *mussels y chorizo Andres*, and *scallops casimiro*.

"No red snapper *adelita?*" Chenoa asked sarcastically.

"No, no, don't want to overdo it," Father Jack said, oblivious to Chenoa's sarcasm.

Chenoa ordered a 1905 salad, which combined iceberg lettuce with julienne of baked ham, Swiss cheese, tomatoes, and olives in a garlic sauce.

"Did you know iceberg lettuce originally was called crisphead," Father Jack said. "Iceberg lettuce got its name from the ice layered on heads of lettuce that were shipped by train to Tampa."

"Jack, I swear to God, if you don't stop pontificating, I'm going to stiff you with the bill — or, sorry, I meant *'la cuenta'*."

Probably would, too, Father Jack thought.

Go ahead, Jack, see if I'm bluffing, Chenoa thought.

Father Jack raised his hands in surrender.

"Okay, Chenoa, enough bloviation on my part," he said, as he gave her his five-star smile.

Man oh man, Jack is a charmer, Chenoa thought. And one heck of a good lay in tight spaces.

The server brought Chenoa her salad and Jack his four plates of Spanish food.

Father Jack said grace while Chenoa stared out the window.

"So I'm not allowed to wax poetic on these lobster croquettes?" Father Jack said.

"Not unless you want to pay for them," Chenoa said. She forked an olive and a piece of *crisphead* lettuce.

"Think I'll just eat," the priest said. He picked up his fork and knife.

For the next fifteen minutes, he and Chenoa ate their lunch in silence.

Father Jack put down his fork, wiped his mouth with a white cloth napkin, and proceeded to order two *cafe con leches* — an exquisite combination of espresso and steamed milk.

Chenoa nodded her approval.

This lunch is going to cost Reed a hundred fifty dollars, she thought.

"So what do you have for me, Jack?" Chenoa said, as she stirred sugar into her *cafe con leche*.

She purposely leaned forward to afford Father Jack a view of her splendid cleavage.

The priest first gazed down at the former nun's breasts, then said, "You gave me pretty short notice, Chenoa, but you've lucked out."

"How so?" she asked, as she lightly ran an index finger across her right breast. It was an overt ploy on her part, yet Father Jack was well on his way to being hypnotized by her sensuality.

Holy Viagra, I could make a habit of this, he thought. The heck with my parishioners, my church, and my vows.

"You told me yesterday that time was of the essence, that two young women were quite possibly in grave danger," Father Jack said, as he shifted uncomfortably in his chair. "Though you wouldn't tell me their names, I figured out you were talking about the Cutler twins, Morgan and Cecelia."

"How did you know that?"

"Clive Cutler and his daughters have been faithfully attending Sacred Heart for many years, though I've never once met the mother."

Chenoa finished her *cafe con leche*, then ordered two more for her and Father Jack.

"And send a *cafe con leche* to the elderly gentleman who's sitting next to that young woman," she said to the server. "Looks as if the old guy is falling asleep."

Again, the young woman overheard Chenoa, and waved enthusiastically to the former nun. Her aged date had no idea of what was going on, though he was pleased when the coffee arrived at his table.

"Jack, you get a cookie for figuring out that the Cutler twins are involved — though I emphasize it's a *metaphorical* cookie, because I'm not buying you anymore food."

"Whatever, Chenoa," the priest said. "You asked me if there have been any middle-age or older men hanging around Sacred Heart with young people in general, or with two young women in particular."

"And . . . ." Chenoa said.

"And among the handful of candidates, one gentleman stands out. I first noticed him attending high Mass on Sunday. He's strikingly hand-some for a man in his fifties. He has a magnificent mane of silver hair, and wears a long-sleeved *guayabera*. Say, did you know *guayabera* shirts originated in the Philippines, then migrated first to Spain and then to Cuba and Mexico?"

"Jack!"

"Sorry, sorry," Father Jack said sincerely. "Afraid I can't resist a teachable moment. Anyways, this gentleman, whose name is Fernando Gonzalez, in recent weeks began attending *daily* Mass — at about the same time Morgan and Cecelia began attending *daily* Mass at Sacred Heart. Interestingly, Clive Cutler never went to daily Mass with his daughters, and Fernando Gonzalez always sat in a pew directly behind the twins."

Chenoa had pushed her chair back, sat slightly askew, and crossed her legs. Her right leg was slowly rocking up and down, and the short sundress exposed her milky white thigh.

At that point, Father Jack was a goner, completely under Chenoa's sexual spell.

"Did you yourself ever see Fernando Gonzalez and the twins at daily Mass?" Chenoa said. "And if so, did you speak with them?"

Father Jack continued to squirm in his chair. He appeared in need of the restroom; in reality, he was trying to deal with an erection under his cassock.

"Yes and yes," he said. "I saw the three of them after a daily Mass. They were leaving Sacred Heart together, with Gonzalez walking ahead of Morgan and Cecelia — the twins couldn't have been more than three feet behind Gonzalez. I said hello to Morgan and Cecelia, and introduced myself to Gonzalez, who was courteous yet distant with me. Frankly, he made me feel as if I were an interloper. The twins were barely communicative, and looked first at Gonzalez before answering my one and only question, which was concerned with the well-being of their parents."

Chenoa put her right elbow on the table and rested her chin in her right hand.

"Your tone toward Gonzalez is rather negative," she said. "Did he do something to upset you? Now be honest, Jack. You're talking with an intimate friend, a *very* intimate friend."

Father Jack no longer cared that he had pitched a tent in his cassock.

"All right, I'll tell you, though I don't like to speak ill of people. When that sonuvabitch was leaving our holy church, he pulled out an enormous cigar and threw the plastic wrapper in the holy water font. And he made sure that I saw him do it."

Chenoa reached over and held Father Jack's hand.

"I'm so sorry, Jack, I'm sure that obscene gesture deeply offended you," she said. "So when did all of this happen?"

Father Jack held on to Chenoa's hand. The young woman at the table next to them was mesmerized by this passion playlet.

"Two weeks ago, and that was the last time I saw them," Father Jack said.

Chenoa untangled her legs and sat straight up.

"Jack, you've been a huge help, you really have. I'll divulge that my employer has been engaged to find Morgan and Cecelia. Our client may give you a generous reward if this pans out."

Father Jack found Chenoa and her offer of a reward enticing.

"Humph, well, let's see, if my information bears fruit, and Morgan and Cecelia come home safely, then Clive Cutler can get a me a lifetime membership to Palma Ceia Country Club."

Chenoa laughed loudly.

"Jack, you're one cagey priest who has very big balls. But you know what, I think we probably can work something out, okay?"

"All right, but tell Cutler that it has to be a *lifetime* membership."

"You're very greedy, but I can live with that," Chenoa said. "Funny though, I thought for sure you were going to ask to screw me again as your reward."

"Oh, don't tempt me, Chenoa. But I have to admit that, being a card-carrying member of the *hoi polloi*, it would be sweet to take those elitist assholes' money on their own golf course."

"I respect that, I really do," Chenoa said.

She paid the lunch tab with her American Express Platinum card. Father Jack admired her high-end credit card.

"My, how we've come up in the world," he said.

Chenoa accepted the compliment with a brief nod.

"Chenoa, before we go, may I ask you a very personal question?" Father Jack asked.

"Sure, why not, you've earned it."

But not if you ask me about the priest murders, she thought.

"When you were a nun, you once told me that you never wore panties under your tunic," Father Jack said. "Was that true?"

"Abso-fucking-lutely," she said.

As the pair rose from their table and started to leave the Columbia, the young woman waved to Chenoa.

"Excuse me, hon, I'm sorry to bother you, but is priesty here your boyfriend?" she asked.

Standing closer to the woman, Chenoa realized she wasn't as attractive as she had first thought.

Good from far, but far from good, she thought.

"Absolutely not, *hon*," Chenoa said.

Just before she left the bar, Chenoa handed her business card to the handsome bartender.

"*Llamame, el guapo*," Chenoa said to the young man.

"*Si, por supuesto, la senorita bonita*," he answered.

10

———

At about the same time Chenoa was leaving the Columbia Restaurant in Ybor City, Reed arrived at the Cutler mansion on Bayshore Boulevard in South Tampa.

She had had a productive morning at her law office, calling several clients, working on the restraining order requests and divorce filings for the five women laying low at The Spring, even interviewing a talented, energetic woman for the commissioner position of her proposed basketball league.

Unfortunately, she didn't have time to fine tune a stock purchase agreement that had to be ready in three days. But time definitely was of the essence with the Cutler case, and the sooner she spoke with Elin Karlsson Cutler the better.

Swedes are cold weather people who tend to button up, she thought. Hope the Tampa tropics have loosened up Elin.

Approaching the front door of the Cutler mansion, she was impressed with its Greek revivalist architecture and precisely mani-cured landscaping that featured massive azalea hedges, a perfect St. Augustine lawn, and six-feet-high ilex schilling hedge rows that bordered the front property.

Feel like Dorothy arriving at Oz, she thought. Only where's my scarecrow, lion, and tin man?

Upon Reed ringing the doorbell, which played Beethoven's *Für Elise* piano bagatelle, an attractive woman in her thirties answered the door. She wore a black suit with a white dress shirt and narrow black tie. Her long blonde hair was in a tight bun, and she wore no make-up. The woman's eyes were the color of green olives.

"Good afternoon, Ms. O'Hara, we've been looking forward to your arrival," the woman said. "Miss Elin is waiting for you in the library."

Now I know how Phillip Marlowe felt, Reed thought. And this woman is one good looking mortician.

Reed entered a grand foyer that could bivouac a platoon in a pinch.

She had to admit that the woman's black high heels went well with the suit, though the heels tapping on the white marble floor was annoying.

"Bet you don't sneak up on too many people in those pumps, do you," Reed said.

"No, I don't, but that's the idea around here," the woman said with a Scandinavian accent.

"Are you a butler?" Reed said. "And what's your name? Where are you from?"

The woman stopped walking.

"I guess that's the nature of a private investigator, isn't it, asking a lot of nosy questions," she said. "All right then, since you're here to help find Morgan and Cecelia, I'll answer your questions."

She stood in front of Reed. Her arms were folded across her chest and her heeled left foot was slightly askew.

"I am indeed a butler, though we prefer to call ourselves household managers, since that title better describes all of our duties," she said. "My name is Mala Karlsson, and I'm from Stockholm, Sweden."

Reed was taken aback at Mala's response.

"Did you say 'Karlsson'?" Reed said. "Are you related to Elin?"

Mala gave Reed a smile that would have inspired Leonardo da Vinci.

"Well, you get a *vaniljkakor*," Mala said.

Reed frowned, then tilted her head.

"A *vaniljkakor* is a Swedish cookie," Mala said.

Both women laughed.

Talk about a Kodak moment — a Swede actually laughing, Reed thought.

"So yes, I am related to Miss Elin," Mala said. "I am her first cousin."

Feigning a Southern drawl, Reed said, "Well, around these parts, you're what we call 'blood'."

"A Blood, not a Crip?" Mala said, as she raised her blonde eyebrows and smiled mischievously.

"Now you get a *vaniljkakor*," Reed said.

Again both women laughed.

"Seriously, though, while Miss Elin is my older cousin, we keep it on a very professional level while she is my employer."

Nice touch, her slipping in she's the younger of the two cousins, Reed thought.

Definitely have to introduce this clever woman to Ravel and Sierra.

As the two women walked together, Reed saw an amazing sight out in the large backyard: four black labs were splashing around in an immense swimming pool while a lifeguard watched over them.

Reed and Mala eventually made it down the basilica-length hallway to the library.

The mansion library was large enough to meet the needs of a small college. The walls were twenty-feet high and lined with oak bookshelves. There literally were thousands of books on the shelves. A stairway led to a narrow balcony that wrapped around the entire library. The centerpiece of the library was a ten-foot wide Francesco Molon Presidential Executive desk. In front of the desk sat two Acacia leather reading chairs. There was a Tiffany floor lamp positioned next to each reading chair. Off in a corner was a contemporary Daydream chaise lounge. It, too, had a floor lamp — its chrome globe and arching steel cable pole made it resemble a spermatozoon astronaut.

That chaise lounge is way too modern for this room, Reed thought. Bet it's Clive's concession to Elin.

"If you're wondering if my chaise is one of the few instances where

I actually got my way around this museum, you're exactly right," Elin said.

She was standing in front of the desk that was the size and style of a *Titanic* lifeboat.

"Ms. Reed O'Hara, allow me to introduce you to Mrs. Elin Karlsson Cutler, spouse to Mr. Clive Cutler and mother to *mademoiselles* Morgan and Cecelia," Mala said.

Reed and Elin Cutler met at the halfway point of the library and shook hands.

All right, shake hands and come out fighting. And let's have a clean fight, Reed thought.

"So I get to finally meet the famous Reed O'Hara," Elin said. Despite her reddened eyes and obvious stress fatigue, she was a stunningly beautiful Scandinavian woman — statuesque, tan complexion, dark brown eyes shaped like almonds, long flaxen blonde hair.

"Equal parts famous and infamous, I'm afraid," Reed said. "I'm very glad to meet you, or should I say, *jag ar glad att se dig.*"

"I haven't heard Swedish in so very long," Elin said. "I don't even allow Mala to speak Swedish around our home — don't want Clive to feel excluded, you know."

Mala looked away. She wasn't smiling.

"I understand, Elin, so I won't inflict any more of my bad Swedish upon you," Reed said. "I just wish it were under better circumstances for us to meet."

"I agree, but come, let's sit down in these wonderfully comfortable chairs and talk, as I feel my maternal worry clock is ticking away relentlessly," Elin said.

After settling into an overstuffed leather reading chair, Reed said, "So, Elin, no word yet of your daughters?"

Elin exhaled slowly.

"No, not a word," she said, resignation darkening her tone. "And that will be all for now, Mala."

Mala nodded to Elin, walked out of the library, stopped and turned around and slowly closed the library's massive pocket doors.

"So Mala is your cousin," Reed said.

"Yes, but it was unprofessional of a household manager to divulge personal information to a guest — I overhead you two talking," Elin said.

"Even if the guest is a private investigator trying to find your daughters?" Reed asked.

Elin paused, then said, "No, you're right, you need any and all information about us. I guess sometimes I forget that Mala is related to me."

"How do you and Mala get along?"

Jiminy Cricket, what's a person gotta do to get a glass of water around here, she thought.

"We get along just fine, we maintain a strict employer and employee relationship," Elin said. "Why do you ask? Do you suspect Mala?"

Whoa, slow down there, little lady, Reed thought.

"My approach as an investigator is to suspect everybody — even myself," Reed said, hoping a bit a levity might relax Elin.

It worked: Elin giggled ever so slightly.

"Excuse me, but I have not laughed since my girls disappeared," Elin said. "But seriously, do you suspect Mala — no evasive jokes this time."

"Not necessarily. I'd simply like to know if your butler resents your obvious wealth and high social station."

"Household manager."

"What?"

"I dislike butler, household manager better describes Mala's many responsibilities."

"Fine, does your household manager slash cousin seem jealous of your success?"

"Not at all, in fact, she's very appreciative of my bringing her over here and giving her such a fine chance for success," Elin said. "Tell me, have you read Stieg Larsson's *The Girl with the Dragon Tattoo?*"

"No, should I?"

"Yes, because that novel captures the real Sweden," Elin said. "You know, Sweden is not all snow skiing and saunas and fjords, there's dwindling opportunity for young Swedes there."

"Which is why you came here, and why you brought Mala here?"

"Exactly, though I admit I was very lucky to meet my Prince Charming while I was slinging cocktails in the Palma Ceia clubhouse lounge," Elin said. "But wait, please forgive my bad manners, would you like something to drink?"

Well that took friggin' forever, Reed thought.

"Yes, some sparkling mineral water, please."

Elin rose from her chair, walked over to that desk on steroids, and pressed a button on the console.

"Have some Saratoga brought in, Mala," said Elin, who then returned to her chair.

"Saratoga mineral water, in the cobalt blue bottle?" Reed said.

"That's the one," Elin said with a *soupcon* of smugness.

"Saratoga is so hard to find in Tampa Bay."

"I'll send a case over to your office."

Yeah right, Reed thought, it's just like in the movies — rich people never follow through on their gestures of generosity. Guess I'll have to get off my butt and find Saratoga online. That cobalt blue bottle is very cool.

"So let's shift our focus to you and the twins," Reed said. "Being in their late teens, have Morgan and Cecelia shown any signs of rebellion, especially of late?"

Elin attempted to lean forward in her leather marshmallow of a chair.

"That's what is so odd, Reed, my girls have never given me any real trouble. I admit Morgan and Cecelia have always had a stronger bond with Clive, but so much of that has to do with the fact that he's the pamperer, while I've been the *de riguer* enforcer."

Hmm, have to check with Jake to find out if she's using *de riguer* correctly, Reed thought. Goodness, where's a French orthographer when you need one? Or is it French grammarian? French usage specialist? Focus, Reed, focus.

"How were the twins before they disappeared?" Reed asked.

"Quite distant and uncommunicative to the both of us."

Just then, a maid, carrying a tray with a large bottle of Saratoga and two ice-filled tumblers, walked into the study. She made it look easy opening one of the large pocket doors while holding the tray.

"Did you make the ice with Saratoga?" Elin asked the African-American woman, who wore a peach pincord tunic.

"Yes, ma'am," the maid said.

"Please put the tray on the council table," Elin said. "And that'll be all."

"Yes, ma'am," the maid said.

She placed the tray on the table and, as she was leaving, gave Reed a playful wink without Elin noticing.

Elin poured herself and Reed a glass of water. She gave Reed her glass, then returned to her chair.

Reed took a hearty drink of the chilled mineral water.

"So in recent weeks, Morgan and Cecelia kept their distance from you and Clive," Reed said. "Did they interact with anyone else in your household?"

"Yes, with Mala, that was when I'd overheard the three of them talking about that Spanish novel, *Don Quixote*, of all things."

"Have you had a chance to take a look at *Don Quixote*, perhaps finding a clue or two in the novel as to why the twins and Mala would talk about it?"

"Yes, of course, just look around you, Clive and I are avid readers," Elin said. "We couldn't find anything helpful — it doesn't make sense why my girls would be interested in the very long story of an insane, meddlesome old man who thought he was a knight in shining armor."

"There's more, though, right?" Reed said.

"You are very observant, Reed. I don't believe for one second that Mala read *Don Quixote*. She once bragged to me that she has read only two books in her life --- *The Wonderful Adventures of Nils* --- twice."

"And has Morgan, Cecelia, or Mala been in contact of late with any middle-aged Hispanic gentlemen?" Reed asked.

Elin took two sips of her water.

"Not that I'm aware of," Elin said. "But I'll speak with Peggy, our maid — if I learn anything, I'll call you immediately."

Well, isn't that a subtle bum rush, Reed thought.

"Elin, I have all I need for now," Reed said. "Thank you so much for your time. You know, I could advise you not to worry too much, but that would be pointless. I can tell you are in agony over your daughters. And so is Clive. All I'll say is that I am an absolute pitbull when it comes to missing women, and I'm optimistic Morgan and Cecelia will come home."

Tears welled in Elin's eyes.

"Thank you, Reed, it is a real comfort having you involved," she said. "I'll have Mala show you out of this labyrinth of ours."

Clip, clop, clip, clop went Mala's heels as she walked Reed to the front door.

Reed kept stride for stride with Mala. She was convinced that if she slowed down at all, Mala would leave her behind.

"So, Mala, have you ever read *Don Quixote*?" Reed said.

She lengthened her stride, refusing to allow the Swedish butler to win this impromptu footrace.

Sure as hell won't be bested by a woman in heels, she thought.

"No, I haven't read *Don Quixote*," Mala said. "Why do you ask?"

"It's nothing, really, only Elin told me that she overheard your talking with the twins about *Don Quixote*," Reed said.

"I really don't recall," Mala said. "I have so much stuff to keep track of, I don't remember every idle conversation I may have had."

Goodness, Mala, I'm not interrogating you, Reed thought. At least not yet.

"Well, don't worry about it, it's nothing," Reed said. "But hey, I would like to toss out an idea to you."

"Yeah, and what's that?" Mala said, taking a cautious tone with Reed.

"Sierra is one of our performers at our cabaret Namaste," Reed said. "She's originally from Stockholm, so I bet you'd enjoy talking with her in Swedish, and she's just a lovely person."

Mala lit up like the Aurora Borealis.

"How old is she?" she asked.

"Twenty seven," Reed answered.

"Single?" Mala said.

"Mostly," Reed replied, a bit evasively.

"And is she hot?" Mala said.

"As hot as a Swedish sauna," Reed said.

"Well, you're on, then," Mala said eagerly. "Why don't you give me her digits."

Reed complied by giving Sierra's cell phone number to Mala.

Damn, I'd better call Sierra from my car, Reed thought. I bet this woman isn't going to waste any time reaching out to Sierra.

When Mala opened the drawbridge-size front door, Reed practically sprinted to her black Mustang GT.

11

———

S on of a bitch, Don Coyote thought, why can't people stick to a plan? Everyone would have such an orderly and productive life if only they followed my orders. Really, they'd thank me later.

Fifteen minutes earlier, Don Coyote was on the phone with Lucia Da Rosa. He had been relaxing in the comfortable study of his palatial estate in South Tampa. He was smoking another American cigar and sipping on a double espresso. Lucia's phone call abruptly interrupted his nicotine and caffeine fueled ruminations.

"I'm sorry, *señor*, but we're having great difficulty in amassing four-million dollars in cash *and* in finding a trustworthy courier," Lucia said in Spanish to Don Coyote.

"Well, who owns that problem, *senora?*" he said in Spanish as well.

"We both do," Lucia answered curtly.

Hija de puta, don't push me, Don Coyote thought.

"Then how are *we* going to solve this problem?" he said. "After all, delays are unacceptable, and may result in your incurring late fees."

"Like hell it will, Fernando," Lucia said.

Don Coyote finished his espresso, then stamped out his cigar in the large crystal ashtray. He was so angry, he crushed his expensive cigar into pieces.

"How dare you address me as Fernando," Don Coyote said. "You are to call me only by my professional name, *Don Coyote*. I've a good mind to raise my price by a million dollars."

"*Please*, I apologize for my bad etiquette, Don Coyote," Lucia said, as she could not afford another million dollars added to the price, and she didn't want those two beauties to slip through her wantonness fingers.

He purposefully exhaled loudly over the telephone.

"Very well, I accept your apology," Don Coyote said.

"Thank you, Don Coyote," Lucia eagerly responded.

Before I'm done with this woman, she'll become my personal bitch, Don Coyote thought.

"Now that we're being so agreeable, let's reach a compromise," he said. "For every day that the cash payment is late arriving, I will charge you an additional fifty-thousand dollars."

"I can live with that, Don Coyote," Lucia said. "But there's another wrinkle."

Don Coyote paused thirty seconds, allowing himself time to contain his anger.

"What now?"

"We're uncomfortable transporting so much cash all the way to Tampa — there's just too great a chance for something bad to happen."

"And how did you plan on getting my payment to Tampa?" Don Coyote asked.

"We were going to use our Gulfstream — our pilot is very trustworthy," Lucia said. "We thought we'd have him land at the Tampa Executive Airport, which is only a few miles east of downtown Tampa."

"Something tells me that security there is less strict than at Tampa International," Don Coyote said. "For Christ's sake, you could even land at the Ocala airport up in shithole Marion County. The security at Ocala is virtually nonexistent."

"That's all well and good, *senor*, but we would still need a courier that's as reliable as a Mormon," Lucia said. "We haven't yet found anyone here, and we're certainly not going to hire a courier in Tampa. This much money would turn the head of a saint."

Shit, a saint could get his head turned for five bucks, Don Coyote thought. I'm beginning to smell a rat here. Are the Da Rosas trying to set me up?

"I think I understand your predicament, *senora*," Don Coyote said. "So what is it you would like to do?"

"Mateo and I would like to transport the cash ourselves — we would act as our own couriers."

"Would you still fly to Tampa?"

"No, we actually had Tucson, Arizona in mind," she said. "But we wouldn't fly directly into Tucson — Tucson International is a civil-military airport, so the security is tighter than an altar boy's butt."

Crude, but I get her point, Don Coyote thought.

"So . . . ?" he asked.

"So we're going to fly our Gulfstream from Puerto Vallarta to Nogales, then drive across the border and head north to Tucson."

Yes, yes, Lucia, I'm well aware you and that *pendejo* husband have a private jet, Don Coyote thought. Probably lease it, same as I do with this McMansion.

"I suppose that would be acceptable from my standpoint," he said in a patrician tone. "But how will you get so much cash across the U.S. border?"

Lucia didn't miss a beat in responding.

"Simple really, since those ICE and Border Patrol idiots are on the lookout for Mexicans bringing in drugs, not millions in cash, we're going to hide the cash in several crates of Spanish bibles."

"Bibles? Spanish bibles?" Don Coyote asked, feeling embarrassed he hadn't thought of that idea back when he and his dear deceased mother used to smuggle cocaine and heroin into the U.S.

"Yes, bibles, *senor*, it's really quite clever," Lucia said. "We tell the border officials that the Spanish bibles are for the illegals detained in the federal prison camps in southern Arizona."

"Do you think your scam will work?" Don Coyote asked.

"I know it will, because we did a trial run that went off without any problems," Lucia said confidently. "Those morons at the Nogales border examined only one crate, which amounted to opening and closing the crate once they saw the bibles. And their dogs, of course, didn't smell drugs. We even followed through and delivered the bibles to a detention camp."

My God, this has been their plan all along, Don Coyote thought. There's an awful beauty to their scheme — meet in the Sonoran Desert, eliminate me, keep the cash and the twins, and I'll bet pesos to churros that there won't be a single Benjamin in those crates of bibles. It's brilliant, really, just exactly what I'd do.

"You have it all thought out, don't you, Lucia," he said. "I'm curious, did Mateo contribute to this scheme, er plan?"

Lucia giggled over the phone. It was the giggle of a small child.

"That useful idiot contributed nothing with regard to this *plan*," she said. "I am the brains of the marriage, while Mateo provides the working capital, which mostly came from his family. You know, of course, I get the first taste of Morgan and Cecelia."

Creepy, but very hot, Don Coyote thought. She actually thinks she's going to pull this off. Won't *she* be surprised when I blow her brains out all over a saguaro cactus.

"So where are we going to meet?" he asked. "I assume that Tucson proper is out of the question — you understand, there's way too much CCTV in the city."

"I quite agree, señor, that's why we're going to meet at Tanque Verde Ranch, which is nestled in Saguaro National State Park West," Lucia said.

"I *know* where Tanque Verde is," Don Coyote said. He immediately felt a horrible pang of loss.

Ah, my sweet mother, a true saint, Maria Gonzalez, I feel your loss every second of my existence, he thought.

Only during business operations did Maria, known as "La Patrona" in the smuggling world, address her son as "Don Coyote". In private she called him "my Fernando", and he called her "sweet mother."

Maria got her son's name from the old story of Fernando the bull, who preferred smelling flowers in the pasture to fighting in the bull-ring. Even as a young adult, Fernando the human shied away from the violence of the family business — he'd much rather listen to jazz and rap, endlessly watch American television, and read *People* magazine and

American mysteries. Fernando's one concession to traditional Mexican culture was to wear *guayabera* shirts, at his mother's insistence.

In fact, it was Maria who held Fernando's hand as they aimed a handgun at the head of Fernando's father, Roberto Gonzalez. The father was Mexican-American. It was he who had connections with the Mexican drug cartels and with the U.S. Border Patrol. It was he who had come up with the concept of *La Frontera*, the garage door section of the border wall that became the family's portal to wealth and power. The Gonzalez family became the ultimate interlocutors, charging prohibitively high fees for the guaranteed delivery of Mexican illegals and narcotics into the United States. Seven days a week, young Mexicans carried backpacks filled with *llelo y chiva* into the Arizona section of the Sonoran Desert. Upon delivery of the backpacks, *los Mexicanos jovenes* were sold off as sex slaves and domestic indentured servants. And there was an endless supply of naïve young Mexicans, as well as cocaine and heroin, available for transport into the United States.

Happy days it was for the Gonzalez family, until Maria discovered that Roberto had an *esposa gringa* in Phoenix.

"Bad enough you got a second wife, *pendejo*, but an *American* bitch?" Maria said to her husband. "What's her name, 'Sally?' "

"'Babs', actually, it's short for 'Barbara,' " Roberto said.

He instantly regretted being so casual and flippant with Maria.

As two *soldados* held tight to Roberto, who was on his knees crying like a two-year-old, Maria and Fernando stood side by side holding the nine-millimeter pistol together.

"This *hijo de puta* deserves to die for his unforgivable betrayal, *querida madre*, but I don't know if I can shoot him," Fernando said.

"Please, please, *mi hijo*, let me live," Roberto screamed. "I will divorce that American whore, and I will dedicate my life to you and Maria."

Roberto struggled with the *soldados*, but to no avail.

Fernando took sole possession of the handgun.

"You will never say the Christian name of my dear mother ever again, *engano bastardo*," Fernando yelled at his father.

He fired six rounds into Roberto's head and torso.

Maria held her shaking son and kissed him passionately on his lips.

She then looked at the dead body of her husband and at the two *soldados*.

"Put that *mierda* in a barrel of acid and bring it to *Babs*," she said. "Then kill the bitch after fucking her."

Consequently, when Lucia Da Rosa mentioned Tanque Verde Ranch to Don Coyote over the telephone, he instantaneously felt a longing for his mother.

Once a year, Maria and Fernando vacationed for a week at Tanque Verde. The pair shared a luxury casita, which had no television, only a large fireplace and a king size four-post bed.

Tanque Verde was a guest ranch that had the largest herd of riding horses in Arizona. Maria enjoyed a variety of quarter horses to ride, while Fernando preferred a hinny, which was the offspring of a male horse, a stallion, and a female donkey, a jenny.

In the evenings, the pair would partake in a cookout that featured grilled ribeye steaks and barbecue beans in a nearby cottonwood grove. There always was a bonfire in the center of the picnic area, and javelinas would circle about in the shadows of the black cottonwood trees.

Good times, good memories, Don Coyote thought. I'll always treasure them. I do so miss *querida madre*.

"*Senor*, are you all right, you've grown as silent as a corpse?" Lucia said.

Talk about Puck's evil twin, he thought. You know, I rather like this woman, reminds me a bit of dear mother.

"I'm fine, *senora*, just doing a bit of reminiscing," he said.

"*Muy bien*, so shall we meet at Tanque Verde in one week?" Lucia said. "I've already taken the liberty of making us all reservations."

Such *huevos rancheros* on this woman, Don Coyote thought. Jesus, am I getting smitten?

"That's fine, but I have a demand that's disguised as a polite request," Don Coyote said.

"And what is your request — notice I am asking politely," Lucia said.

"Said the wolverine in lamb's clothing," Don Coyote replied.

"*Senor*! Are you flirting with me?" Lucia exclaimed. "After all, I am a married woman, though that hasn't stopped me before."

Truer words, you *puta*, Don Coyote thought. Enough of this coyness, back to business.

"Regardless, *senora*, I will require an additional one-hundred-thousand dollars for the change of location, though I'll waive the daily late fee because, well, you're such a pleasure with which to do business."

He could hear Lucia breathing heavily over the phone.

I'm either turning her on or royally pissing her off, he thought. Probably both.

Finally, Lucia spoke.

"I accept your *demand*, senor," she said. "I'll probably regret this, but is there anything else you require?"

Look at that, she's asking a condemned man for his final request, Don Coyote thought. I might bed this woman before we close the deal.

"Actually, there is," he said. "I will need to see photographs of the cash in your possession at Tanque Verde Ranch. Upon receipt of these photos, and once I'm satisfied that my money is at the ranch, my twin virgins and I will travel to Arizona."

Lucia became breathy again.

"Your request has been granted, *senor*," she said. "We will arrive at Tanque Verde two days before your arrival, at which time we'll send you photographs, all right?"

"*Claro*," Don Coyote answered with casual indifference.

"Let's conclude this conversation, all this talk of money and virginal twins has gotten me hot and bothered," Lucia said. "I need to go find where I put my *vibrador*."

That's right, *cona*, one last tease to get me off track, Don Coyote thought.

"Just try clap on, clap off," he said.

"What's that?" Lucia said.

Don Coyote chuckled.

"Never mind, *senora bonita*. I look forward to hearing from you in five days."

"Very well, *adios, senor guapo*," Lucia said.

She disconnected before Don Coyote could respond.

Gazing at the tattered remains of his American cigar in the crystal ashtray, Don Coyote slowly overcame his anger.

Come to think of it, this change of plans may work out very well for me, he thought.

He lit another cigar.

Be lovely to leave Tanque Verde with both the cash and the twins, he thought. *Querida madre* would be so proud of me. But first, I must make a phone call.

Don Coyote sat in his easy chair in the study and dialed a number on his cell phone. He puffed on his cigar as his phone rang for a connection.

"Benecio? Very good, it's me, Don Coyote," he said in Spanish. "Turns out, I have a little extra work for you. Interested?"

12

R avel was preparing for her solo expedition into Tampa's seamier nightlife. She carefully slid her prized laptop into a dark green satchel, which she slung over her right shoulder. She wore a freshly laundered white tee shirt that read, "You Had Me at Gay." She stuffed her cell phone, cash, and cigarettes into the large pockets of her dark brown cargo pants. The cigarettes weren't for her — while employed by Reed and Jake, she abstained from tobacco, alcohol, and illegal drugs. Rather, she sometimes offered cigarettes to keep conversations going while she was analog data hunting. She bent down and laced up her scuffed Doc Martens.

Just before leaving her West Tampa apartment, she paused to look at herself in the full-length hallway mirror.

"Ravel, darling, you are one bitchin' good looking woman," she said aloud to herself.

And Ravel was a strikingly attractive woman. Only twenty-six years old, she stood a smidge under five feet and weighed but ninety-nine pounds. She kept her black hair short, and she had an angular face that featured large violet eyes, a ski slope nose, and high cheekbones. She maintained an athletic figure, and playfully described her large breasts as "ro-bust-a-licious."

Ravel hadn't always appeared so fetching and attractive. She had come a long way from being virtually homeless, drug addicted, and in the United States illegally.

After demonstrating her inestimable computer skills, Ravel convinced Reed to hire her as Jake's assistant office manager at the Namaste cabaret. She also was instrumental in working on Reed and Jake's private investigations.

The only hitch was that Ravel was deeply in love with Reed, though Ravel enjoyed her friends-with-benefits relationship with the Swedish Namaste performer Sierra. And Reed, being a highly principled woman completely in love with Jake, did not respond to Ravel's overtures.

Ravel knew, though, that she was as much Reed's close friend as she was an employee. And that was why Ravel rarely objected to Reed sending her out to Tampa Bay's dark underworld to mine for information. And besides, Reed understood that Ravel was far better suited than she for this kind of investigation. As she sometimes said to Ravel, "Sherlock Holmes had his Baker Street Irregulars, but I have my brilliant Swiss renegade."

Ravel took one last glance at herself in the mirror.

"Reed, sweetheart, you really don't appreciate what you're missing here," Ravel said, as she lightly caressed her breasts over her tee shirt.

After making certain her front door was securely locked, Ravel walked down the three flights of stairs to the apartment complex's parking garage. And there was her red Porsche Boxster backed into reserved parking space number six-nine.

She revved the three-hundred-seventy-five horse powered engine, then peeled out of the parking garage like a gazelle escaping from a cheetah.

Her first stop was the Hub, a bar on Franklin Street in downtown Tampa. Ever since it opened in 1946, the Hub enjoyed a rather infamous reputation. Before the City of Tampa tore down its nearby jail, the first place that recently released inmates visited was the Hub. The freed inmates often were joined by courthouse lawyers, hipsters, hobos, and curiosity seekers. The bar had a jukebox and pool table, walls covered with fliers and graffiti, classic chrome barstools with red pleather cushions, and a dark, shadowy ambience that shrouded its Fellini-esque patrons and all their beatific troubles.

In other words, it was the kind of alt dive bar that twanged Ravel's buds.

As she entered the Hub, Ravel thought of Reed and how worried she was that Ravel was going to check out the Hub.

"Ravel, I wonder how safe you'll be by going into such a dreadful place," Reed said.

"No worries, Mommie, I'll be just fine," Ravel said. "I'll keep in mind a piece of advice you once gave me."

"And what was that?" Reed said. She was genuinely puzzled.

"You told me to never let 'em see you sweat, 'cause sometimes you just have to go for it," Ravel responded.

"Ravel, you know full well I was talking about how to get through Malfunction Junction on the Interstate," she said.

"Oh really?" Ravel said. "Certainly applies here doesn't it."

"I suppose so, but don't forget your Mace," Reed said.

Yeah, right, Ravel thought, as she entered the bar where a less than friendly middle-aged bartender was wiping down the countertop.

Mace is just what I don't need in these close quarters, better to just hit him with a bottle, like I had to do here last month, she thought.

"Ravel, are you going to behave yourself tonight?" the bartender said.

"Long as no one fucks with me."

"Fair enough, so what'll you have?" the bartender said.

"My usual, Rip, a glass of Fiji on the rocks — and make sure the ice was made from spring water," Ravel said.

"Fuck sake, woman," Rip the bartender said.

He started to walk away.

"I'm kidding, Ripster," she said. "Gimme a Sprite with a lime."

"Okay, but don't fucking call me 'Ripster'," Rip the grouchy bartender replied.

"So sorry, *Rip*," Ravel said. "Man, you're one ornery son of a bitch tonight, don't you realize it's still a white man's world out there?"

"Out there, yeah," Rip said. "In here, not so much."

Rip was correct: the Hub was peopled with African-Americans,

Asians, Hispanics, even a couple of Seminoles. There were gay, straight, and questioning patrons, as well as people of means and of means by no means. Surprisingly, most everyone got along, at least until the Hub's signature strong drinks started kicking in full bore.

Ravel grabbed her Sprite and gave Rip an Andrew Jackson.

"No change, Rip," Ravel said. "But could I get a receipt?"

Rip the happy bartender laughed loudly.

"Sure, why not," he said, as he scribbled out a receipt on the back of a water-ring stained flyer. "And thanks, Beautiful."

"Anytime, you handsome old Neanderthal," Ravel said.

Time to reconnoiter, she thought. I got a feeling this is the only stop I'll need to make tonight.

She looked over the clientele, some of whom were sitting at the bar, others standing in the pool room, and several more seated at tiny scarred tables.

Two lawyers, wearing wrinkled dress shirts and loosened ties, were having a heated argument over which Beat writer had more influence on American literature, Jack Kerouac or Allen Ginsberg.

An African-American homeless man, who was allowed by Rip to bring in his shopping cart filled with his worldly belongings, was teaching a young Asian couple how to play dominoes — as long as the couple kept buying him shots of Patron.

And off in a dark corner sitting by herself was Ravel's prey, alt diva Veronica Lake. Her birth name was Walter Davis, but damn if Walter didn't look just like the forties *feme fatale* actress, Veronica Lake.

This version of the starlet was dressed in a red silk dress with coordinated red pumps. Her hair, obviously a wig, was long, wavy and blonde. Even though smoking technically wasn't allowed in the Hub, Veronica held a lit cigarette in a silver snake cigarette holder. Her silver elephant cigarette case was next to her martini on the table. An empty martini glass, still with an olive in it, served as her makeshift ashtray.

Rip the horny bartender let her smoke in the bar and drink for free in exchange for oral sex in the Hub's store room after last call.

Ravel strolled over to Veronica's table.

Veronica smiled at Ravel, then her arm slipped off the table and her long blonde hair fell over her right eye.

"Wait, wait, don't tell me, I know this one," Ravel exclaimed. "Straight out of *I Wanted Wings*, right?"

Veronica smiled dreamily. She appeared to have consumed several very dry martinis.

"Peek-a-boo, peek-a-boo, Ravel dear, you're exactly right, though I don't know how straight it is," Veronica said.

Both she and Ravel laughed quietly and politely, as neither wanted to upset the lost-soul ambience of the Hub.

"What brings you out here to my stomping ground, Ravel dear?" Veronica said. Her speech was slightly slurred.

"Oh, well, I've been avoiding the Hub ever since I smashed that guy's beer bottle over his head," Ravel said. "Think I've given it enough time to make my triumphant return."

"I was here that night, sweetie, you liked to have killed that poor man," Veronica said. She puffed on her cigarette holder, then exhaled a long plume of smoke.

"Rip didn't say anything too much just now, so I think I'm in the clear," Ravel said. "May I sit down, Veronica?"

"It's a free country, Betty Boop," Veronica replied indifferently.

Jesus, the breasts on this woman, Ravel thought. If I didn't know she was a trans with a full package . . . .

Ravel sat down at the tiny table. There was barely room enough on the table top for her highball glass filled with Sprite.

"Still drinking like a little girl, I see," Veronica said.

"Yeah, doctor's orders, you know," Ravel said sheepishly.

"Hmm, Doctor Reed O'Hara's orders?" Veronica said.

"Yup, and I always do what my doctor tells me," Ravel said.

"I have to admit, Ravel dear, ever since you went to work for that Reed and her gorgeous hunk of a man Jake Dupree, you're a changed woman, almost a goddamn Girl Scout," Veronica said.

She leaned toward Ravel so far, her breasts practically tumbled out of her low-cut dress.

"Funny you'd say that, Veronica, because I've gotten myself hooked on Thin Mints," Ravel said.

"And do you still dine only at the taco truck?" Veronica asked impishly.

"Yes indeed, the spicier the better," Ravel replied.

"All right, well, then let's set this scene properly, Ravel dear. I'm drunk and you're sober, and we're sitting all by ourselves in the dark. Even though you easily could afford me, I say with all confidence that you're not ready for the Hollywood starlet trans experience. So what exactly are you up to, my petite ingenue?"

Ravel drank some of her soft drink.

"I know better than to play games with you, Veronica, so I'll put it all on the table, with no fucking bullshit. I'm looking for a middle-aged guy, a real smarmy asshole who probably persuaded eighteen-year-old female twins from South Tampa to run off with him."

Veronica finished her martini. She opened her cigarette case and took out the last cigarette.

She looked at Ravel and raised her eyebrows.

"Oh sorry, Veronica, here, let me fill up your case with these Newports, and I'll get you another martini — very dry, right?" Ravel said.

"Thank you, sweetie, so thoughtful of you," Veronica said. "Goodness me, you're being uncharacteristically charitable — must be really serious about the old guy and the Cutler twins."

Ravel finished re-stocking Veronica's cigarette case, then held up Veronica's martini glass, signaling to Rip that Veronica was ready for another.

"I am *very* serious, Lady V, but wait . . . how did you know the twins' name?" she said.

Veronica smirked at Ravel.

"Oh, the places I've been and the things I've done," Veronica said. "So tired and sore, yet so very well informed, darling."

Is she doing Dietrich? Garbo? Madeline Kahn as Dietrich, maybe, Ravel thought. God, sometimes I really love this place. Any second now, Freddie Mercury and George Michael are going to walk into the Hub holding hands.

"So how do you know about the Cutler twins?" Ravel asked.

Veronica smirked again.

"No way, Mandalay," she said. "My lips stay sealed until you pry them open with a thick stack of Splanklin' Franklins."

"You're kidding," Ravel said.

Veronica became very serious and employed her deep masculine voice when she said, "Look, you little twit, in my line of work I can't afford to kid, not unless I want to end up being dog food for a pack of black labs."

Ravel was starting to wish she had brought her Mace with her.

"All right, sorry again, Veronica," Ravel said, perhaps too quickly. "So what kind of donation can I make that would loosen those beautiful pouty lips?"

Veronica gave Ravel a toothy grin.

Yikes, she's got the chompers of a Taipei cannibal, Ravel thought.

"Gimme a thousand, darling, and I'll open up to you in every which way imaginable."

Figured as much, Ravel thought. Just should give her what she wants, long as she delivers the goods.

"Here's how we'll do this, Veronica. I'll ask you a question, you give me a convincing answer, and you get a hundred-dollar bill. Ten questions, ten good answers, a thousand dollars."

While Veronica was considering Ravel's proposal, Rip walked over to the table and gave Veronica a fresh martini.

Will wonders never cease — Rip got out from behind the bar and brought a drink to a customer, Ravel thought. Didn't even know the man had legs.

"You can start a fresh tab for Veronica, Rip, and I'll take care of it," Ravel said.

"Veronica don't need no tab," Rip said. He winked at Veronica, who returned the gesture with the eye that wasn't covered by her long blonde hair.

Veronica sipped daintily from her fresh martini, then she had Ravel light another cigarette with a silver tiger Zippo.

"I like your idea, sweetums, so I say let's do this," Veronica said in a sultry whisper. "Only don't take all fucking night — got a gentleman coming by shortly, a courthouse bailiff who looks just like Alan Ladd."

"Lies take longer than the truth, *sweetums*," Ravel said.

Veronica started to lose her temper, then recovered quickly.

"I take it question number one is how do I know about the Cutler twins," Veronica said.

"That's a good starting point," Ravel said. She noticed that the Hub was starting to get busy.

Veronica again sipped from her martini.

"I *could* just say it was scuttlebutt I overheard here or at the Honey Pot or at El Castillo, but that wouldn't get me my Benjamin Franklin, now would it," she said.

"Nope," Ravel said with Swiss succinctness.

"Well then, I first came across Morgan and Cecelia over at Metropolitan Ministries," Veronica said. "The twins were volunteering in the thrift shop, where I find some of the most divine evening wear and shoes that have been barely worn at all. Last week, for instance, I found these very pumps I'm wearing, as well as . . . ."

"Veronica, please, stay on point," Ravel interjected.

"Sorry, Zoot Suit, I get distracted when the topic of fashion comes up," Veronica said. "Anyway, I spotted those Cutler girls at the thrift shop — I mean, goodness gracious, so young and beautiful and blonde . . . like me, right?"

"Most certainly," Ravel said. "Go on."

"Well, I introduced myself and we chatted away while they helped me find a dress," Veronica said. "Funny, they were doing that twin thing, you know, standing side by side and answering questions together — if they weren't so cute, it'd be kind of creepy."

"Keep going, Veronica, you're doing great," Ravel said, as she lit Veronica's cigarette.

"Anyway, I'm thinking how fun it'd be to have a threesome with these twins, but decided it'd take too much time and effort to get these princesses in bed. Then it hit me, as if Bogey himself had slapped me in the face, these tasty twin-kies better watch out for someone who has more patience and more money than I got. I was more sad than surprised when I heard Morgan and Cecelia had disappeared. Such a shame, the twins were born targets."

Ravel put a hundred-dollar bill on the table. Veronica whisked it away into her red knock-off Chanel purse, then she raised her empty martini glass in the direction of Rip.

Rip nodded his head at Veronica and, in less than two minutes, brought her a fresh martini.

"Rip, darling, would you put 10cc's 'I'm Not in Love' on the juke-box," Veronica said.

"Yeah right, I got ten cc for you," Rip the comic bartender said.

"Good, I look forward to it," Veronica replied coquettishly.

Rip ambled back to the bar.

Ravel tapped on the table.

"Sorry to break up this budding romance, but you mentioned an old guy," she said.

"Is that question number two?" Veronica asked.

"Yup," Ravel said.

Veronica appeared nervous as she gulped down the rest of her martini.

"I think this man had something to do with the twins running off. He shows up in town and starts hanging around El Castillo. He's even been here a couple times. He said his name is Don Quixote, would you believe it?"

Ravel laid down a second hundred-dollar bill. Veronica missed in her first attempt at grabbing the money; in her second attempt, she secured it and speedily put the bill in her purse.

"Sounds as if you ran into this guy," Ravel said.

Veronica nodded.

"So what'd you think of him?" Ravel asked.

"Is that number three or four?" Veronica said in a slurred voice.

"Number three," Ravel answered.

"One of the classiest creepos I've ever met — and that's saying something," Veronica said. "He asked a lot of questions and listened with a lot of interest to my answers. I could tell he wasn't into me. He seemed really fixated on young, preferably virginal, daughters of wealthy families."

Ravel placed a third hundred-dollar bill directly into Veronica's purse.

"Saves time this way," Ravel said.

"Thank you, Cupcake, my coordinates is a bit off, don't know why," Veronica said.

Don't correct her, just don't do it, Ravel thought.

"All right, Veronica, here's a three-part question that's worth three-hundred dollars."

Veronica smiled.

"Will I be in jeopardy if I don't answer in the form of a question?" Veronica asked.

"I'll relax the rules this time," Ravel said.

Pretty clever for being so drunk, Ravel thought.

"So, Veronica, what does Don Quixote look like, do you know anything about his background, and what does your gut tell you about him?"

Rip the thoughtful bartender brought over another martini without Veronica having to ask for it.

Veronica smiled at Rip, who then gave her a slight bow.

She sipped from her fresh martini.

"Don Quixote is in his fifties easy queasy, he has a full head of longish silver gray hair, he's definitely Hispanic, his English is perfect, he has a nice body for an older gentleman, he has impeccable manners, but unfortunately he smokes the most disgusting cigars," Veronica said with remarkable rapidity and preciseness.

Ravel committed all of these valuable details to memory.

"And do you know where he's from?" she asked.

"Um, huh, he said he was from Mexico, where he ran an export company called La Frontera. He decided to — I think it's the right word — expatriate to the U.S. to seek out — and these are his exact words — 'new hunting grounds'."

Jesus, what a ballsy guy, Ravel thought.

"And what did you think of this guy?" she asked.

"I was offended at first that he wasn't attracted to me — doesn't happen very often, you know," Veronica said. "But I realized that Don Quixote has a pretty unhealthy mommy fixation, and besides, the dude is all about the money. One other thing, my hot little lollipop, Don Quixote has got a secret agenda that I'm guessing is pretty dark, dark, dark."

Ravel put three hundred-dollar bills in Veronica's purse.

"That's six hundred dollars total, Veronica," she said. "So my next question is, did he try to enlist you in finding girls or young women?"

Veronica polished off what Ravel hoped would be her last martini.

"No, he didn't ask me directly, because I suspect he didn't think I traveled in the lofty social circles he had in mind."

"You said not *directly?*"

"Well, he asked me if I knew anyone who could put him in contact with some young things," Veronica answered.

Ravel leaned forward and stared directly at Veronica.

"Let me take a wild guess, you mentioned someone, didn't you — who was it?"

Veronica sat in pouty silence and scowled at Ravel for a full minute.

This is what it must be like when Serena Williams stares you down, Ravel thought.

"Fine, I'll tell you, long as I get my thousand dollars," Veronica said. "I told Don Quixote that he should contact Mala, the Cutler's butler, to get an introduction to Morgan and Cecelia. And that bitch is just cray-cray evil enough to do it, though I have to say Mala is pretty good in bed. Not too proud of it, but I gave the Mexican geezer Mala's phone number."

This time, Ravel sat in silence for a full minute.

"Veronica, I can't believe I'm actually uttering this, but did you say the butler did it?"

Veronica smiled at Ravel.

"Yes, but it was more that the household manager did it," she said.

Ravel laid four one-hundred-dollar bills on the table. Veronica had no problem picking them up and squirreling them away in her purse.

Ravel stood up.

"Veronica, three remarks before I leave you to Alan Ladd. First, you have been a huge help tonight. Second, I've never seen anyone put away so many martinis and still be conscious. Third and last, I hope you feel deeply ashamed of helping Don Quixote make off with those young women."

"Thanks for the cash, but do really piss off, you midget Euro trash," Veronica said with vitriolic clarity.

Ravel slowly shook her head, then said, "*Ciao*, baby."

She turned and walked out of the Hub.

About five minutes later, a Hispanic man rose from a table located from across the bar floor and ambled over to Veronica's table.

He wore a Tampa Bay Rays baseball cap, sunglasses, and had a full black beard. His orange tee shirt read, "*No Mas Los Tacos, Pendejo.*" His jeans were filthy and he sported green flip flops.

In other words, the man blended in perfectly at the Hub.

"So, *la puta hermosa*, did everything go good with that bitch Ravel?" he asked.

Veronica stood up quickly and faced the man.

"Yes, everything went *well*, Benecio," Veronica said. "But call me a whore again — even a good looking whore — and I'll cut off your cock and have it for breakfast."

"Stop, *mamacita*, you're turning me on," Benecio said. "Damn, you got some pep in your step. Looks like it helped what with Rip giving you watered down martinis and all."

"Whatever, errand boy," Veronica said. "Now *vamoose*! My date just came in."

Sure enough, in walked the bailiff. He was wearing a gray double-breasted suit with a yellow dress shirt, a floral tie, and black derbies. And damn if he weren't the spitting image of Alan Ladd.

13

Don Coyote left his home in South Tampa and drove in his black Cadillac Escalade to La Teresita, a Cuban coffee shop on Columbus Avenue in West Tampa.

He expected to meet Benecio there at one p.m. As usual, he was on time, as he wound his way north on Bayshore Boulevard, which ran parallel with Tampa Bay. He had factored extra time for the drive, as Bayshore Boulevard was slightly out of his way. He simply couldn't resist the view of the bay on his right and the five-mile-long row of elegant mansions on his left.

And Don Coyote was equally enamored with La Teresita, as it was the story of Cuban exile Maximino and Coarlia Capdevila coming to Tampa in 1962 and going on to open first a grocery store, then a coffee and sandwich shop named La Teresita, and eventually a four-teen thousand square foot restaurant, eponymously named Capdevila's.

Don Coyote preferred the twenty-four-hour coffee shop with its three horseshoe-shaped counters, its bright fluorescent lights and its overall conviviality — the vast majority of the regulars were Hispanic men who opted to speak only Spanish in the coffee shop. While Don Coyote enjoyed *cafe con leche* and Cuban sandwiches at La Teresita, he thoroughly enjoyed the *puerco asado, pescado relleno, vaca frita*, and *pollo a la plancha.*

Nothing like doing business while feasting on genuine *la comida Hispanica*, he thought.

When Don Coyote walked inside La Teresita at precisely one p.m., he noticed that Benecio already was seated by himself at the less busy counter to the left.

Good, Benecio got us a spot where we can keep an eye over the coffee shop and have an emergency exit door behind us. Knew this boy had his act together, Don Coyote thought.

He took the seat next to Benecio's left. Benecio already had ordered two cups of *cafe con* leche for the both of them. He held a copy of *La Gaceta* newspaper and pretended to read it with interest.

"Young man, how is the world treating you?" Don Coyote said.

"Like a hooker with AIDS," Benecio said in a near whisper.

Don Coyote produced a guttural chuckle.

"Well, aren't we just a ray of sunshine today," he said.

Benecio sipped from his cafe *con leche.*

"Yeah, sorry, I just get all froggy being back in this shithole town."

The two men, though both Hispanic, spoke in English at La Teresita, as they figured very few of the fellow customers and wait staff would understand them.

"When we're done with our projects here, you'll feel differently about Tampa — you will experience a sense of closure, I guarantee it," Don Coyote said.

"I hope so," Benecio said.

Indeed, Tampa had not worked out so well for Benecio. A while back, he was the assistant manager of security at Namaste. He enjoyed his work — he was paid well to help maintain order at the cabaret and to protect the Namaste performers. Since the clientele at Namaste was upscale and sophisticated, Benecio never got into a brawl and only rarely resorted to calling the police. He and Andre, chief security officer at Namaste, kept theft to a minimum, and break-ins didn't happen because of Namaste's state-of-the-art security system that Ravel installed.

Where it went south for Benecio was when the Russian mobster

Victor Petrov bribed him to assist in the kidnapping of Ravel — Petrov planned to use Ravel as a bargaining chip in his hostile takeover attempt of Namaste. It didn't take a lot of persuading on Petrov's part to get Benecio involved in the kidnapping: he hated with misogynistic passion that sarcastic, know-it-all Ravel. Fortunately for Ravel, she was rescued; unfortunately for Benecio, Reed and Jake figured out he was a party to this scheme. They did not have him arrested. They also told Andre he could not, in Andre's words, "hurt Benecio really, really badly." Instead, Jake fired Benecio and had Andre put Benecio on a bus to his hometown, Paris, Texas. But before he Rode the Dog, he had to sign over the title to his prized silver Ford F-150 STX to Ravel, who promptly sold it to Carvana.

"Really, Reed, do you see me driving around in a *pick-up truck?*" Ravel said. "I'm not ready to go *that* native."

From Benecio's standpoint, he lost his job and his truck all because of Ravel. So when Don Coyote reached out to him in Texas, Benecio jumped at the chance to make some good money back in Tampa and possibly exact revenge on Reed, Jake, Andre, and, most of all, Ravel.

Don't really care how this guy found me, but I'm sure as shit glad he did, Benecio thought.

"Young man, stop day dreaming," Don Coyote said. "How'd it go at the Hub?"

Benecio finished his *cafe con leche*, then asked in Spanish for another.

"It went grand, simply grand at the Hub," he said, again in English and in a low voice. "Veronica really worked Ravel, making her think she was drunk, when she wasn't, acting reluctant about saying anything about you and the girls, probably made a grand off Ravel for that performance."

"And did you let Veronica keep the money?" Don Coyote asked. He, too, had finished his *cafe con leche* and asked for another, along with a plate of *masas de puerco con arroz frito*, which was fried pork chunks with fried rice — as a courtesy to Benecio, he ordered a plate of *masas de puerco* for him as well.

"Yeah, I let her keep most of the money," Benecio said. "I mean, of course I took my manager's cut. That's all right, isn't it?"

Don Coyote smiled at him.

"Of course, shows initiative, my good man," he said.

And that much less I have to pay this little twit, Don Coyote thought.

"Was it good to see Ravel?" he asked.

Benecio saucered his coffee cup.

"Yeah, like herpes flaring up," Benecio said.

Boy's got a flair for the similes, Don Coyote thought. Perhaps one day I shall make him my Boswell. A man who does great things needs a biographer, after all.

"And you don't think Ravel recognized you."

"No way, the Hub was a fucking cave, and I was wearing a Rays cap and sunglasses, and she's never seen me in a beard."

"That's excellent, because everything I hear is that Ravel is a clever little bitch," Don Coyote said.

"And has she got a set of tits on her," Benecio mused.

"Why, my dear boy, do we have a bit of a crush on our Ravel?" Don Coyote said.

"No way, sir, I'm not into that dyke bitch," Benecio said unconvincingly.

"And the dyke bitch, in turn, is not into you, which makes her all that more desirable, right? Truly, fruit from the forbidden tree is the juiciest and tastiest."

Benecio looked at him quizzically.

"I really have no idea what you're talking about," he said.

At that moment, the server brought their food to them. He was an elderly Hispanic man who haphazardly laid down paper thin napkins and cheap silverware next to the plates of pork and rice.

"*Gracias, senor*," Don Coyote said.

"*De nada*," the old man mumbled, then shambled off.

Gentleman reminds me of those ancient waiters at Mallorca's in *San Juan Viejo*, Don Coyote thought.

For several minutes, both men sat in silence and ate their food.

Finally, Don Coyote used four paper napkins to wipe his mouth. He emitted a quiet belch, then he ordered two more cups of *cafe con leche* for himself and for Benecio.

"Do you think Ravel found Veronica to be reliable?" he asked.

"Absolutely," Benecio said. "Otherwise, she wouldn't have kept giving Ronnie all those Benjamins."

Don Coyote paused and stared reproachfully at Benecio.

"'Ronnie,' huh?" Don Coyote said. "Do I detect the scent of romance in the air?"

Benecio grinned slightly.

"I don't know, maybe."

"Hmm, a diminutive Swiss lesbian, a trans Veronica Lake look-a-like," Don Coyote said. "Looks as if you have a taste for the exotic."

"Maybe, yeah, probably, okay, definitely," Benecio said.

Don Coyote smiled broadly.

"Well, I certainly approve, as long as it in no way interferes with our business."

"Roger that, Kemosabe," Benecio said. "But listen, how did you know Ravel would end up talking with Ronnie, I mean, Veronica?"

Don Coyote finished his *cafe con leche*.

Drink these all day, I could, he thought.

"All a matter of visualization, really," Don Coyote said. He brushed some fried rice off his pink *guayabera*.

"What do you mean?" Benecio asked.

"It was a gamble on my part, but a pretty safe one," Don Coyote said. "I visualized that Clive Cutler would enlist Reed O'Hara's help in finding his missing daughters — they're good friends, after all, and Cutler knew that O'Hara and her *hijo de puta* husband Jake Dupree would do a thorough job of searching for the twins. Why, you yourself know how good O'Hara and Dupree are."

"True that," Benecio said. "But please, go on."

"Of course," Don Coyote continued in a hushed voice. "I purpose-fully sought out Veronica Lake to get the skinny on Mala Karlsson, you know, the Cutler's butler and caretaker of the twins. Once O'Hara was on the case, I figured she'd send out Ravel to call on her, shall we say, less conventional sources. And who better to chat up than Veronica Lake — she and Ravel hang out at the Hub, wouldn't say they're friends per se, but they get along, and Ravel appreciates that Veronica will give up reliable info for the right price."

Don Coyote seemed very proud of himself.

"I must say, sir, I'm very impressed, it's all turned out the way you visualized it. What's next?"

"Normally I keep my plans to myself, but I am beginning to trust you, Benecio, and trust among men can be an unshakable bond," Don Coyote said.

Tears actually welled up in Benecio's eyes.

"Thank you, sir, for trusting me," he said. He struggled to maintain his composure.

"You're very welcome, I know you won't let me down, because no son wants to disappoint his father," Don Coyote said.

Benecio looked at him with joy and surprise.

"Yes, yes, I know you never knew your father, and that it is a constant source of pain for you, so I want you to understand that I've come to look upon you as a son," Don Coyote said.

"And I've come to look upon you as my father," Benecio answered. Tears rolled down his cheeks.

Mother of God, even I'm starting to believe this bullshit. Don Coyote thought. And that can be very dangerous.

"Benecio, wipe your tears and listen very carefully to me."

Benecio wiped his face with a handful of paper napkins. He nodded his head, signaling he was composed and ready to listen.

"If all goes according to my master plan, we will have four-million dollars in our possession and still retain the twins," Don Coyote said in a voice laced with menace. "And the *coup de grace* will be that we exact revenge on Jake Dupree by taking away from him that which he most cherishes — Reed O'Hara. I intend to make Dupree fully comprehend the horrifying nature of personal loss."

"That is so awesome, Father — may I call you Father?"

Don Coyote nodded yes.

"What do you want me to do?" Benecio asked eagerly.

"You are to help me set the trap for Reed O'Hara," Don Coyote said. "It won't be long before she gets to Mala Karlsson. We'll allow O'Hara to get just enough of a confession from Mala that she will pick up my trail."

Benecio practically saluted Don Coyote.

Good, this young idiot is totally invested in my project, Don Coyote thought. What a triumph to make people have faith in their own false reality.

"Do you still want me to go with you to Arizona?" Benecio asked.

Don Coyote made the mistake of drinking from his clear plastic tumbler of Hillsborough County water.

This water tastes like pond scum, he thought. You'd think we could get some filtered water. Oh well, that which doesn't kill me makes me stronger.

"I most assuredly want you to come with us to Tucson," Don Coyote said. "I'll certainly need your expertise in eliminating the Da Rosas and finding them a suitable resting place in the Sonoran desert."

Benecio began to drink his water, but Don Coyote put his hand on Benecio's arm and shook his head no.

"That bad, huh?" Benecio said.

Don Coyote nodded yes.

"Thanks for the heads up, Father," Benecio said. "So will I be rewarded for my work?"

Don Coyote smiled warmly at his newfound son.

"Benecio, you will be rewarded very handsomely for all of your efforts."

I should say, you'll be most *appropriately* rewarded, you little prick, he thought.

"Now, let me take care of *la cuenta*, so that we can get out of here and get back to our work," Don Coyote said in his very best paternal voice.

14

———————

Jake Dupree hated to speed, especially on the Interstate. He preferred leaving the kamikaze driving to Reed and her Mustang GT. But he was running late for his tennis match with Tom Murray, his good friend and former CIA colleague. Their plan was to meet at the tennis courts next to the soccer stadium at the University of South Florida. He knew Tom would be on time; he also knew he'd never hear the end of it if *he* were late.

Jake pressed pedal to metal as he whooshed through the passing lane in his brand new yellow Lamborghini Urus. After donating his Range Rover to The Spring's live auction, Jake received the Lamborghini SUV as a birthday gift from Reed.

"So, Reed, does this mean I don't get my usual birthday present, if you know what I mean."

"I know exactly what you mean, my greedy Frenchman, so no, there won't be no *oirish scuttle* for you, not if you want to keep the Lamborghini."

"Didn't you say my Lambo has six-hundred-fifty horses, top speed of one-hundred-ninety, and rips zero to sixty in three seconds?"

"That's right, lad," Reed said in a sultry voice — for she, far more than Jake, enjoyed driving a fast car almost as much as having sex.

"Well then, I'll take the Lamborghini," Jake said. "But any chance we can make love next Sunday?"

"You got that right," Reed said with enthusiasm. "If I can hold off that long."

"Find me irresistible, don't you," Jake said with a devilish grin.

"I do, my handsome husband, I do," she said without a hint of sarcasm — at least Jake couldn't detect any.

He finally was able to exit on the Fowler Avenue off ramp and speed east to the university campus.

As Jake steered into a parking space next to the tennis courts, he spotted Tom Murray standing next to a blue Honda Element. Tom, looking very fit for a man in his fifties, shook his head at Jake while tapping his index finger on his Tissot chronograph.

Jake quickly grabbed his tennis bag off the front passenger seat and climbed out of the SUV.

"Tap that Tissot and it tells you how the markets are doing, that's what you're doing, right, Tom?" Jake said.

"No, Jake, it's my way of signaling that you're as late as an Italian train."

"So very sorry, Oh Great One," Jake said. "How about I spot you the first couple of games, you know, as a way to make up for my tardiness."

"Do that and we're done here," Tom said with a smile that in no way diminished how serious he was about Jake's patrician proposal.

The two seasoned warriors laughed, then shook hands with sincere warmth.

"Damn fine to see you, Tom," Jake said.

"And you as well, Jake," he said. "Now that we got the niceties out of the way, what say we play tennis — I can't wait to run your sorry self all over the court."

"No problem, my friend," Jake responded.

Both men stretched behind a baseline of their court.

"Why'd you rent the Element, Tom?" Jake said.

He tried to stretch thoroughly, without looking like a dork.

"Because the back of the Element converts into a full bed," Tom replied. "After I'm done whipping you in tennis, I'm heading down to

Alafia River State Park to camp for a couple nights before flying back to North Carolina."

Tom grabbed hold of the tall chain-link fence and stretched his hamstrings.

"Got that Smith & Wesson with snake shot?" Jake said.

"Yes sir," Tom said. "In a state park, never know what you're going to encounter, a fat diamondback or a varmint of the two-legged variety. Rattler or parolee, my Smith & Wesson will take care of business quite nicely."

He and Jake finished stretching and began warm-ups on the court.

Forehand to forehand, backhand to backhand, flat returns met with wicked topspin returns, rallying switched to volleying, finishing with practice serves.

Jake and Tom were ready. Though it was only a friendly match with no money on the line, the two men approached tennis as a clash of will and skill and stamina.

I love this game, Jake thought.

I must dominate, Tom thought.

Turns out, neither player truly dominated, as Jake and Tom had always been evenly matched, though their styles differed greatly — Tom loved to serve and volley, while Jake stayed behind the baseline and crushed powerful cross courts. Jake struggled with his first serve, but his kick serve saved him on the second try. Tom blasted flat first serves that were accurate and tricky to return. He took the first set, six games to four.

During the break between sets, Jake and Tom decided that, tennis etiquette aside, they'd take off their tee shirts — it was a sunny afternoon, and the more sun they soaked up, the more serotonin their brains released, keeping them focused and relaxed.

Just before they started the second set, a young woman, probably a USF student, walked by their court. She carried a tennis racket.

"Excuse me, sir, but are you the tennis pro here?" she said to Jake. "I'm ready for my lesson."

Jake couldn't help himself from flexing his well-defined abdominals.

You, sir, are totally shameless, he thought.

"Why yes, yes I am," Jake said to the young woman.

Tom shook his head in mock disgust.

"For goodness sake . . . ." he exclaimed.

"Sheesh, all right," Jake said. "No, young lady, I am *not* the tennis pro here. Sorry, I was just having a little fun."

The young woman smiled pleasantly at Jake.

"No worries," she said to him. "And thanks for your honesty, *grandpa*."

Game, set, and match for the young woman. She took her time walking away.

"First time you've been called 'grandpa'?" Tom asked.

Jake sulkily nodded yes.

"Better get used to it, if you insist on being a wise guy with these co-eds," Tom said.

Both men thought it prudent to put back on their tee shirts — increased serotonin be damned.

Jake took control of the second set by getting in his first serve. Tom maneuvered Jake away from the center of the baseline, but Jake moved effectively from side to side, and he dug for every drop shot. Jake won the second set, six games to two.

During the break, both men gulped down chilled Gatorade.

"So what's up with that, what is it, a Lamborghini, a bright yellow Lamborghini sport-ute?" Tom said, as he wiped perspiration from his face with a white hand towel that Jake gave him.

Good sign, Tom's syntax is stuttering some, Jake thought. Even tired out, Tom's a dangerous player — time to step it up.

"Yeah, it's a birthday gift from Reed," Jake said. "I kinda dig that yellow."

"Well, happy birthday and all, but it's not exactly keeping it low profile, is it," Tom said. He walked over to the fence, grabbed fistfuls of chain link, and again stretched his hamstrings.

"Reed thought the car reflected my personality — you know, sophisticated, sporty, unnecessarily complex."

Tom chuckled.

"I agree with Reed on the last part," Tom said. "So are we going to play, or just horse around for the rest of the day?"

Jake leapt out of his chair.

"We're gonna play, my man," he said. "Let's do this."

"Now you're talking, Pilgrim," Tom answered.

The decisive third set was frenzied and competitive. Neither player would give up on points, resulting in extended rallies and ferocious volleys. Tom resorted to first serves with top spin, thereby giving him more accuracy. Jake's kick serve jumped wickedly. By unspoken agreement, drop shots in the final set were abandoned for safety's sake — this late in the match, digging out a drop shot could cause hamstring pulls or sacroiliac tears. The third set ended with a tiebreaker, which Tom won, eleven points to nine.

Both players, exhausted and dripping with sweat, met at the net and shook hands.

"Heck of a match, Tom, congratulations," Jake said.

"Thanks," Tom said. "I have to admit, you're making me work harder and harder to win. That bed in the back of the Element is starting to look good right now."

For several minutes, Jake and Tom sat in wobbly plastic chairs, which thankfully were under a cantilever shade. At first, they didn't speak, preferring instead to savor the athletic battle that just occurred.

Finally, Jake broke the silence.

"Find out anything about Don Coyote?" he asked.

Tom smiled at no one in particular.

"You mean *senor* Fernando Gonzalez?" he said. "Yeah, it took some doing, but I found out plenty about that son of a gun."

Tom Murray was something of a double threat. On one hand, he was a renowned marine biologist and consultant. He provided expert testimony for the seafood fisheries that sued British Petroleum over its disastrous Deepwater Horizon oil spill. On the other hand, Tom had enjoyed a long career as a CIA field analyst, traveling throughout the Asian Pacific, Europe, and the Caribbean. He was adept at boots-on-the-ground field research. And sometimes it was rather pleasant work, as he got to night fish off the Jamaican coast, hike New Zealand's South Island, and snow ski in the Austrian Alps. Oftentimes, Tom provided remote support to Jake as he carried out his deadly assignments. Over time, the two men grew to like one another, and a lasting friendship formed.

Even though Jake no longer was associated with the CIA, he didn't think it presumptuous to ask Tom for background on Don Coyote. And Tom didn't hesitate to help Jake.

"What can you tell me about *Fernando Gonzalez?*" Jake asked.

Tom took a long pull of blue Gatorade.

"Gonzalez is from Nogales, Mexico, and for the last twenty-five years has been human trafficking and drug smuggling," Tom said. "For a while, he'd been working with his mother, Maria Gonzalez, until she upped and got herself killed in the Arizona desert."

Jake lowered his head.

"Yeah, I may have heard something about that," he said.

"I'm sure you have, and you know what, may Maria Gonzalez rot in Hell and Serg Garcia rest in Heaven," Tom said.

"Thanks for that thought," Jake said. "What else can you tell me about Don Coyote?"

Tom finished his Gatorade.

"He's stayed pretty much under The Company's radar, mostly because we're a bit preoccupied with watching over the Mexican drug cartels — Don Coyote is a fathead minnow compared to the killer whale cartels."

"Hmm, doesn't a fathead minnow live in fresh water and a killer whale live in salt water?" Jake said. "Seems like a faulty metaphor."

Tom grinned at Jake in a manner best described as threatening.

"Been reading *Field & Stream* again?" Tom said. "Well, smart guy, a fathead minnow and a killer whale could conceivably encounter one another in brackish water, so my marine life metaphor remains in play."

"Fair enough," Jake said. "Sorry for the interruption."

"No worries," Tom said. "So I dug a little deeper and found out Don Coyote has changed his business model."

"How so?"

"He has moved his base of operations from Nogales to somewhere in Tampa Bay," Tom said. "He's no longer smuggling drugs. Don Coyote is completely into human trafficking, but with an ingenious twist."

"You have my attention."

"What he does now — and he's making millions from it — is take upper-class young American men and women and sell them into slavery to Mexican buyers."

Jake's jaw literally dropped.

"Red-ass world out there, isn't it," Tom said.

Instead of Gatorade, he pulled out a can of Bud Light from his cooler; he knew better than to offer Jake a beer, so he gave him an ice-cold bottle of Zephyrhills water.

"Hey, it's not Fiji, but it'll do, right?" Tom said.

"Most definitely, thanks," Jake said.

He cracked open the bottle of water and gulped down all of it.

"Sure fire way to get cramps, my friend," Tom said.

"I don't know if I'm hydrating or trying to drown my disgust," Jake said. "I really thought I'd put all of this putrid ugliness behind me when I left The Company."

"No you didn't, Jake, you thought you could just hide from it by living among the normals."

"Yeah, I guess you're right," Jake said. "Tom, you seem as if you've got more to tell me."

"Afraid I have," Tom said. "Don Coyote has been in Tampa Bay for only a few months. Before that, he plied his new trade in Central and South Florida, where he sold off young women *and* men. Here, he's focusing solely on young women."

"Why only women now?" Jake said. "Oh, no . . . . "

"That's right, my man," Tom said. "Ensnaring young women exclusively in Tampa Bay was the best way to get your attention and Reed's. I'm pretty certain that he has those Cutler twins, and he's using them to make a tidy profit while enticing you all to come after him."

"It's all about Maria Gonzalez, isn't it?" Jake said.

"Signed, sealed, and delivered, my good man," Tom said. "Now this is just speculation, but I suspect it's pretty reliable — when you shot and killed Don Coyote's mother, you shot and killed his lover as well."

"Jesus Christ . . . ." Jake exclaimed.

"Jake, do *not* blaspheme around me, you know full well that Jesus is my Lord and Savior," Tom said with a censuring tone. "But I have to say, you're in double jeopardy with Mister Fernando Gonzalez."

"He's coming after me, isn't he."

Tom put his racket and can of tennis balls in his athletic bag. Then he thought better of it, took the can of tennis balls out of the bag, and left the can next to the court.

"He's coming after you *and* Reed, Jake. Want me to stick around and provide field support?"

"Decent of you to offer, Tom, but that would turn this into a Company operation, and I can't let that happen," Jake said. "Reed and I can handle it, and we've got good people to back us up."

"I know you do — that Ravel is a real pistol," Tom said.

"Know about her, huh?" Jake said.

"Of course," Tom said. "Now, you know where I'll be for the next couple of days — contact me if you change your mind about my getting into the mix."

"Will do, and thanks, Tom."

The two men stood and shook hands.

As Tom walked toward his makeshift camper, Jake sat back down. He wanted to savor the remains of this beautiful sunny afternoon in Tampa Bay. He also wanted to sketch out a plan for finding the Cutler twins and getting Don Coyote reunited with his dear, dead mother.

15

It was eight a.m. on a gorgeous Friday morning in downtown Tampa. Reed and Jake were stretching in their yoga room. Sunlight from the east flooded the room. Giuseppe Tartini's *Violin Sonatas, Opus One* was playing over the yoga room's sound system.

Jake admired Tartini because the Baroque musician turned himself into a virtuoso violinist by living in a monastery for three years and perfecting his technique.

Now *that* is what I call dedication, Jake thought.

He promised Reed that, after Tartini, he would put on the music of contemporary jazz saxophonist Richard Elliot.

As the couple stretched vigorously, Jake marveled at Reed's impressive flexibility. Though he was improving his own flexibility, he knew he'd never match Reed's.

"I swear, Reed, do you have extra vertebrae?"

Reed was in a complete side split as she lowered her head first to her left knee and then to her right knee, finishing with touching the floor in front of her with her forehead.

"You mean extra vertebrae like a cat?" she said.

Reed then executed a perfect front split followed by a lotus knee press.

"Afraid it has nothing to do with additional vertebrae," she said. She was mildly out of breath.

"What, good genes combined with gymnastics, basketball, and *tae kwon do*?" Jake said.

He was doing a series of knee twists that felt wonderful, though he appeared to perform the Hokey Pokey.

"I think you're right on the mark," Reed said. "Plus, it helps to stretch my butt off once a day, every day."

"So when are you going to do a back arch?"

Jake knew immediately he sounded over eager. But he couldn't help it — he loved watching Reed arch her body toward the ceiling and hold the pose for a full minute.

Reed stopped stretching and frowned at her husband. She also noticed his staring at her erect nipples poking through her sports bra.

"Is nothing sacred to you, Jake — for God's sake, this our yoga room," Reed said in a tone more serious than Jake would have preferred.

"Sure, Reed, what's sacred to me is Baroque music, Monet's paintings, Italian roast espresso, Mephisto sandals, the complete works of John LeCarre."

Reed raised her eyebrows.

"What about our marriage?"

Crap, I did it again, Jake thought.

"Our marriage is so sacred to me that mere words do not suffice — I'll let my actions speak for themselves."

Reed laughed heartily.

"You are so full of *merde, mon amour*," she said. "However, I'll reward your surprisingly quick retort by letting you off the hook this time, though you don't get to see me do a back arch."

"Fine," Jake said petulantly. "How about we start my *tae kwon do* lesson — everybody's going to be here in an hour."

"Righto," Reed said.

Jake admired her white sports bra and baggy white martial arts pants.

Such a beautiful warrior, he thought.

Jake loved that she was barefoot, as she possessed exquisitely petite feet, and he only recently discovered he had something of a foot fetish. Every morning, he gave Reed a foot massage using Argan of Morocco lotion — it was a toss-up as to who enjoyed the foot massage more.

"Jake, quit staring at my feet — focus, focus. So let's just do *poomse* together, all right?"

Jake nodded yes.

Poomse are *tae kwon do* forms where martial artists engage in a strict set of synchronized strikes, blocks, and kicks in different directions. The idea behind *poomse* is to train martial artists to deal with an array of attacks from multiple directions. *Poomse* instill confidence and discipline through precise repetition of proper form.

Since Reed was a third-degree black belt in *tae kwon do*, she was a most suitable instructor for Jake. Jake already was a lethal weapon; what he sought from Reed was the discipline and control inherent in *tae kwon do*.

Since she no longer fought in tournaments, *poomse* became almost an obsession in refining her martial art.

Reed and Jake bowed to each other, then stood side by side about four feet apart.

"Since we're tight on time, Jake, we'll do *tae qeuk el-jong, tae qeuk e-jong*, and *tae qeuk sam-jong*."

"So, forms one, two, three, right?" Jake said.

"Yes, and I'm suitably impressed, now let's go."

At Reed's lead, she and Jake performed *tae qeuk el-jong*, which involved punches and front kicks, complemented with low, middle, and rising blocks, all the while stepping forward, turning side to side, and pivoting completely around. It was the simplest of *poomse*, yet still required concentration and proper form.

Jake was impressed with Reed's ability to strike with her hand or foot with such controlled and ferocious velocity.

Tae qeuk e-jong included all the moves of the first *poomse* while adding inside forearm blocks and wicked high-section punches.

Reed and Jake moved fluidly and in perfect synchronicity.

Both were beginning to perspire.

Jake particularly enjoyed *tae qeuk sam-jong* because the *poomse* required an inward knife-hand strike to the side of the neck. This strike can be lethal if applied correctly — Jake lustily envisioned using the knife-hand in a real-life situation.

Reed and Jake took a short break before repeating the three *poomse* four more times. Not once did they bump into each other, and Reed didn't have to correct Jake at all.

As they caught their breath, they drank greedily from bottles of Voss water.

"So when do I get to break some more boards?" Jake said.

From his viewpoint, there was nothing quite so pleasurable as smashing his hand, elbow, or foot through pine boards. It was for him a kind of roughhouse physical therapy.

Pity the board that isn't afraid of me, he thought.

"Maybe next time," Reed said. "Now it's time to hit the showers, Grasshopper."

She took Jake by his hand and led him to their master bath.

The steam shower had upper and middle shower heads on each side, as well as a large rain shower head in the center. Reed walked over to a keypad next to the shower and programmed all five shower heads to turn on.

She then faced Jake and deftly took off her sports bra, exposing her perfect breasts and erect nipples.

"Jake, you did so well in your *tae kwon do* lesson today, I've decided that you may kiss my breasts."

Jake happily complied, noticing that Reed's nipples tasted salty from perspiration.

The couple disrobed and entered the shower together.

As Reed shaved her legs, she noticed that Jake had an impressive erection, one that resembled a divining rod wangling about for water.

"Any luck finding water?" she asked with a giggle.

"Huh? What're you talking about?" Jake said.

Then he looked down at his erection.

"*Now* I get it," Jake said. "Very funny, wise guy."

"Sorry, I couldn't resist — am I the only woman who thinks male genitalia is funny sometimes?"

"You are one among many, my dear," Jake aid.

To show there were no hard feelings over Reed's joke, Jake shampooed Reed's gorgeous blonde hair. He made sure his diving rod didn't poke her in the back.

Reed returned the favor by shampooing Jake's curly brown hair. She stood on her tippy toes and leaned against Jake's backside.

And then nature took its course.

Jake arched his back and pressed his buttocks into Reed, who then began grinding her hips against Jake.

She began to breathe heavily.

Reed reached around and held Jake's manhood.

Jake began to breathe heavily.

The couple climaxed together.

Jake turned around and held his beautiful and sated wife. She rested her head on Jake's shoulder.

Hot steam enveloped the couple.

Gradually, their breathing steadied.

"Guess I couldn't wait for Sunday," Reed whispered.

"My divining rod and I are glad you couldn't wait, my sweet Reed."

Then she reached around Jake again — this time to smack his left buttock.

"All right, Mister, we need to towel off, get some clothes on, and get ready for our meeting."

"Roger that, Cap'n."

Jake kissed Reed, then stepped out of the shower and pressed three buttons on the keypad to shut off the water.

He turned and admired Reed, who was still standing in the shower. Rivulets of water ran down her body. Steam formed a halo around her.

God, I do so love that woman, Jake thought.

16

———

Reed O'Hara's posse arrived right on time. As she held open the massive oak front door, Judi Ploszek, Ravel, Chenoa, and Sierra walked in single file into the living room. Jake stood in front of the living room's picture window and welcomed the women to sit down, which they did. Judi and Chenoa sat together on one sofa, Ravel and Sierra on the other. Reed settled into an over-stuffed armchair, while Jake sat across from her in an identical armchair.

Jake had placed a Bodum of French roast coffee, diner style coffee mugs, sugar and cream containers, and bottles of Evian water on the coffee table.

In collective acknowledgement of Reed's leadership role, no one talked until Reed spoke.

"Thanks to all of you for agreeing to come to our home on such short notice," she said. "I want to especially thank Judi for joining us — she doesn't have a dog in this fight, at least not yet."

Everyone laughed politely.

"Thanks, Reed, but I'm here only to listen and perhaps make an observation or two," Judi said. "This is the first time I've had the chance to mingle with a group of intelligent people since I retired, so I'm truly glad to be here."

It had been only six months since Judi retired as Chief Financial Officer of Tampa General Hospital. For several years, she had been Reed's friend, confidant, and ally. Though she hadn't been directly involved in Reed's private investigations, Judi provided crucial insights to Reed and Jake as they solved the case of the perished priests.

When Reed invited her to attend this meeting, Judi jumped at the opportunity to spice up her day.

Reed pushed down the plunger to the Bodum, then poured coffee for everyone.

"Mind making us another pot of your delicious coffee, Jake?" Reed said, holding the empty Bodum.

"Get right on it," Jake said.

Anything for the woman who has sex with me in the shower, he thought.

"Jake, what's with your always making coffee?" Judi asked playfully.

Jake was busy in the kitchen scooping out the coffee grounds from the Bodum. He always saved the coffee grounds, as they made a wonderful soil fortifier for his rose bush planters that lined both sides of the lap pool on the penthouse terrace.

He smiled benevolently at Judi's question.

"Making coffee is but one of many aspects of doing the domestic," Jake said. "You know very well that I live to serve Supreme Leader."

Judi laughed heartily.

"Make another Kim Jong Un reference about me, Jake, and I'll put you on severe rationing — and you know exactly what I'm talking about," Reed said.

Ravel was sitting on the sofa and using her laptop that was, indeed, on her lap. She only appeared not to pay attention to this exchange between Reed, Jake, and Judi.

"Yeah, right, severe rationing," Ravel mumbled. "As if Reed could stop herself from fucking French Boy."

"Ravel!" Reed and Judi exclaimed together.

"What? What'd I say?" Ravel said defensively.

Sierra sat up and placed her hand on Ravel's inner thigh.

"In her own inimitable way, Ravel is only speaking the truth, Reed," Sierra said. "We know full well that your denying Jake sexual favors is an empty threat."

She gave Reed a Mona Lisa smile, Swedish style.

Well, look who's growing herself a pair of balls, Ravel thought.

In the kitchen, the tea kettle whistled. Jake picked up the kettle and poured boiling water over eight tablespoons of freshly ground Italian roast in the Bodum.

"Hey, Ravel, did you know the Bodum Company was founded in Denmark in 1944 by Peter Bodum; then Jorgen Bodum, the founder's son, moved the company to Switzerland in 1978," Jake said.

"No, I didn't, Mr. Google," Ravel said.

Jake's gambit worked: by gassing on about the Bodum, tension between Reed and Ravel eased.

Reed knew exactly what Jake had done. She gave him a subtle wink as he walked into the living room and placed the full Bodum on the coffee table.

Reed started the meeting, after pushing down the plunger on the coffee press.

"I'll start with a report on my interview with Elin Karlsson Cutler, the mother of twin sisters Morgan and Cecelia."

"You go, girl," Ravel said, as she tapped away on her laptop.

Chenoa rolled her eyes at Ravel.

"While Elin doesn't seem terribly involved now with her daughters, she is genuinely distraught over their disappearance," Reed said.

Reed took a sip of coffee.

"Elin insists that the sisters didn't run away — even though Morgan and Cecelia took their passports when they disappeared. Elin believes with all her heart that her daughters were abducted," she said.

Chenoa was about to speak when Judi put her hand on Chenoa's knee.

"Do you suspect Elin and Clive are involved in any way with the possible abduction?" Judi asked.

"Not for one second," Reed said without hesitation. "and there's no 'possible' about it — these young women were kidnapped."

This time, Chenoa put her alabaster hand on Judi's knee.

"What do you make of Clive and Elin as a couple?" she asked.

"Interesting, to say the least," Reed said. "Clive is considerably older than Elin. He's *nouveau riche*, while she's more working class, though she seems comfortable with the upper-class lifestyle. I mean, for God's sake, she has a lifeguard watch over her dogs as they splash around in the swimming pool."

"What's wrong with that?" Judi asked.

This time, Chenoa rolled her eyes at Judi.

People and their dogs, she thought.

"My point, Judi, is that Elin has transitioned nicely from a cocktail server at a country club to the *doyenne* of a wealthy South Tampa family."

Judi ran her hand through her strawberry blonde hair.

"I see your point, Reed," she said. "But where's the rub here?"

"The rub?" Chenoa asked.

"Yes, the rub, the friction point of discontent and unhappiness in the Cutler household," Judi said in a professional tone. "Somebody in that ridiculously large home had to have played a role in the disappearance of the twins."

"Well, okay, it's only a hunch," Reed said. She shifted uncomfortably in her armchair.

"Your hunches are usually right on the mark," Jake said. "So tell us about it."

"I think the butler did it," Reed said reluctantly.

Jake, Judi, and Chenoa laughed aloud; Ravel and Sierra stayed silent.

"Reed isn't being flippant here, guys," Sierra said. She still spoke with a heavy Swedish accent. "Go on, Reed, explain it to them"

Reed cleared her throat.

Ravel gave Reed a nod of encouragement.

"I think there's a dark wild card in the Cutler home, and her name is Mala Karlsson," Reed said.

"Who's that?" Judi asked.

"She's the family butler, but for all intents and purposes, Mala manages the entire household — including the care of Morgan and Cecelia."

"Holy shit," Judi said. "And did you say *Mala Karlsson?*"

"That's right, Mala Karlsson is Elin's cousin — and her butler," Ravel said. "Gee, I don't know why anyone would have thought it was a bad idea to hire your cousin to be your servant."

"Ravel, you'll have your turn to report," Reed said. "Let me finish up, okay?"

"Fine, but I can't believe you stole my line," Ravel said. She smiled mischievously at Reed.

"I probably should have credited you for the butler line, Ravel, but what the heck, you probably got it from Agatha Christie," Reed said.

"Playing Clue, actually," Ravel said.

"Can we get back on the point here?" Judi said. For just a moment there, she thought she was back at Tampa General's corporate center.

"Yes, of course, Judi," Reed said.

"Teacher's pet," Ravel muttered.

"Whatever, Ravel," Reed said. "Now, I suspect Mala isn't too happy with the arrangement at the Cutler mansion. She and Elin are both from Sweden and come from humble backgrounds. I'm sure she thought it was fantastic of Elin to bring her to the United States. Reality, though, probably set in quickly. Mala works very long days and gets little time off. Elin doesn't allow her to speak Swedish around the house, and she even makes Mala wear high heels all day long."

"Why high heels?" Sierra asked.

"With high heels clopping on marble floors, Elin can always hear Mala coming," Reed said.

"What a jerk," Sierra said.

"So I suppose Mala sees herself as Cinderella, and Elin as the evil stepmother," Judi said.

"That's very good, Judi," Reed said.

"*Fucking* teacher's pet," Ravel said.

Judi sat straight up. Her face reddened. Almost out of some strange habit, she ran her right hand down her right trouser leg.

Reed knew that Judi kept a rose-gold derringer in her trouser sock. She also knew Judi possessed a fierce Chicago temper.

"Judi, chill, I mean it," Reed said. "Ravel's just baiting you — it's her way of showing how much she likes you."

Judi seemed to calm down.

"Is that true, Ravel, you like me, you *really do* like me?" Judi said.

Ravel actually looked up from her laptop.

"You betcha, Judi," she said. "I think you're one hot little *chica*."

"Yeah, thanks, I think," Judi said. "You know, of course, I'm totally into men, right?"

"A gay girl can dream, can't she?" Ravel said coyly.

"Well, you just keep on dreaming, sweetheart, but it's never going to happen," Judi said.

"Ooh, me thinks you doth protest *too* much," Ravel answered.

Reed had heard enough.

"No more of this *batonnage*, ladies," Reed said. "So if Mala sees herself as a sort of Cinderella figure, then wouldn't she be vulnerable to some smooth-talking Prince Charming who happens to be a predator of upper-class young women?"

"You couldn't have put it more accurately, Reed," Ravel said.

"Why thank you, Ravel," Reed said.

"Fucking teacher's pet," Judi interjected.

Everyone in the living room broke out in uproarious laughter.

"On that note, everyone, let's refill our coffee mugs and relax for a bit," Reed said.

After everyone finished their coffee, Reed re-started the meeting.

"It makes sense to have Ravel give us her report," Reed said. "She has come by some very useful intel on Mala."

Ravel closed her laptop. She drank from her bottle of Evian.

"I'll let it pass that you just stole my thunder, Reed," she said. "Anyway, I spent the better part of an evening with a Veronica Lake trans at the Hub, and she convinced me that Mala Karlsson is up to her neck with the abduction of the twins."

"You've got my attention, Ravel," Judi said.

"After several martinis and a thousand bucks, Veronica told me how she encountered the twins at Metropolitan Ministries, how she hooked up with Mala, and how she got Mala and Don Quixote to meet one another," Ravel said.

Reed marveled at how Ravel built her case against Mala with the steady precision of a funicular ascending Mount Pelerine in Switzerland.

"Any chance Don Quixote is Mala's Prince Charming, whose real agenda was to get at the twins?" Reed asked.

"Oh, there's a hundred-percent chance — at least that's how I see it," Sierra said. With her cascading blonde hair, glacier blue eyes, and a body fit for a full day of downhill skiing, Sierra was a Scandinavian beauty who struggled with people taking her seriously.

"I think you see it exactly right, Sierra," Judi said in a reassuring tone.

"*Tack*, Judi," Sierra said.

For some reason, Jake seemed as if he wanted to speak, yet he remained silent.

"My hunch is that Don Quixote didn't just roll up to the Cutler mansion in a white panel van one late night, break into the mansion, and abscond with the twins," Reed said.

"The way Veronica described him, you know, a cultured and sophisticated middle-aged Mexican *caballero*, that just wouldn't be his style," Ravel said.

Jake rose out of his armchair and walked over to the full length picture windows. He appeared to stare out at the Tampa skyline.

"Everything all right, Jake?" Reed asked.

"Just fine, needed to stretch my legs," he answered.

"Okay," Reed said. "So how do you think he made off with Morgan and Cecelia? I mean, even with Mala's help, he couldn't have spent much time around the Cutler home."

"I think I can answer that," Chenoa said. She wore a Balmain striped six-button cotton blazer with matching slacks. The gold buttons matched nicely with her gold Tag Heuer watch on her left wrist and the gold Christian Louboutin heels on her petite feet. She wore no blouse under her jacket.

"God, even if I could've dressed like that at Tampa General, I don't think I would've," Judi said. "But don't get me wrong, Chenoa, you look great, and I want to hear what you have to say."

Chenoa blushed slightly. She also noticed Ravel staring at her cleavage.

Look but don't touch, dearest, Chenoa thought.

Talk about a lipstick lesbian, Ravel thought. Wishful thinking on my part, I'm sure.

"I had lunch with Father Jack the other day — I used to work with him at Sacred Heart," Chenoa said.

"Work *and* play, right?" Ravel said.

"Screw you, Ravel," Chenoa fired back.

"I really wish you would," Ravel answered.

"Enough, ladies," Reed said. "Chenoa, proceed."

"Yes, ma'am," Chenoa said. "Jack told me that Don Quixote — his real name is Fernando Gonzalez — started hovering around the twins at Sunday Mass at Sacred Heart."

"What do you bet that Mala put this Gonzalez character on to the twins attending Mass at Sacred Heart," Judi interjected.

"I think you're right," Chenoa said. She sat straight up, as she was exposing her breasts a bit too much.

Don't do that on my account, Ravel thought.

"Jack also told me that Gonzalez and the twins started attending daily Mass together, and Clive Cutler was never there," Chenoa said.

"When was this?" Reed asked.

"Maybe three weeks ago," Chenoa said. "And Jack actually met Gonzalez after a daily Mass."

"What does Father Jack think of Gonzalez?" Reed said.

"Jack found him polite but standoffish, and Gonzalez was very controlling with Morgan and Cecelia," Chenoa said. "Jack also was deeply offended by Gonzalez's passive-aggressive behavior — he tossed a cigar wrapper into the holy water font."

"Did he make certain that Father Jack saw him do it," Sierra asked.

"Jack said Gonzalez wanted him to see his sacrilegious stunt," Chenoa said.

"So Don Quixote is one ballsy guy," Ravel said.

Jake exhaled loudly, then covered his face with his hands.

"Goddamnit it, it's not Don *Quixote*, it's Don *Coyote*," he said.

"You mean like the animal?" Judi asked.

"I mean more like the two-legged coyotes who traffic in human beings — more specifically, those predatory assholes who charge an exorbitant amount of money to get very desperate Mexicans across the U.S. border," Jake said.

"So Don Coyote is a human trafficker?" Judi asked.

"He and his mother used to smuggle Mexicans into the U.S.," Jake said. "They were a real piece of work — they'd force their fellow Mexicans to backpack heroin and cocaine across the border, then they'd sell off these poor souls to the highest bidder in Arizona."

"Was it a lucrative business?" Judi asked.

"Maria and Fernando Gonzalez made millions," Jake said. "And there was an air of mystery about them, people were allowed to address them only as '*La Patrona*' and '*Don Coyote.*' "

"How do you know all this, Jake?" Sierra asked.

"I happened to run into the mother and son back in the day, plus my old CIA buddy Tom Murray provided me some valuable intel this week," Jake said.

"What else can you tell us?" Reed said.

"*La Patrona* was large and in charge," Jake said. "She was based out of Nogales, Mexico, and she referred to her operation as *La Frontera.*"

Chenoa had a studied frown on her face.

"Jake, you keep using past tense when referencing Maria Gonzalez," she said. "Is *La Patrona* no longer with us?"

"No, she's among the departed now," Jake said. "She died eighteen years ago."

"So Don Coyote carried on the family business" Sierra asked.

"Yes, but he eventually changed the business model," Jake said.

"How so?" Reed asked. She was genuinely perplexed as to why her husband hadn't already given her this information — he had been uncharacteristically buttoned up for the past day or so.

"Don Coyote moved his operation to the United States," Jake said. "Apparently, he has been obsessed with American pop culture and consumed with achieving the American Dream."

"You said he changed his business model," Judi said.

"Yes, now he preys on young, well-off American women and men, brainwashes them so that they come under his complete control, then sells these young Americans as sex slaves to wealthy Mexicans."

A cloud of silence, almost like mustard gas, fell upon everyone in the living room.

Reed finally broke the silence.

"Good God, Morgan and Cecelia are in terrible danger," she said.

"Got that right," Ravel said. "Talk about a wicked take on Montezuma's Revenge."

"I'm afraid there's more," Jake said.

"Let's hear it," Judi said.

She already had taken out her rosary beads from her purse, and was praying for the twins — despite the horrific scandals rocking the Roman Catholic Church, Judi remained a Catholic. Reed once asked Judi why she didn't abandon her Catholic faith. Judi told her, "A person isn't finished when she meets defeat — a person is finished only when she quits, and I'm not a quitter."

"Don Coyote had been plying his trade throughout Florida, specifically in Miami, Naples, Boca Raton, Sarasota, and Orlando," Jake said. "But he's in Tampa now, for a specific reason."

"And that is . . . ." Ravel said.

"In 2001, The Company tasked me and my partner Sergio Garcia with taking out *La Patrona*," Jake said.

"You're shitting me," Ravel said.

"No, no I'm not, and this isn't easy for me to talk about," Jake said.

"You're doing great, Jake," Reed said.

"Well, there was a shoot-out at the U.S. border east of Nogales," Jake said. "Maria Gonzalez shot and killed Serg, I shot and killed her, and Fernando Gonzalez got away."

"So am I to infer that Don Coyote is here to sell Morgan and Cecelia as sex slaves in Mexico *and* take revenge on you for killing his mother?" Judi said, still clutching her rosary beads.

"Yes, he's going to make a fortune selling twin American sisters to the highest bidder in Mexico, plus he's doubly motivated to exact revenge on me," Jake said.

"I'm afraid to ask, but how is he doubly motivated?" Sierra said. She was growing more confident by the minute — Sierra was starting to feel as if she actually belonged in this meeting.

"I can't believe I'm saying this: Maria Gonzalez was Don Coyote's mother . . . and lover," Jake said.

"Ooooo, so gross and so cool at the same time," Ravel said, her violet eyes all alit.

"You know, Ravel, I'm going to pray for you," Judi said.

"Never hurts to put in a good word for me with the Big Guy," Ravel said without a hint of sarcasm.

Reed got up from her armchair and walked slowly around the living room. She wore a green *guayabera* embroidered with flowers on the two vertical rows of pleats on the front of the shirt. She discovered the *guayabera* at the San Miguel *mercado* on Cozumel Island in Mexico. Reed found it appealing to wear a shirt traditionally worn by Hispanic men.

"We are getting short on time, ladies and gentleman," Reed said. "So we have to come up with a very pointed and precise action plan."

"Agreed," Chenoa said.

"I mentioned to Mala that she ought to meet Sierra, since they're both from Sweden, and Mala could use the company," Reed said. "I gave Mala your phone number, Sierra, has she contacted you?"

Sierra nodded yes.

"Mala must have called me not five minutes after you left the Cutler mansion, Reed," Sierra said. A seasoned stage performer at Namaste, Sierra was at ease with being the center of attention at this point in the meeting.

"Right, and did you two decide to get together," Reed asked.

"*Absolut*, Mala is coming over to Namaste tomorrow night to watch me perform, then I thought I'd bring her over to my place after work," Sierra said.

"Let me guess, she's another gay Swede," Ravel said jealously. She didn't at all like the idea of Mala intruding on her amorous arrangement with Sierra.

"Don't worry, Ravel, Sierra isn't going to have sex with Mala," Reed interjected. "What will happen is that you, Chenoa, and I are going to throw a little surprise party for Mala at Sierra's apartment."

"Oh, I *like* that," Ravel said. "Can I beat the truth out of her?"

Reed pretended to be annoyed with Ravel, who had herself endured horrible torture by the Russian mobster Victor Petrov.

"There will no enhanced interrogation," Reed said. "Rather, we will explain to Mala that it only makes sense to tell us where the twins and Don Coyote are."

"You know I was joking, right?" Ravel said. She still had scars on her chest from Petrov caning her with a bamboo switch, and there wasn't enough Mederma in the world to make those scars go away.

"Of course I know, my beautiful Swiss genius," Reed said lovingly.

"What should we do in the meantime?" Chenoa asked.

"Ravel, I want you to get on the internet and see if you can find Fernando Gonzalez's financial information — where does he bank and where does he invest. Does he have an accountant, a financial manager, or a lawyer? I want you to dig into his complete portfolio."

"Sounds good, and once I've tracked down this jerk's money, do you want me to clean him out?" Ravel said. "I was thinking maybe I'd donate all of his money to shelters for abused women throughout Florida."

"So tempting, but let's hold off on that for now," Reed said. She understood that Ravel, could clear out Don Coyote's accounts in her sleep, but it was all a matter of timing. Cleaning out Don Coyote now might spook him.

"Jake, get a hold of Nat Doliner and ask him if Don Coyote and the twins have popped up anywhere, particularly in South Tampa," Reed said. "That's the beauty of Tampa, really, we have big-city aspirations, yet we're still small-town enough that everybody is all up in everybody else's business."

"I'll be glad to contact Nat, Reed," Jake said. He appeared at peace with himself.

Nat Doliner was a senior shareholder at the prestigious Tampa law firm of Carlton Fields. He also captained the neighborhood watch programs throughout Tampa. Nat was a good friend to Reed and Jake, and he sometimes assisted them in their investigations. Reed knew that Nat would help out in any way possible regarding the Cutler twins.

"Any time you need me, just call and I'll be there," Nat once said to Reed, not realizing he was actually quoting the Supremes.

"All right, everyone, let's bring this most productive meeting to an end," Reed said.

Jake said goodbye to everyone, then walked out to the penthouse terrace to get some fresh air.

Chenoa, Ravel, and Sierra left.

Judi stayed behind.

"Got something on your mind, Judi?" Reed asked. She finished her bottle of Evian.

"I do, but it has nothing to do with Don Coyote and the Cutler twins," Judi said.

"Good, I'm a little burned out right now over this case," Reed said. "So talk to me."

"How's your co-ed basketball league coming along?" Judi asked.

"Just fine, though Roman's doing most of the work right now," Reed answered.

"I think you should nail down a commissioner as soon as possible, and I'd like to suggest someone who would fill that role nicely."

"I'm all ears," Reed said. "I recently interviewed a strong candidate, but the job remains open."

"Please consider Jean Mayer," Judi said. "And it's not just because Jean's my good friend. You know, she retired recently as senior vice president of strategic planning at Tampa General, so she may be available."

"And Jean's a marketing maven, right?" Reed said.

"You bet," Judi said. "Plus, she has superb organizational skills, and she's politically savvy."

"Considering Jean for league commissioner reminds me of the Brooklyn Nets, who went against convention by hiring their director of player performance from the U.S. Naval Special Warfare Command," Reed said.

"Been reading *Sports Illustrated?*" Judi said.

"Oh yes, I consider *SI* a vital part of my doing research on this new league," Reed said.

"Does Jake or Ravel get the *SI* swimsuit issue?" Judi asked.

"Ravel, of course," Reed said. "Jake says he doesn't need to ogle beautiful women in tiny bikinis because he has me."

"Jake is a lovely man," Judi said.

"Smart, too," Reed quipped.

"So why don't you and Jean have a chat," Judi said.

"Let's do this, we'll have you and Jean over for dinner, and we'll explore her becoming league commissioner," Reed said.

"Who'll cook?" Judi said. Unfortunately, Judi had endured Reed's burned brownies and Christmas cookies. She suspected Reed intentionally burned food in order to get banned from the kitchen.

"Jake will cook, of course," Reed said matter of factly.

"Wow, devoted husband, nightclub manager, private investigator, accomplished pianist and composer, now chef — is there anything that man can't do?" Judi asked.

Reed rolled her Irish blue eyes at her good friend.

"Geez, Judi, *please* don't ever tell that to Jake."

17

———

Don Coyote was having his own special meeting in his South Tampa home and he was none too pleased about it.

The twins approached him to protest over not being allowed to attend daily Mass at Sacred Heart.

Don Coyote suggested that Morgan and Cecelia watch a televised Mass on EWTN, the Catholic Church's Eternal Word Television Network.

Damn cable and streaming services, cost me three-hundred bucks a month, he thought. Least the little brats could do is watch EWTN to get their holy roller jollies.

"But, *El Patron*, watching it on TV isn't the same as being there, especially at Sacred Heart," Cecelia said.

Cecelia was showing increasing boldness, which concerned Don Coyote.

The sooner this deals' done, the better, he thought. Guess I'll have to increase Cecelia's dosages of angel's trumpet and cyclobenzaprine — that'll fix her caboose, or is it wagon? Time to binge watch *Gunsmoke*.

"Sorry, but I can't let you out in public, my sweethearts," he said. "Your ignoble parents have hired an army of henchmen to find you and steal you away, and I won't allow that to happen."

"Why couldn't we go to Mass in disguises?" Cecelia asked.

What, dress you up as nuns, have you wear Ray-Bans, Don Coyote thought. Sure, why not, we'd tell 'em you're visiting from a South Beach monastery. Geesh!

"Too great a risk someone will recognize you, even with fake mustaches, noses, and glasses," Don Coyote said.

"That'd be our disguise, looking like Groucho Marx?" Cecelia asked.

Morgan *tsked* at her sister.

"No, you friggin' idiot, *El Patron* was making a joke," Morgan said.

"Well, I didn't know," Cecelia said. She began to cry, which awakened Goliath the Chihuahua, who had been sleeping peacefully on Don Coyote's lap.

Don Coyote gently stroked Goliath. The tiny dog promptly went back to sleep.

"Cecelia, darling, there's no need to cry," Don Coyote said. "Now, Morgan should not have used gutter talk, but she was right — I was providing a bit of levity, since you appeared so serious and perplexed."

"I apologize for my gutter talk, my True Father," Morgan said.

That Morgan's a crafty one, Don Coyote thought. Gonna double dose her, too.

Cecelia stopped crying.

"Maybe the problem is we're getting a little stir crazy here," Morgan said.

She put her arm around Cecelia's waist and patted her sister's shoulder.

"Don't I give you free range of this beautiful home, including the pool in the backyard?" Don Coyote said.

He never worried about a nosey neighbor spotting the twins sunbathing in the backyard. They weren't allowed to play music outside; just to make sure, he had taken away their phones, tablets, and laptops. Also, a six-foot-high concrete block wall bordered the backyard. Plus, twenty-foot-high Japanese timber bamboo ran the perimeter of the backyard.

"Yes, True Father, and we appreciate it," Morgan said. "I only wish that we could go for a walk, perhaps late at night and you could accompany us."

In a pig's eye, Don Coyote thought.

He slapped the armrest of his La-Z-Boy recliner. Goliath awoke and squeaked his disapproval. The twins jerked at Don Coyote's display of anger.

"I won't allow it!" he said. "I am beginning to question your commitment, Morgan and Cecelia."

"No, please don't doubt us, *El Patron*," Cecelia said. The last thing we want to do is disappoint you."

She started to cry again.

"We are fully committed, True Father," Morgan said. "I still can't believe how generous you were in offering us a path away from, how did you say it, 'the gilded emptiness of an absurdly privileged life'."

"Do you mean that, Morgan?" Don Coyote asked.

Morgan made prayer hands.

"With all of my heart, *El Padre Verdad*," she said. "Sister and I are prepared to dedicate the rest of our lives to meeting the needs of Mateo and Lucia Da Rosa."

Well, I sure as shit don't know about the rest of your lives, but the Da Rosas probably'll get three or four good years out of you before they move on to their next playthings. That is, if I let those *pendejos* live.

"What about your cabin fever?" he asked.

"We'll deal with it, *El Patron*," Cecelia answered.

"Good, good," Don Coyote said. "It won't be but a few more days until you travel to the paradise that is Mexico."

"We're so happy to hear that," Morgan said. "I promise that we'll be good from here on out."

"Yes, we will, *El Patron*," Cecelia said with eagerness.

"In that case, I shall reward you with an appearance by someone who simply will enthrall you," Don Coyote said.

"Who is it, who is it?" both twins said in unison.

They had returned to their almost childlike temperament.

Don Coyote chuckled, which awakened Goliath.

"Not going to say," he said. "Right now, off to your bedroom and change into something appropriate and tasteful."

Morgan and Cecelia practically ran to their bedroom.

"Don't be in such a rush," Don Coyote called out. "Our guest won't be here for a couple hours."

Plenty of time for Benecio to go shopping, then get himself over here, he thought.

Don Coyote picked up his phone and speed dialed Benecio's phone number.

After speaking with Benecio for a few minutes, Don Coyote decided to nap in his La-Z-Boy with his lazy dog, who steadfastly remained on his master's lap.

OF LATE, HE HAD BEEN EXPERIENCING EXCRUCIATINGLY PAINFUL dreams of his mother. What bothered him the most was the breast-feeding dream. Sigmund Freud and Dr. Ruth would have fought to the death in a steel cage match to get Don Coyote for a patient.

Don Coyote and Goliath were awakened by the doorbell playing Rupert Holmes' "Escape", more popularly known as "The Pina Colada Song".

Difficult to re-program that doorbell, but man, I dig that song, he thought.

As he walked down the hallway, he sang about drinking pina coladas and getting caught in the rain.

Do so love this country, he thought. So many wonderful ways to make a buck.

Don Coyote opened the front door to Benecio standing on the pink flamingo welcome mat.

He was aghast at Benecio's appearance, as he was wearing perhaps the most blatantly inauthentic priest's outfit that Don Coyote had ever seen.

Benecio's priest cossock was made of diaphanous black polyester material. The pope mitre atop his head appeared to be made of cardboard. A white plastic rosary dangled out of a front pocket. And, of course, Benecio was still wearing his green flip flops.

Don Coyote closed the front door as he stepped out onto the front veranda.

"Are you out of your mind?" he exclaimed.

Benecio hung his head.

"I did the best I could, Father," he said.

"Really?" Don Coyote said. "Where's your companion, the whore nun of Babylon?"

"Huh?" Benecio said, thoroughly befuddled.

"Never mind, but where on earth did you find that get up?" Don Coyote said. "At the El Castillo gift shop?"

A former late nineteenth-century Ybor City hotel, where some of Teddy Roosevelt's Rough Riders stayed in 1898 as they prepared to invade Cuba, El Castillo now was a gathering place for transexuals, bisexual swingers, occultists, psycho sexual infantilists, and practitioners of bondage and sadomasochism. The club was a veritable free-for-all marketplace of freakiness and, indeed, had a gift shop.

"No, El Castillo's wasn't open this early," Benecio said, totally oblivious to Don Coyote's sarcasm — as usual. "There wasn't exactly a Priests & Things at Westshore Mall, Father, so I had to go to Party City over by USF."

"For God's sake," Don Coyote said. "At least lose the mitre."

"The what?" Benecio said.

"The *hat*, you moron," Don Coyote said.

But before Benecio could take off the mitre, a postal carrier approached with that day's mail. The carrier said good afternoon to the two men, pausing just long enough for her to soak in this unusual scene, then put the mail in the veranda mailbox.

"Allow me to explain," Don Coyote said.

"Don't wanna know, not part of my job description to judge," the postal carrier said.

She hurriedly walked away.

"Have a nice day," Benecio called out to her.

"Shut the hell up," Don Coyote said. He grabbed the cardboard mitre off Benecio's head, crushed it, and tossed it into a nearby azalea bush.

"And what's with the rubber sandals?" he asked.

"The flip flops?" Benecio said. "Father, I'm fighting some wicked hardcore Athlete's Foot — I'm airing out my feet."

"You know that doesn't work . . . oh, never mind," Don Coyote said. "Just come inside and hide out in the front room for a while, and I'll give the twins some, shall we say, extra fortified tea. Man, you creep me out."

Benecio smirked as the two men walked inside the mansion.

Smile away, fuckwit, 'cause your days are numbered, Don Coyote thought.

Benecio ambled into the front sitting room and plopped down in a chair.

Don Coyote went to the kitchen and prepared an especially strong batch of angel's trumpet tea. He determined that ten angel's trumpet blooms would be sufficient, without poisoning the twins, of course. He crushed eight fifteen-milligram tablets of cyclobenzaprine in a stone mortar and pestle, then sprinkled the powdered muscle relaxant into the steeping angel's trumpet tea. He stirred the concoction.

This tea'll make the girls as cool as the center seed in a cucumber, Don Coyote thought.

He called out to Morgan and Cecelia, who promptly came into the kitchen. They were wearing matching white pantsuits and white dress slippers.

"Time for your tea, my beauties," Don Coyote said.

"No vitamins?" Morgan asked.

"Only tea today, my dear," Don Coyote said. He figured that the crushed cyclobenzaprine, dissolved in the hot tea, would work much faster than taking it in pill form.

The twins dutifully drank all of their tea.

"That was tasty," Cecelia said. "Did you put extra honey in it?"

"Very observant of you, Cecelia," Don Coyote said. "Now let's go into the living room and relax — our guest will be here shortly."

For the next fifteen minutes, the twins lounged on the living room sofa. In a low voice, Don Coyote sang Foghat's "Slow Ride" to them.

The twins and Goliath were getting droopy eyes.

The time has come, Don Coyote thought. The tea has taken, now Benecio needs to make his grand entrance.

"Father Benecio, please come to the living room," Don Coyote called out. "I want you to meet my angels, Morgan and Cecelia."

Benecio flip-flopped down the hallway. The closer he came, the more ridiculous he appeared, what with his shimmering, almost see-through, cassock and askew priest collar.

I can see his tee shirt and Spiderman boxers under that cassock, Don Coyote thought. Thank God the twins made it up the stairway to heaven.

"Morgan and Cecelia, sit up, right now!" Don Coyote said.

The twins sat up. Their shoulders slumped, and their eyes were half opened. They appeared quite happy and dreamy — the tea had had its desired effect on them.

"Please say hello to Father Benecio," Don Coyote said. "He has come here today to bless you in your travels to Mexico."

Not going to make 'em get up, he thought. Probably'd go down like dominoes.

"Hello, Father Bagnelli, how're you," Morgan slurred.

"That's Benecio." He said.

"Hmm?" Morgan said, trying to get her bearings.

"I'm Father *Benecio*, child," he said in a paternalistic tone, though he was only seven years older than the twins.

"Hi, Father Benecio!" the twins exclaimed loudly.

Goliath had had enough and padded off to his bedroom.

"Children, I have come here to ask for God's blessing and spiritual protection as you embark on your exciting new life in Mexico," Benecio said. "Please, down on your knees to show obedience to God."

Morgan and Cecelia awkwardly got down on their knees. Cecelia giggled a bit.

Benecio looked at Don Coyote, who gave him a thumbs up.

"Lord, we ask you to be Morgan and Cecelia's guide and protector on the journey they are about to take," Benecio said. "Watch over them, protect them from accidents, keep them free from harm to body and soul, keep them always mindful of Your presence and love. Amen."

"Amen," the twins said as they made the sign of the cross.

"Amen," Don Coyote said and hurriedly crossed himself.

"Morgan and Cecelia, go on this journey in the name of God,"

Benecio said. "May God the Father be with you, may God the Son protect you, and may God the Holy Ghost be by your side. Amen."

"Amen," the twins said as they again crossed themselves.

Don Coyote uttered a half-hearted "amen" and didn't bother to cross himself.

"Thank you, Father Benecio," he said. "Now, Morgan and Cecelia, please say goodbye to the priest, then return to your bedroom."

Don Coyote and Benecio helped the twins to stand up.

"Thank you, Father Bagnelli," the twins said as they wobbled back to their bedroom.

"Father, those are two messed-up chicks," Benecio said. He started to unbutton his polyester cassock.

Don Coyote grabbed Benecio's wrist.

"Stay in character, my son, at least until you leave the house, which you're going to do right now," he said.

Benecio re-buttoned his cassock.

"How'd I do?" he whispered.

Goliath came back out to the living room and looked disapprovingly at Benecio.

No, my beautiful furry baby, it's not Halloween yet, Don Coyote thought.

"You did very well, despite that asinine costume, my son," he said in a low voice. "Got those prayers off the internet?"

Benecio smiled.

"Yes, Father," he said.

"Well done, my son," Don Coyote said. "Time now to leave, and get rid of that ridiculous costume, *pronto*."

"Yes, sir," Benecio said. "And can I get reimbursed for the priest outfit — cost me fifty bucks."

"Of course, just keep the receipt, and I'll reimburse you once this deal's done, all right?" Don Coyote said.

"Okay, Father," Benecio said. He obviously was disappointed in not getting cash today.

Don Coyote ignored his disappointment.

Benecio carried his crumpled pope's mitre as he walked down the sidewalk. He passed the postal carrier, who appeared to be sorting mail in her parked mail truck.

Only she wasn't sorting mail. Turns out, Alexa was a member of Nat Doliner's network of volunteers who looked out for suspicious activity in Tampa neighborhoods.

Alexa excitedly called Nat.

Nat answered on the first ring, "Lex, what's going on? Are you okay?"

"I'm fine, Nat," she said. "Listen, I think I know where that Don Coyote character might be hiding out — I'm pretty sure I just saw him with the phoniest looking priest I've ever seen, or maybe a hippie Pope helped kidnap the twins."

18

———————

Saturday night at Namaste was fast approaching, and Sierra was about to give the performance of her lifetime, a performance requiring her to channel her innermost Mata Hari.

And it was no small task set before her: she was to employ her Swedish beauty and alluring dance moves to seduce Mala Karlsson into confessing her role in the kidnapping of the Cutler twins.

The set-up had gone well. Only a few minutes into her phone conversation with Mala, Sierra persuaded Mala to be her special guest at Namaste on Saturday night.

"I need to forewarn you, Mala — my performance involves some nudity," Sierra said over the phone. "Will my naked breasts offend you?"

"No, your bare breasts won't offend me, Sierra," Mala said in a throaty voice. "Just as long as you let me kiss them."

"Mala, please, Namaste isn't that kind of night club."

Indeed, Namaste wasn't a strip club. It was a cabaret that featured tasteful stage performances, jazz and classical music, live piano performances by Jake Dupree, a bar featuring exclusively premier liquor, and a restaurant menu showcasing international cuisine.

Reed named the nightclub Namaste because *namaste* is Indian Sanskrit that means "the light in me honors the light in you." She saw Namaste as a safe harbor for the female performers struggling with alcohol and drug abuse, with unhealthy and abusive relationships, and with giving up altogether.

Namaste's success stories were innumerable, involving brave and beautiful women, including Sierra, who overcame horrible addictions, earned a high school diploma and a college degree, and enjoyed a handsome living by performing at the cabaret.

"Well, Sierra, if I'm not allowed to touch you at Namaste, perhaps you'll let me make love to you later on," Mala said over the phone.

She couldn't recall the last time she had been so aroused — and she hadn't yet met Sierra in person.

"Such directness, you're turning me on," Sierra said. "Tell me, Mala, what are you wearing right now?"

Mala still had on her conservative butler suit.

She was sitting poolside at the Cutler mansion — she had ordered the lifeguard to dry off the dogs and take them inside.

Damn dogs, such a pain in the ass, she thought. And that life guard better stop flirting with me. Boy's barking up the wrong tree.

"I'm in my bedroom, Sierra, and I'm wearing only some pretty pink lace panties. And what are you wearing *alskling?*"

Sierra had on a workout outfit, as she was getting ready to meet Ravel at their executive athletic club for some intense exercise and a therapeutic soak in the whirlpool.

"I'm absolutely naked, *bebis,* cause I'm gonna take a bath in the Jacuzzi tub," Sierra said.

"Oooh, *hur himmelsk,*" Mala said. "Find the strongest jet and think of me, will you?"

"Already there, *bebis.*"

"*Tanker du pa mina brost i min vagina?*" Mala asked.

"Of course," Sierra said dreamily.

Actually, she was cleaning her white Nike Air Force 1 sneakers.

"All right, stop right now, *min skonhet,*" Mala said. "You're not allowed to cum until we're in bed together."

What a control freak, Sierra thought.

"Yes, ma'am. Here, let me turn off the jets," she said.

"*Duktig flicka.* So what time should I come to Namaste on Saturday?"

"No earlier than nine p.m. Tatiana and Sehar will perform first, then I'll come on. I'll leave your name at the front desk and make sure you get a front row table. You'll be my VIP guest."

"I should come alone, right?"

"No, Mala, I don't want you sitting all by yourself, so a friend of mine, her name is Ravel, will keep you company."

"I'm not sure I like that," Mala said angrily. "Is Ravel competition, is she one of your lovers?"

"Heavens no, Ravel is all about the dick."

Sierra had had to rehearse that line several times before she could stop laughing.

"Gross," Mala said.

"Yeah, I agree," Sierra said.

"Then I guess it's okay for Ravel to sit with me," Mala said. "At least I won't get hit on, which I know would happen if I were all alone."

I don't know, your Viking vibe probably would scare off most people, Sierra thought.

"Listen, Mala, I have to finish my bath and get ready for tonight, which takes friggin' forever. And I want to look *perfect* when I perform — which I will be for you on Saturday."

"Perfectly delicious?"

"Perfectly, exquisitely delicious."

Sierra finished tying her sneakers, stood up, and admired herself in the mirror.

Ravel's not going to be able to keep her hands off this tasty Swede, she thought.

"Until Saturday night, then," Mala said. "*Ciao*, Sierra."

"*Ciao, Bella.*"

Ravel's all about the dick, that's a good one, Sierra thought. Hope the gym isn't too busy, so we can play a bit in the whirlpool.

Before heading out for her workout, Sierra thought it best to

contact Reed and fill her in about her successful conversation with
Mala.

She and Reed spoke over the phone for about ten minutes.

I kind of like being the honeypot, Sierra thought. Just hope I don't
anger Ravel. Oh well, sometimes a woman's gotta do what a woman's
gotta do.

19

Swedes tend to be as punctual as the Swiss. And sure enough, Mala and Ravel arrived separately at Namaste, exactly at nine p.m.

Ravel approached Mala in the cabaret lobby.

"Mala?" Ravel said.

"Yes, hi, you must be Ravel," Mala said.

Ravel had on a wrinkled white tee shirt whose front read, "Sprezzatura". She wore black cargo pants and black leather Koio high-tops. Her satchel bag, containing her laptop, was slung over her right shoulder.

By contrast, Mala wore a little black dress, which she found on sale at Macy's in Westshore Plaza earlier in the afternoon. The LBD showed off her fit figure and long shapely legs. Her black high heels allowed her to tower over the diminutive Ravel.

Mala wore her long blonde hair down. She had a full face of make-up — the dark eyeliner made her green eyes pop.

Since she wasn't wearing a bra, her nipples protruded prominently.

Mala caught Ravel looking at her breasts.

Talk about a dyke in denial, Mala thought.

Jesus, I could tap that right here and now, Ravel thought.

"What say we head on in?" she said. "Performances are going to start soon."

"All right," Mala said. "I can't wait to see Sierra on stage."

Said the fly to the spider, Ravel thought.

"By the way, Ravel, nice kicks."

"Why thank you, Mala. These Koios are elemental to my evening wear ensemble."

Good God, Ravel, just come over to the other team already, Mala thought.

The two women sat down at a front-row table marked, "Reserved for Mala".

Mala picked up the reservation card.

"Isn't that just so thoughtful," she said.

"Yuppers, Sierra is the bestest," Ravel said.

A young female server approached their table. She wore a white linen long-sleeve blouse with matching slacks, complemented by black Sketchers Desert Kiss sandals. Her complexion was an alabaster white. The woman's long black hair contrasted dramatically with her complexion and her outfit.

Nice touch with the white outfit, black hair, and black sandals, Ravel thought. Talk about a nun gone *Nehru*.

Indeed, it was Chenoa, undercover.

"Evening, ladies, I'm Athena . . . ."

"Of course you are," Ravel interjected.

Athena smiled benignly at Ravel.

Reminds me of the Bond villain who smiles just before feeding you to the sharks, Ravel thought.

"What will y'all have to drink?" Athena asked. "Remember, there's no minimum — or maximum — drink order for y'all, and Sierra's picking up the tab."

"In that case, I'll have a tall glass of Sprite with *three* lime slices, *two* orange slices, and *one* cherry," Ravel said.

You little brat, Athena thought.

"And I'll have a Moscow Mule with Absolut Elyx," Mala said.

Athena smiled warmly at Mala.

"You know something, hon, two days ago Sierra ordered Absolut

Elyx specifically for you," Athena said.

"How thoughtful of her, but don't call me 'hon' ", Mala said. "You may address me as Miss Karlsson."

Damn, what a bitch, Ravel thought.

"No worries, Miss Karlsson, I'll just get your drink orders in," Athena said. "*Namaste*, y'all."

"Whatever," Mala mumbled.

"Guess you won't be hitting on our cocktail waitress, will you?" Ravel said.

"Oh, I don't know, Ravel, some women you simply have to bend to your will before you bed them — but anyway, I'm here to see Sierra."

Within three minutes, Athena served the women their drinks. She gave Ravel a sly wink.

Ravel looked out over the nightclub and admired its peaceful, relaxing ambience.

God, I re-charge my zen batteries every time I come here, she thought.

In fact, Namaste's layout fostered a meditative state of mind. There were only thirty small tables in the nightclub. A lit waterfall was in each corner. Floor-to-ceiling sheer drapes covered the beige walls.

There was a Bluthner grand piano to the left of the stage, and a small DJ booth to the right — and DJ Koala did not take requests. Center stage was four-hundred square feet, more than ample room for the performers' dance routines. The long granite bar was located across the room from center stage. The bartenders and bar backs weren't allowed to use blenders or make a noisy show of shaking martinis and juggling liquor bottles.

The kitchen's entrance was next to the bar. Chef Glenn subscribed to the concept of a quiet kitchen — foul language wasn't permitted, and no one was permitted to yell out food orders or bang dishes, pots, and pans. He played Tibetan music in the kitchen, and urged his staff to first meditate after clocking in for the night.

"I kind of like this place," Mala said. "But I'm tempted to take a nap."

She picked up her copper mug and drank some of her Moscow Mule.

After eating the two orange slices and the single cherry, Ravel squeezed the three lime slices into her Sprite, then took a healthy drink.

"Don't get too sleepy, Mala, because Tatiana's coming on stage in a few minutes."

" 'Tatiana', huh? What is she, some Russian bitch?"

"Ukrainian, actually. She doesn't do a thing for me, of course, but Sierra thinks she's hot as hell. Plus, Tatiana's seven-months pregnant."

"Now, that *is* hot," Mala said. "You've probably never done it with a pregnant woman, have you?"

"Nope, never, haven't even done it with an un-pregnant woman," Ravel said casually.

Last count, I've had at least three pregnant women, she thought. Un-pregnant women? Too many to count, really.

Mala polished off her Moscow Mule and waved her copper mug to Athena for a refill.

Curiously, Athena was standing close by, and she made it to the table in seconds.

"Athena, my love, be a good girl and bring me another Moscow Mule," Mala said. "And make it a double."

"Yes, ma'am, anything else you wish?" Athena asked seductively.

"Yeah, you, if it doesn't work out with Sierra," Mala said.

Athena ran her black gel polished finger down Mala's forearm.

"In that case, I hope it doesn't work out with Sierra," Athena said.

Her eyes actually twinkled from the recessed lighting.

Turning around so that Mala could see her backside, Athena slowly walked away.

Now just where did *that* nun pick up *that* swish, Ravel thought.

"God, I've died and gone to Valhalla," Mala said, almost out of breath. "So Sierra says you're all about the dick. That true?"

"Of course it's true, there's nothing I like more than a big stiff one," Ravel said with conviction.

Yeah, a big stiff one that vibrates and isn't attached to a guy, she thought.

"So you have no problem with my shagging Sierra?" Mala said.

"Have at it, my friend," Ravel said with indifference.

"Excellent, my little friend," Mala said.

Girl, I so want to Mace you, Ravel thought.

At that moment, track lights lit the stage and the recessed lights dimmed throughout the rest of the nightclub.

Jake walked over to the grand piano and sat down.

Everyone applauded, and Jake nodded in acknowledgment.

Tonight, Jake wore a Theory navy blue short-sleeved shirt, Brunello Cucinelli gray linen slacks, and Bruno Magli white loafers with tassels. Reed had done a superb job of dressing her husband.

"I'm going to perform my own composition, which has its foundation in the Baroque tradition," Jake said.

Someone from the audience yelled, "If it ain't Baroque, then fix it!"

It was Tampa Police Detective Peter Langdon, who was sitting with his wife Rebecca.

Jake recognized Langdon's voice.

"Hey, Pete, that's *my* line," he said good naturedly.

Everyone laughed.

"You know, 'Baroque' initially was a negative term used to describe European art and architecture from about four-hundred years ago," Jake said. "It lost its pejorative connotation once music scholars adopted 'Baroque'."

The audience appeared to appreciate Jake's mini-lecture.

Except Mala.

"Blah, blah, blah," she said. "When are we gonna see some titties?"

Andre was nearby and he caught Ravel's eye.

Ravel slyly shook her head at Andre, signaling to him that she'd handle this situation.

"Mala, hush. We're gonna get in trouble if you keep it up," Ravel said.

"Okee, dokee, I be a good girl," Mala said.

Man, those Moscow Mules must have a mean kick to them, Ravel thought.

"Anyways," Jake said. "What I truly love about performing Baroque-style music is I'm allowed freedom to embellish and improvise within the melodic theme — sort of reminds me of jazz, in a way."

"What're you playing tonight?" Rebecca Langdon, Peter's wife, asked politely.

"Becca, I title my composition 'Earth Goddess', and I dedicate it to Tatiana, who's going to perform for you right now."

Jake began playing the piano as Tatiana stepped onto the stage.

Loud applause erupted.

Tatiana stood at attention on center stage. She was nearly six-feet tall, and had long, straight brunette hair and brown eyes as dark as roasted coffee beans.

She wore a green silk robe over black yoga pants.

Tatiana slowly took off her silk robe and tossed it to the right of the stage.

The audience gasped.

She was not wearing a top, and she had applied baby oil to her engorged breasts and large, round stomach, making her glisten under the track lights.

Truly, Tatiana was a fecund and voluptuous Earth Goddess on center stage.

"Holy Mother of God," Mala said, this time in a whisper. "I wish I could have put that oil on her."

She finished her second Moscow Mule.

Athena magically appeared with Mala's third Moscow Mule.

"Was I right to assume you wanted another double, Miss Karlsson?"

"Yes, of course, and call me Mala, you gorgeous piece of ass," Mala said, also in a whisper.

Mala ran her finger along Athena's inseam. Athena didn't flinch.

Might have to cut her off, Athena thought. Any second now, she's going to grab my breasts.

"Mala, please, you're getting me all hot and bothered, I won't be able to concentrate on my work."

Athena walked away a bit more briskly than last time.

With Jake deftly playing the piano, Tatiana broke out into a slow-motion Ukrainian folk dance. Despite being seven-months pregnant, she flawlessly executed the twists and turns and kicks she learned as a little girl in Kiev. She moved in sync with Jake's piano playing. The audience clapped to the same beat.

Tatiana's dance was over after fifteen minutes. It was her last performance before going on maternity leave. She wouldn't return to the stage for six months, so several members of the audience rushed to the front of the stage and filled her tip bowl with hundred-dollar bills.

Both Tatiana and Jake received a standing ovation.

Andre brought Tatiana her silk robe. She put on the robe and left the stage. The stage lights dimmed as the recessed lights came back on

Athena approached Mala's table.

"Ready for another, Mala?" She asked.

"Fuck yeah, baby," Mala said.

Off in the distance, Andre frowned at Mala. As Chief Security Officer for Namaste, he worried Mala would cause an unpleasant scene, one that might mar Namaste's peaceful harmony.

The son of a Russian mother and an African-American father, Andre reveled in the cabaret's international quality — performers and guests came from all over the world. At Namaste, he felt at ease with his mixed heritage. Andre prided himself in learning other languages, since he believed it built bridges of communication. He was fluent in Russian and French. Sierra was teaching him Swedish; Reed was introducing him to Irish Gaelic; and Sehar already had taught him various Hindi expressions. He was a true open-minded intellectual, and a budding polyglot.

Physically, Andre was six-foot, five-inches tall. He weighed in at a chiseled two-hundred-fifty pounds. His daily exercise regimen included free weights, battle ropes, stair climbers, treadmills, and long sessions in the steam room. And he never took performance-enhancing drugs.

Though he was a born fighter, Andre was a considerate and gentle man.

And Mala's coarse behavior was testing his patience.

Athena, who as Chenoa was very attracted to Andre, walked by him.

"I got it under control, Handsome," she said.

"I sure hope so, Miss . . . Athena," Andre said.

Goodness, she's a beautiful woman, he thought.

Athena gave him a re-assuring smile, then brought Mala her third Moscow Mule.

"Thank you, Athena darling," Mala said. "But please bring Ravel another one of those little girl drink."

"Sure enough, Mala," Athena said as she sashayed away.

"Ravel, don't let me forget to get Athena's phone number from her," Mala said.

Ravel couldn't resist being a wily minx.

"I have Athena's number on my phone," she said. "Let me give it to you."

"Text it to me, Little Sweetie," Mala said.

She gave Ravel her phone number.

Little Sweetie dutifully texted Athena's phone number to Mala — and it was Chenoa's actual number.

Athena promptly served Ravel a fresh glass of Sprite with three lime slices, two orange slices, and a single cherry.

"Thanks, Athena," Ravel said. "Hope you don't mind that I gave Mala your digits."

Mala looked eagerly at Athena.

"No problem Ravel," Athena said. "I'll be disappointed if Mala doesn't call me."

Before walking away, Athena subtly glared at Ravel, who bore a self-satisfied smile.

"So, Mala, what'd you think of Tatiana?" Ravel said.

Mala took a long pull from her Moscow Mule.

"That's one beautiful pregnant chick," Mala said. "So who's up next . . . Seema? Simba?"

"It's *Sehar*," Ravel said. "She's from a very wealthy family in India. She ran away from some arranged marriage her parents set up for her. Namaste is trying her out as Tatiana's temporary replacement."

"Jesus, this place is like the United Nations," Mala said.

"More like, this is the new America, and I kind of dig it," Ravel said.

"Not if you have to be a slave for your bitch of a cousin."

"Buck up, Mala, it's almost time for Sehar, and you-know-who comes after her."

Mala finished her third Moscow Mule. She raised her copper mug, yet Athena appeared not to notice her.

"Athena better not be ignoring me," she said. "But whatever — bring on the Hindu bitch."

A Hispanic lesbian couple sitting behind Mala *tsked* at her crudeness.

Just then, DJ Koala played the music of Anoushka Shankar, the daughter of Ravi Shankar and half-sister to Norah Jones.

DJ Koala chose Anoushka's CD *Breathing Under Water* as Sehar's walk-up music since it blended traditional Indian *sitar* play with synth-pop beats and melodies.

Sehar, all of four-feet ten-inches tall and weighing about ninety-five pounds, stepped tentatively onto the stage.

She wore a fuchsia pink *salwar kameez* outfit, consisting of a long-tailed shirt and matching pants. Sehar was barefoot and wore silver anklets. *Mehndi*, temporary *henna* tattoos, adorned her hands and feet. She displayed the decorative *bindi* white dots on her forehead. Her long, straight hair was as black as midnight in Delhi. She wore an ornate gold necklace as well as several gold bracelets.

"Wow, she puts the 'hot' in 'ex-hot-ic'," Ravel said, realizing immediately she had slipped up.

Mala raised her eyebrows at Ravel.

"What? What'd I say?" Ravel said.

"Don't worry about it, you tasty Swiss treat," Mala said. "It's a girl's perogative to swing both ways whenever the mood hits her."

Ravel reached over and lightly pinched one of Mala's nipples.

"Guess I'll have to get in line, huh?"

Mala held Ravel's hand against her breast.

"Yes, but for right now, you're behind Sierra, and ahead of Athena."

Mala had never felt more desired in her life.

For Sehar, though, standing all alone on center stage, she had never felt more frightened in her life.

Should I just make a run for it, she thought.

Taking a deep breath, Sehar caught the rhythm of Anoushka's sitar playing. She began performing *Bharatanatyam*, a classic Indian dance dating back to 1000 B.C. Rooted in *Hindu* arts and religious practices,

Bharatanatyam celebrates *Hindu* spirituality. Originally, it was a temple dance for women — which was a clever choice on Sehar's part to perform at Namaste.

For twenty minutes, Sehar kept her legs bent while her feet maintained rhythm. She used her hands to make a series of *mudras*, or symbolic hand gestures.

And damn if she didn't showcase a Mona Lisa smile throughout the performance.

Sehar's goal in performing *Bharatanatyam* was to evoke a *rasa*, or strong emotion, among the audience.

Judging by the loud applause from the audience at the conclusion of her dance, Sehar did, indeed, achieve *rasa*.

She stood frozen on the stage. Tears welled in her eyes. She laughed nervously.

The applause wouldn't end. Several people came forward to place fifty- and hundred-dollar bills in the tip bowl.

Finally, Andre had to come on stage, take Sehar's hand, and escort her off stage left. The Afro-Russian gentle giant and tiny Hindu performer made for a most extraordinary pair.

Athena brought Mala her fourth Moscow Mule. This time, the cocktail had only a modest splash of vodka.

Got to slow down this woman, she thought.

After sipping from her drink, Mala slid her hand under the table and began stroking Ravel's crotch. Ravel obliged by opening her legs slightly. She became aroused.

Sometimes, I just *love* my job, she thought.

"If you could taste only one, me or Sehar, who'd it be?" Mala said.

Ravel exhaled slowly.

She tried to calm herself by thinking of Jake Dupree sitting at the grand piano and wearing only a gold silk thong.

That'll stifle the old libido, she thought.

"Sehar would be my appetizer and you'd be my main course," Ravel said.

"And dessert?" Mala said. She slowed her stroking of Ravel's crotch.

"That's easy, it'd be that chocolate molten lava cake over there."

Ravel pointed to Andre, who had no idea of what Ravel was up to

— as usual.

"My, such a big appetite for a little lady," Mala said.

She stopped touching Ravel.

"Enough of that for now, Ravel --- don't want to spoil you."

Crap, and I was so close, Ravel thought.

"Besides, isn't it time for the main attraction?" Mala said.

She finished her fourth drink, then waved to Athena to bring her another.

Athena acknowledged her request.

"Funny, Athena doesn't seem to have any customers other than us," Mala said.

"As per Sierra's instructions," Ravel said. "Now get ready, Sierra's about to come out."

Mala drunkenly giggled.

"No pun intended?"

"Nope, we Swiss tend not to pun around," Ravel said. "We're all about taking care of *bidness*."

And right now, you Swedish asshole, you're my one and only *bidness* at hand, she thought.

Suddenly, the stage lights brightened and the nightclub lights receded.

It was show time for Sierra.

DJ Koala, an expatriate from Agadez, Niger, put on Euge Groove's "Born 2 Groove", a sexy smooth jazz composition featuring seductive tenor sax wailing with plucky lead guitar funkadelics.

Sierra made her entrance wearing a golden yellow sports bra and royal blue yoga pants. As she walked on stage, she kept pace with the rhythmic beat of "Born 2 Groove".

The audience applauded enthusiastically.

"Nice touch, she's wearing the Swedish national colors," Mala said.

And on Sierra, Sweden's yellow and blue never looked sexier.

Bet Mala doesn't get Sierra's message, Ravel thought. The yellow represents generosity, but blue — that symbolizes truth and justice. Sierra's such a Sneaky Pete.

Sierra's routine was comprised mostly of challenging yoga moves. It was a demanding performance, requiring the Junoesque Sierra to be fit and focused. Happily, she was all of that: at six-feet, two-inches tall, she weighed in at a healthy and muscular one-hundred-sixty pounds. She exercised two hours daily, and she ate responsibly. And somehow, she found time to earn a first-degree black belt in *tae kwon do*.

"Christ, does that woman have even an ounce of fat on her?" Mala said.

None that I've even been able to find, Ravel thought.

Sierra struck a warrior's pose as DJ Koala played Keiko Matsui's inspiring composition, "Prism". With support from her percussionist and bass player, the beautiful Japanese jazz pianist riffed up and down the piano keys, hitting crisp and confident notes.

And Sierra was doing the same on stage, expertly blending modern dance with traditional yoga. Preceded by twirls and kicks, she executed a triangle yoga pose, followed by crescent moon and eagle poses.

Yoga enthusiasts in the audience wildly applauded each pose.

As "Prism" concluded, Sierra returned to the warrior's pose.

This time, the entire audience erupted in raucous applause, and several came forward to place gratuities in the bowl.

Everyone knew what was coming next, except Sierra had planned a little surprise.

She undid her ponytail, allowing her long blonde hair to flow down her back and over her shoulders.

She then removed her yellow sports bra, tossing it to Mala in the front row.

Sierra's full, shapely breasts glistened in the stage lights.

"Oh my," Mala and Ravel said in unison.

Sierra winked at Mala, who blew a kiss to Sierra.

Then Sierra did something she never before had done at Namaste.

She removed her yoga pants.

The audience gasped.

Sierra stood on center stage wearing only a smile and a pair of canary yellow boy short panties.

"Holy shit," Ravel said.

"What she said," Mala said.

Displaying her usual perfect timing, DJ Koala, her deep black skin contrasting sharply with a solid white track suit, put on Richard

Elliot's "Moomba". Having earned his chops playing tenor sax with Tower of Power, Elliot was a veteran sax player who produced tsunamis of lush, rich sound. And Elliot was at his most seductive with "Moomba".

Sierra had asked DJ Koala to play "Moomba" because she thought the jazz composition enhanced the sensual nature of her yoga moves on the stage.

Earlier in the day, Sierra and DJ Koala sat together at Namaste and listened to a wide variety of songs. After an hour, both women agreed upon Richard Elliot.

"Sierra, 'Moomba' — *c'est un choix magnifique*," DJ Koala said.

"*Merci beaucoup, ma belle princesse africaine*," Sierra said.

On stage, Sierra caught Elliot's rhythms and performed a cat pose, a wide-leg stretch, a three-limbed forward bend, and a sage twist.

Virtually her entire body shimmered in perspiration.

The audience seemed as if it were in a trance.

Even Mala was silent and mesmerized. She didn't touch her Moscow Mule. Instead, she tightly clutched Sierra's yellow sports bra — the gay couple behind her appeared jealous over Sierra playing favorites with Mala.

As Richard Elliot continued to wail on his saxophone, Sierra went into warrior II, followed by a camel pose and a hare pose.

She concluded her performance with sun salutation.

Sierra was playing to a very friendly home crowd, which responded with boisterous cheers.

Amid this positive uproar, audience members filled the tip bowl to overflow. The Hispanic gay couple, in particular, put five hundred-dollar bills in the bowl.

Sierra bowed and said quietly, "*Namaste*, everyone. You are so beautiful and kind."

Stage lights dimmed once again. Recessed lights in the nightclub brightened once again.

The overall mood in the cabaret was festive and upbeat. Guests began ordering drinks and food — they'd have thirty minutes before the next performance.

Then Sierra had yet another first at Namaste: normally, she walked directly backstage to the dressing room after a performance; but there was nothing normal about this evening, so she stepped off the stage and made a bee line to Mala's table.

Sierra put her yoga pants on, making certain that Mala was watching her.

Using both thumbs, Sierra popped the waistline of her yoga pants.

"Mala, any chance I can get my sports bra back?" she said. "The twins are chilled."

You clever beauty, Ravel thought.

Mala was admiring Sierra's bare breasts when she frowned momentarily.

"What? Sure, why not," she said. "Christ, I don't know who needs toweling off more, you or me."

Mala begrudgingly returned the sports bra to Sierra, who promptly put it back on.

Mala drank the rest of her cocktail.

"So why don't you sit down, Sierra," she said.

"Sure, I could sit down with you two, we could have some dinner, then watch the other performances," Sierra said. "Or we *could* just go back to my place — my manager said I could have the rest of the night off."

"Is Ravel coming?" Mala said.

"Oh, I'm sure she is, but not with us," Sierra said.

"In that case, let's go to your place — *right now*," Mala said. "You know, I expect you to give me the sports bra and boy shorts as souvenirs."

Creepy *and* sexy, Ravel thought.

"Give me a few to freshen up and throw on a tee shirt" Sierra said.

"Don't freshen up on my account," Mala said.

Sierra smiled alluringly and walked away.

"Ravel, it's been real and it's been fun, but it hasn't been real fun," Mala said.

She's actually sending me down the road, Ravel thought.

"Message received, Mala," she said. "Sooner or later, we'll hook up."

Ravel got up and walked away.

It'll be sooner, rather than later, my little pretty, she thought.

20

––––––––––

As Sierra and Mala walked through the Namaste lobby, Andre met them at the front door.

"Leaving early, Sierra?" Andre said. "Did Jake or Ravel approve it?"

"Actually, Jake and Ravel both approved my getting off early," Sierra said. She wore over her yoga outfit an oversized Of Monsters and Men white tee shirt — she loved the Icelandic indie folk band. She also had on white Chuck Taylor Converse high tops.

"*Spasibo, krasavitsa,*" Andre said.

"*Dobro pozhalouat, krasavets,*" Sierra answered.

Sierra and Mala went out to the nightclub parking lot.

"What was that about Ravel, of all people, letting you leave early?" Mala said. She walked at such a fast pace, her large breasts practically popped out of her little black dress.

"Ravel's the assistant manager here," Sierra said casually.

Damn it, I forgot to tell Andre not to bring up Ravel, she thought.

"Odd, Ravel never mentioned that to me," Mala said.

It was good and bad Mala's head was clearing: good that she wasn't going to pass out, bad that she was more alert.

"No biggie, *alskling*," Sierra said. "So whose car do we take, yours or mine?"

Mala appeared embarrassed.

"It'll have to be yours," she said. "I took an Uber here."

"All righty then, that's my car over there," Sierra said. She pointed to a caldera red Jaguar F-Type sports car.

"You're fucking kidding me," Mala said.

"What?" Sierra said.

"I gotta get a job here," Mala said enviously.

"No problem, I'll be glad to mention you to R . . . Jake, okay?" Sierra said.

The two women climbed into the Jaguar. Sierra showed off by burning a little rubber as she sped out of the Namaste parking lot.

While she drove, Sierra slid her right hand between Mala's legs. Mala offered no resistance; in fact, she pulled up her dress a few inches.

"Mala Karlsson, you're not wearing panties," Sierra said.

"Commando is the only way to go-go," Mala said.

Sierra turned on the Jaguar's stereo. Contemporary jazz came on from Sirius XM's *Watercolors*.

"We'll be to my place in just a few," Sierra said.

Mala was enjoying Sierra's intimate touching.

"Take your time, *babe*," she said. "I'm really enjoying this fine ride."

I bet you are, Sierra thought. Wow, this woman's a hot thermal spring down there.

Sierra exited off Interstate 275 and took Ashley Drive into downtown Tampa. She crossed a short bridge to Harbour Island and entered the parking garage of the Icon luxury apartment complex.

Extra five-hundred a month is worth it for a reserved space next to the elevator, Sierra thought.

As she and Mala rode the elevator up to her twelfth-floor apartment, Sierra gathered Mala in her arms and kissed her.

"I have a feeling this is going to be a very special night," Mala said.

"I have the same feeling, Mala," Sierra said. "As the Barracuda used to say, perhaps tonight you will be my *especial* lady."

"The Barracuda?" Mala asked.

"It's from *Frasier*, but never mind," Sierra replied.

As they stepped out of the elevator, Sierra cupped Mala's buttocks.

Here's hoping Miss Beatrice doesn't spot me doing this, Sierra said. She's a lovely old lady, but she might turn me into the board.

Sierra opened the apartment's front door for Mala.

"*Apres toi, petite bombasse,*" she said.

"*Merci beaucoup,*" Mala said.

She walked down the darkened hallway toward the lighted living room.

Sierra stayed several feet behind Mala. She stopped at a sideboard table in the hallway, quietly opened a drawer, and pulled out a fully loaded Browning nine-millimeter semi-automatic pistol.

Mala stopped just short of entering the living room.

She gasped at the scene before her.

Reed, Ravel, and Chenoa stood in the living room. It was a classic ambush — the three women might as well have worn cowboy hats and six-shooters while dangling a hangman's noose in front of Mala.

Sierra came up behind Mala and poked her pistol in Mala's back.

"Go on in and sit down, asshole," Sierra said. She surprised herself with her testosteronic aggressiveness.

"Reed O'Hara? Ravel? Athena?" Mala cried out. "What're you doing here?"

Chenoa sauntered over to Mala.

"I'm Chenoa, hon, not Athena," she said. "Sorry about the trickery, but we really need to talk with you tonight."

God bless Reed for letting me be the good cop, she thought.

This time, Sierra gave Mala a firm shove from behind.

"I *said* go sit down, Karlsson," Sierra said.

That's so sexy, Ravel thought. Who would've thunk Sierra could be such a badass.

Mala obliged Sierra by sitting on the brown leather living room sofa.

Reed, Ravel, Chenoa, and Sierra continued to stand.

Sierra slipped the Browning behind her back and secured the pistol in the waistband of her yoga pants.

I just don't know this woman anymore, Ravel thought.

"Mala, we don't intend, necessarily, to hurt you," Reed said. "But one way or the other, you're going to tell us where Fernando Gonzalez, aka Don Coyote, is hiding the Cutler twins."

"This is bullshit," Mala said. "This is kidnapping, pure and simple. I want to call the police."

"Sure, you can call the police," Chenoa said. "But there's so much evidence against you, I worry the police would be a lot rougher than we'd ever be, Mala."

"Oh, I don't know about that," Sierra said. "I'm in the mood for kicking some ass."

Ravel put her arm around Sierra's waistline. She was careful not to touch the Browning — it would be a scandal of international proportions for the Swiss Ravel to accidentally shoot the Swedish Sierra in her perfectly round buttocks.

"Come on now, Sierra, chill," Ravel said reassuringly. "Save some of that savage energy for when we hook up tonight."

Mala jumped up from the sofa.

"I knew it!" she yelled. "You two *are* a couple, aren't you."

"Sit your flat ass back down, bitch," Ravel said.

"Did you say 'fat'?" Sierra said.

"*Flat, flat*, as in flat as a board, as in no round mounds of renown," Ravel said.

Mala sat back down and began to cry.

"I am *so* fucked," she moaned.

Reed crossed her arms.

Tonight, she wore a black Armani business suit, an open-collar white dress shirt, and black cowboy boots.

"Yes. Yes you are, Mala," Reed said. "But you'll get a much better deal with us than with the police."

"Yeah, hon, you may be able to avoid prison time if you cooperate with us," Chenoa said. "It's really for the best, so please calm down, it's going to be okay."

Sierra rushed toward Mala and slapped her in the face. She then turned toward Chenoa.

"Chenoa, stop acting like Mr. Rogers," Sierra said. "Mala conspired to have her cousins kidnapped — she deserves to get her tail kicked."

Just had a nice little orgasm, thank you very much, Ravel thought.

The left side of Mala's face was the color of Sierra's Jaguar. Her nose was bleeding. She started crying again.

"Why did you hit me, Sierra?" she said in a whimpering voice. "Morgan and Cecelia are adults. They left their home of their own accord. All I did was introduce Fernando to the girls."

Reed put her hands on her hips.

"Now we're getting somewhere," she said. "Appears Sierra slapped some sense into you."

Chenoa gave Mala a warm, moistened hand towel. Mala applied the towel to her bloodied nose.

"Did you get that hand towel from my guest bathroom, Chenoa?" Sierra asked indignantly.

"Sure, it didn't look too expensive," Chenoa said.

"Oh, that's nice, real nice," Sierra said. "All this creep deserves is a wad of toilet tissue."

"I looked at the toilet tissue in your bathroom, it was single ply," Chenoa shot back.

"Sometimes, Chenoa, you can be such a bitch," Sierra said. "Think I'll just take it out on Mala."

Mala cringed at Sierra's threat.

"Time to ratchet down, ladies," Reed said with the authority of a head mistress. "After all, we don't want to kill Mala, just hurt her a little bit."

"Oh, Christ!" Mala exclaimed.

"He isn't gonna help you," Ravel said. "Ain't nobody but us gonna get you out of this briar patch."

Really, Ravel, a double negative, Reed thought. She has to stop treating *Deliverance* as her American Rosetta Stone.

"A question, Mala, and a very easy one," Reed said. "Just how did you get involved with Don Coyote?"

Mala collected herself. She barely sniffled now. She understood she had to be straight-forward and honest with Reed, or Sierra probably would hit her again.

Sierra nodded knowingly at Mala. A bit of a psychic, Sierra practically could read Mala's mind.

"Let's hear it, Mala," Ravel said. "You can ill *fjord* to lie."

Everyone, including Mala, laughed at Ravel's awful pun.

"I did it because I hate Elin," Mala said. "She's no better than I am, but she acts so high and mighty. I mean, she was a fucking cocktail waitress before Clive married her."

Sierra glared at Mala.

"Go on, Karlsson, say another swear word and I'll punch you in the pussy," Sierra said.

Ravel bent over slightly, unable to contain the sexual energy coursing through her body.

Thanks, everybody, for a great show, she thought. And don't forget to tip your waitresses.

"I'm sorry, I'm a little upset right now," Mala said. "I f . . . , hooked up with Veronica Lake, she introduced me to Don Coyote, he gave me ten thousand dollars to introduce him to the twins."

Recognizing the floodgates of truth had opened, Reed decided to take complete control of the interrogation.

She stepped forward and hovered over Mala, who trembled with well-founded fear of Sierra.

"I won't let Sierra hurt you anymore, as long as you keep telling the truth, Mala," Reed said.

The tips of her black cowboy boots almost touched Mala's feet.

Man, that's Joan Crawford from *Johnny Guitar*, right? Ravel thought.

"I don't see what I did wrong," Mala said. "So Don Coyote went to church a few times with Morgan and Cecelia, it was no big deal, and he made the girls feel empowered."

"How so?" Reed asked.

"The twins felt useless, like pampered princesses with no direction in life," Mala said. "He gave them purpose — like going to Mexico and being personal assistants to a wealthy family. The girls thought they'd be actual players, that they'd be relevant."

"You mean, sort of how you thought it'd be for *you* coming to the United States and working for Elin?" Ravel said.

"Yeah, sure," Mala said tentatively.

"How has that worked out for you so far?" Reed asked in a stern voice.

Mala paused.

"Not so well, I guess," she said.

"Indeed," Reed said. "And do you know why Fernando Gonzalez calls himself 'Don Coyote'? Do you know what a 'coyote' is?"

"I thought he was being cute, you know, being playful with 'Don Quixote'."

Reed tapped the toe of her right cowboy boot on the washed-oak floor.

"There's nothing cute about it, you idiot," she said. "A 'coyote' is a Mexican trafficker in human beings."

"Oh, God no," Mala exclaimed.

"Oh, God yes," Reed replied. "And Don Coyote added a perverted little twist to the human smuggling business — he sells wealthy young American women to well-off Mexicans who use these women as sex slaves."

"No, no, no," Mala moaned. "My baby cousins, I didn't know that would happen to them. I only wanted them to get away from their controlling parents."

"And make a few bucks while you're at it," Reed said.

"I'm going to use that money to go back to Sweden and get set back up in Stockholm," Mala said.

"Money that comes from a sex slaver," Reed said. "Money that comes from a man who brainwashed your cousins into being sex toys for the rich and famous in Mexico."

"Veronica and Benecio never told me about that sex slave stuff, and Fernando never brought it up — I just didn't know, can't you believe me?" Mala pleaded.

"Wait a minute, did you say 'Benecio?' " Ravel said.

"Yes, Benecio met me one time at El Castillo, and he was very nice, but he wasn't my type," Mala said.

"Guy with a penis kind of type?" Ravel said.

Reed's instincts told her to let Ravel have the floor.

"Yeah, exactly," Mala said. "But he introduced me to Veronica Lake, and I found *her* a very interesting change of pace."

"Chick with a dick?" Ravel said.

"Yes," Mala said. "I had no idea Veronica would be so . . . delightful."

"Back to Benecio, Mala," Reed said impatiently. "What does he look like?"

"He's a nice boy, sexy smile, maybe twenty-two or twenty-three, Mexican, gorgeous black hair and beard, terrible dresser, kinda short," Mala said.

"Is his last name, by any chance, 'Flores?' " Reed asked.

"Yes it is, I remember because he said he's a flower child," Mala said. "Get it, Flores, flowers."

"Yeah, we get it, you piece of shit," Sierra interjected.

Nice touch, Sierra, Reed thought. She's not letting Mala get too comfortable.

Reed looked at Ravel.

"Go ahead, *mon petit fromage suisse*, ask her about the tattoo," Reed said.

Ravel cleared her throat.

"Does this Benecio happen to have on his left forearm a tattoo of an eagle eating a snake on top of a cactus?" Ravel asked. She was almost too afraid to hear the answer.

"Yes he does," Mala said. "I asked him about the tattoo — he said it was Mexico's national symbol and proof he's a true patriot. A little wacko, huh?"

Reed and Ravel looked at each other.

"Can you believe that little shit had the balls to come back here?" Ravel said.

"*And* he's working for Don Coyote," Reed said.

Sierra hugged Ravel.

"It's going to be okay, baby," Sierra said. "We're going to make Benecio regret he came back to Tampa."

Ravel held on to Sierra and began to cry.

Sierra shielded Ravel from Mala's prying eyes.

"Mala, look at me and me only," Reed said. "Now's the time for you to tell us where the twins are."

Mala sunk her face into her hands.

"I can't tell you, Fernando took me into his confidence," she said. "Besides, Benecio said if I told *anybody anything*, he'd cut me up in little pieces and feed me to the sharks in Tampa Bay."

Still holding Ravel, Sierra said, "For Christ's sake, Reed, let's do that ourselves, I'm tired of this bitch."

Well played, Sierra, Reed thought.

"Sierra, please, don't frighten Mala," Chenoa said, almost on cue.

"Thank you, Athena . . . I mean, Chenoa," Mala said, grateful to have at least one friend in the room.

"Now don't worry about Benecio and Don Coyote," Chenoa said. "We will protect you from those *men*. We girls have to stick together, right?"

Sierra shook her head in feigned disgust.

"I suppose we do, Chenoa," Mala said.

"So I don't think I'm out of line here to offer you a deal," Chenoa said.

That's right, Chenoa, always be closing, Reed thought.

There appeared a glimmer of hope in Mala's eyes.

"Really? What kind of deal?" she said eagerly.

"First, you'll have to tell us *exactly* where the twins are," Chenoa said. "Once we rescue the twins, we'll help you go home to Sweden. Might even give you extra funds for expenses and such. You'll have no involvement with the police. And we'll protect you the entire time — you'll stay with me at my place."

"What's the catch?" Mala said.

"*Catches*, actually, two of them to be exact," Chenoa said. "First, you have to apologize to the entire Cutler family before you leave — got a problem with that?"

"No, no I don't, it's the least I could do," Mala said. "Elin won't forgive me, though."

"Mala, never doubt our capacity to forgive," Chenoa said. "Ready for the second catch?"

"I suppose," Mala said.

"You have to donate the entire ten thousand dollars you got from Don Coyote to Metropolitan Ministries," Chenoa said.

"What? All of it? And why Metropolitan Ministries?" Mala exclaimed.

"Yes, you're to donate all ten thousand dollars," Reed said. "And the money's going to Metropolitan Ministries because Elin told me her daughters loved volunteering there."

"I just don't know," Mala said.

"Little missy, you have ten seconds to make up your mind," Reed said. "If you don't agree to our terms, I'll let Sierra go all primal on you."

Sierra smiled at Mala.

"C'mon, shithead, turn down the deal — please, for my sake," she said.

Reed began a countdown, "Ten, nine, eight, seven, six . . . . "

"You're not really going to sic Sierra on me, are you?" Mala cried out.

"Five, four, three, two . . . "

"All right, all right, you got a deal," Mala said.

"That's good, Mala, that's very good," Chenoa said. "Now, where are Morgan and Cecelia?"

"They're staying at Fernando's house, two streets over from the Cutlers," Mala said.

"The hell you say," Sierra said.

"It's true," Mala said. "I found it comforting that the girls were so close by."

Mala gave Reed Don Coyote's street address.

"Reed, please let me drop kick her, just once," Sierra said.

"Relax, Sierra, your work's done here — for now," Reed said.

"Looks as if Nat's intel was on the mark," Ravel said. "Jesus, that Don Coyote is one ballsy guy."

"Got that right," Reed said. "All right, Chenoa, escort Mala to your place, and stay in contact with me."

"Will do, Reed," Chenoa said. "Let's go, Mala."

Totally resigned to her fate, Mala didn't say a word as she left Sierra's apartment with Chenoa.

"Golly, that went swell," Ravel said.

"It did, didn't it," Reed said. "I'm heading out, ladies, got to meet up with Jake and work up a game plan."

"Tell Jake for me that he looks pretty good in a thong," Ravel said.

"Using my husband again to delay orgasm, right?" Reed said.

She smiled lovingly at her protégé.

"Maybe," Ravel said. She returned Reed's warm smile.

"Ravel's gonna hang out here for a while," Sierra said. "Let me walk you to the front door."

As she and Reed walked down the hallway, Sierra paused to put her Browning back in the sideboard drawer.

When she returned to the living room, Ravel was stretched out on the sofa — completely naked.

"Feel like fucking?" Ravel said.

"Oh god yes," Sierra answered.

21

———————

Don Coyote was relieved the Da Rosas texted him photos of themselves and the money in Tucson. The photos depicted Mateo and Lucia standing behind a large SUV with its rear hatch up. Inside the SUV's cargo area were six plastic storage boxes filled with cash. The Da Rosas had parked on the shoulder of Speedway Boulevard in front of an Arabian horse farm just a half-mile down from Tanque Verde Ranch. Mateo held that day's *Arizona Daily Star*.

It was a proof trifecta — location, date, and four million dollars.

Pleasure doing business with you, Lucia and Mateo, you sick degenerates, Don Coyote thought. Almost feel sorry for my twins, but Morgan and Cecelia will be fine, at least until the next time I sell them.

Don Coyote was on his third American cigar of the day. That morning, he drank an entire pot of percolated Chase & Sanborn coffee. He was so nervous over whether the Da Rosas would deliver, he couldn't even watch *The Price Is Right*.

Now that the pressure was off, he was going to stream episodes of *Family Feud* on Hulu.

Might check out *Let's Make a Deal*, too, he thought. You know, when Monty Hall was the host.

All of a sudden, the Pina Colada song came on over the intercom system.

Ah, Benecio, right on time, Don Coyote thought.

Carrying Goliath, he ambled to the front door and opened it.

And there was Benecio — clean shaven and wearing a yellow polo shirt, pleated black khakis, and camo check Old Skool Vans.

"Who are you, and what have you done with my Benecio?" Don Coyote said playfully. "Goodness, I don't recognize you without those awful green flip flops.."

Even Goliath yipped approval.

Benecio grinned sheepishly.

"Well, you told me to clean up my act, so I decided to take your advice, literally," he said. "What do you think, do I look professional enough, Father, to be a permanent member of your operation?

"*Absolutely*, my son," Don Coyote said.

Never gonna happen, he thought.

"May I come in?" Benecio asked. "As you can see, I am early for my appointment with you."

"Of course, my son, come in, come in," Don Coyote said with feigned warmth.

He and Benecio came into the living room and sat down, Don Coyote and Goliath in the La-Z-Boy recliner, Benecio on the sofa.

"How are the twins, Father?" Benecio asked. He didn't seem entirely comfortable in his new clothes.

"Fine, just fine," Don Coyote said. "They're getting anxious to travel to Arizona."

"Are we still going to drive to Naples, then fly to Tucson?" Benecio said.

"That remains the plan, except with one small change, my son," Don Coyote said.

Benecio sat forward on the sofa.

Goliath growled at him.

"What's the small change?" Benecio said anxiously.

You're out of the goddamn loop, Junior, Don Coyote thought.

"It's nothing serious, my son," he said. "I'll need you to stay behind briefly to take care of a little business.

"I'm listening, Father," Benecio said.

Don Coyote then explained to Benecio what he needed him to do.

"You're kidding me," Benecio blurted out.

"Don't be impertinent, young man," Don Coyote said in a scolding manner. "You need to remember that you are elemental to the effective execution of my plan."

"I know, but . . . " Benecio whined.

Don Coyote cut him off.

"Enough Benecio, are you in or out?" he said.

"Will I still be able to catch up with you in Tucson?" Benecio pleaded.

"Of course, my son," Don Coyote said. "I will leave you a first-class ticket, as well as five thousand dollars in spending money. And look at it this way, you will be king of the castle while I'm gone."

"What about the f..., that dog?" Benecio said. He hated Goliath more than his itchy new threads.

"Goliath goes with me, all right?" Don Coyote said.

"Then I'm in, *mang*," Benecio said, trying to sound like Tony Montana in *Scarface*.

You little smartass, Don Coyote thought.

"That's wonderful news, my son. Because after all, the key here is cooperation from all those involved."

"I'm all about the cooperation, Father."

"I believe you, my son," Don Coyote said.

"When do you and the twins — and Goliath — leave, Father?" Benecio asked.

"In two days."

"Should I go ahead and stay with you until you leave?"

"No, I really don't want the twins to figure out who you are — even without the beard, you still very much resemble our priest friend."

Benecio chuckled.

"Yeah, that was a fun little bit of theater, wasn't it," he said.

"Fun *and* effective," Don Coyote said approvingly. "You did a good job of calming down the twins."

"Speaking of which, where *are* they?"

"Napping in their bedroom," Don Coyote answered.

"In the same bed?" Benecio asked.

"Yes, they always sleep together," Don Coyote said. "But don't let that imagination of yours run amok — their sleeping together is an innocuous twin thing. I find it rather charming."

"Oh sure . . . me, too," Benecio said unconvincingly. "So when do you want me to come back?"

"Tomorrow at midnight," Don Coyote said. "We'll leave at four a.m. the next morning, since we have a three-hour drive to Naples and a nine a.m. flight to Tucson. But don't take any chances — stay in the guest bedroom until we're gone."

"Yes, sir," Benecio said. "Do you want me to shut down the house, you know, before I leave?"

"No, just lock up," Don Coyote said. "Got six more months on the lease — we might come back for awhile."

"Do you think that's smart, after what I'm supposed to do?" Benecio said.

"Look, we were away on business," Don Coyote said. "We have nothing to do with what goes on here while we're gone, all right?"

"Sure, but I gotta say, it's nice to hear you using 'we' so much," Benecio said.

Enjoy it while you can, Sancho Panza, Don Coyote thought.

22

It was three-thirty in the morning. Reed and Jake sat together at a table in Namaste. Most of the performers and staff had gone home. Except for Chef Glenn, who had prepared truffle mac and cheese side dished with dragon fruit and honeydew melon for his employers. And Andre was busy closing down the nightclub while Ravel kept him company — though mostly she was playing the videogame *Frozen* on her laptop. Ravel was feeling very mellow after having made love with Sierra.

Reed called out to Chef Glenn, who was attempting to close his kitchen.

The chef came out of the kitchen and walked over to Reed and Jake's table.

"Need anything else, folks?" he said. "Is the food okay?"

"Just wonderful, Glenn," Reed said. "Thank you so much for staying."

"Happy to do it, Reed."

"Please, Glenn, head on home," Jake said. "We'll clean up after ourselves."

"You're sure?"

"Yes, time to doff your *toque blanche* and go home to Guillermo," Jake said.

Reed smiled at Jake.

"Couldn't just say 'chef's hat', could you?" she said.

"Yeah, a bit late for showing off, isn't it," Jake said sheepishly.

"Well, anyway, I'm heading out," Chef Glenn said. "Good night."

He returned to the kitchen. In fifteen minutes, he'd be out the door and on his way home to his husband.

"So I want to make sure I got this straight," Jake said. He had finished eating. "Don Coyote and the Cutler twins are holed up in a house not three blocks from the Cutler mansion, and Benecio Flores is assisting the creep."

"As usual, my love, you're accurate *and* succinct," Reed said. She, too, had finished her late-night meal.

"My impulse is to rush over there right now, shoot Don Coyote and Benecio in the back of the head, and rescue Morgan and Cecelia," Jake said. "But my gut is telling me that isn't a smart move."

"Please listen to your intuition," Reed said. "We need to come up with a sensible plan."

"Aren't you afraid Don Coyote is just going to take off?" Jake asked.

Reed twirled a paper straw in her glass of iced pomegranate juice. She was lost in thought.

Jake took this opportunity to admire his beautiful and brilliant wife.

God, I am one lucky man, he thought. I wonder if she'll let me massage her feet later on.

"Sure, baby, you can give me a foot massage," Reed said.

"How in the heck . . . " Jake exclaimed.

Reed gave Jake her Mona Lisa smile.

"I can hear you think, my love," she said.

"Oh really, then what am I thinking now?" he said.

Reed squinted her azure blue eyes at Jake.

"Hmm, let's see . . . no, Jake Dupree, I *won't* wear my cowboy boots to bed," Reed said.

"That's *amazing*," Jake said. "But I don't know why not — boots'll let you dig in real nice like."

That ersatz twang of his is almost kind of sexy, Reed thought.

"Dig in where, you or the bed?" she said.

"Your choice," Jake said.

"Not happening, buddy," Reed said. "But let me tell you why Don Coyote isn't in a rush to leave."

"Proceed, please," Jake said. He sat back in his chair and crossed his legs. He was ready to listen.

"I'll be straight up with you, Jake, I suspect Don Coyote is waiting for us to find him," Reed said.

"Interesting," Jake said. "and what makes you think that?"

Obviously excited about her analysis, Reed leaned far forward in her chair and placed her elbows on the table.

"He has had the twins for nearly two weeks, and Mala said they are still holed up in his house," Reed said. "What is he waiting around for?"

"Tsk, tsk, ending a sentence with a preposition," Jake said.

"*Touché, mon amie*," Reed said. "Okay, what's keeping him here?"

Jake cleared his throat in an attempt to buy a bit of time before responding.

"Maybe his business deal has got a hitch in its gitalong," he said.

"It's my cowboy boots, isn't it," Reed said. "They're making you go all country on me."

"Maybe," Jake said.

"Well, *maybe* there has been a hitch in his . . . whatever," Reed said. "However, Don Coyote came to Tampa as much for revenge as for trafficking sex slaves to Mexico."

"If I were a drinking man, I'd turn stone cold sober right now," Jake said. "I really don't want to turn this affair into being about me, but I have to admit, I do think Don Coyote wants to get even for my killing his mother."

"And his lover," Reed said.

"Thanks, there's an image I won't get out of my already crowded mind for the next century," Jake said.

"Sorry, but we have to be candid and clearheaded about what motivates Don Coyote," Reed said. "I think he gambled on Clive Cutler hiring us — Benecio probably knew I'm good friends with Clive."

"Makes sense, Reed," Jake said. He kept hitting his mental delete button on the image of Don Coyote and his mother in a lover's embrace — but to no avail.

"You know full well that Benecio arranged for Veronica Lake to seduce Mala," Reed said. "Ravel knows Veronica, so Don Coyote figured Ravel eventually would track down Veronica in connection with the twins missing — I mean really, Veronica Lake has been South Tampa's plaything for years, she has the skinny on everyone south of Howard."

"Veronica's straight out of *Midnight in the Garden of Good and Evil*, isn't she," Jake said.

"Yes, but you're back to showing off, Professor," Reed said.

"Sorry," Jake said. "Sometimes, I really can't help myself."

"No worries, my erudite Frenchman," Reed said.

"So Don Coyote is setting a trap for us," Jake said.

"*My* gut is saying that's *exactly* what he's doing," Reed said.

Jake unfolded his legs and sat straight up in his chair.

"So what do you want to do?" he asked.

Reed stared at her husband for a few seconds.

"Exactly what Don Coyote wants us to do: we're going to walk right into this trap," Reed said.

"A little reckless, isn't it?" Jake said.

"Sure, but we're going to do this on our terms," Reed said.

Andre and Ravel approached Reed and Jake's table.

"Time for us to join you?" Andre asked.

"Right on time, Andre," Reed said. "Please, the two of you sit down with us."

Andre and Ravel did just that.

Ravel smiled warmly at Reed.

"So what's happening, Momma?" Ravel said.

"Well, Sweet Pea, what's happening is that we're going to map out our apprehending Don Coyote and bringing the twins home to their parents."

"Will your plan include kicking Benecio's ass?" Ravel asked.

"I sure hope so," Andre said. He'd never forgiven Benecio for betraying his trust by putting Ravel, his "Baby Bird", in grave peril.

"Ask, and ye shall receive," Jake said. "Seek and ye shall find."

"Oh, for Christ's sake," Ravel said.

"Ravel, yes, we're going to take care of Benecio, once and for all," Reed said.

"I like the sound of that, straight out of the fucking Old Testament," Ravel said.

"Baby Bird, please watch your language, *yesli ty ne protiv*," Andre said.

"No, I don't mind, and I'm sorry, Andre," Ravel said.

"*Spasibo, Ptenets*," Andre said.

"Lady and gentlemen, we're going to come at Don Coyote full bore," Reed said. "In a little over twenty-hours, Jake and I are going to raid Don Coyote's home. We'll be fully cocked and loaded. We'll show absolutely no mercy. If we can take Don Coyote and Benecio alive, then fine and dandy. But if they put up a fight, we'll take them out with extreme prejudice."

"You know you're turning me on, right?" Ravel said.

Reed ignored Ravel's remark.

"No police?" Jake asked.

"No police," Reed said. "We're fully licensed private investigators, and we're going to close this case on our own."

"I think I just orgasmed," Ravel said.

Jake chuckled.

"It that even a word?" he asked.

"It is now," Ravel retorted.

Reed paid no attention to Ravel and Jake's playful exchange — one of her great strengths was staying focused on the matter at hand.

"I'll expect back-up from Andre and Ravel," she said.

"Really? You're not cutting me out of the action this time," Ravel asked incredulously.

"No, I'm not," Reed said. "You and Andre make a superb team. I'll feel very secure knowing that you two have our backs."

"Thank you, Miss Reed, we won't let you down," Andre said.

"I know you won't, Andre," Reed said. "And please stop addressing me as 'Miss Reed.' "

"All right . . . Reed," Andre said.

"We're going in at six a.m., everyone," Reed said. "Jake, we'll take your Lamborghini — it'll fit in better in South Tampa than my Mustang."

"You got that f . . . , you got that right," Ravel said.

Everyone at the table laughed at Ravel catching herself just in time.

"How about I contact Nat Doliner and let him know we'll be in the neighborhood," Jake offered.

"Good idea," Reed said.

"I still say we should consider making Nat part of our team," Andre said.

"Well, I think Nat's got his hands full with his law practice and monitoring the neighborhood watches," Reed said. "But we'll see, okay, Andre?"

"Yes, ma'am," Andre said.

"Tomorrow, or later today, I guess, it will be business as usual for all of us," Reed said. "I have a law practice to tend to, and you all have a nightclub to run."

"Roger that," Jake said.

"Let's go home and try to get some sleep," Reed said. "But first, Jake, you have some dishes to wash."

"I live to serve, my love," Jake said.

"Smart man, Jakester," Ravel said.

23

───────

Reed and Jake's dawn raid on Don Coyote's home went off without a hitch — at least at the start.

They arrived in South Tampa at five a.m. Driving through the residential neighborhoods, the only traffic they spotted was the newspaper deliverers and a handful of go-getters heading to their offices in downtown Tampa, West Tampa, and St. Petersburg.

Reed drove Jake's yellow Lamborghini Urus. He didn't mind that Reed always insisted on driving — after all, she was the superior driver, and this way, he could be an effective spotter.

Gotta go with your strengths, Jake thought.

"I'm really impressed with your SUV's power and handling, baby," Reed said. "And ooh, it's *so* big."

"Stop distracting me, okay?" Jake said, though he enjoyed her playfulness.

Many of the streets in South Tampa were paved in brick, which often made for a bumpy ride. But the Urus' suspension system ensured a smooth ride, which was incredibly important in light of the gear in the back seat.

There was a Glock 19 nine-millimeter and a Browning Hi Power nine-millimeter on the back seat. Both semi-automatic pistols were holstered, and there were several extra ammo clips in a nylon bag on the seat.

Also, an Enforcer battering ram stretched across the backseat. The Enforcer, also known as the Big Red Key, weighs about forty pounds and is three-feet long. The Big Red Key amounts to a steel tube with a handle and a steel pad on the impact end. A favorite of the British police forces, the Enforcer applies over three tons of impact force.

Finally, a Trigger Pouch rested next to the pistols. It contained six flashbang grenades. Using a spring mechanism, the Trigger Pouch facilitates quick and safe deployment of the flash grenades. Each grenade produces seven-million candela units of luminous intensity, while delivering a powerfully loud bang of one-hundred-seventy decibels.

Consequently, Reed and Jake were very glad this gear didn't bounce around in the backseat.

"We get pulled over, Reed, we got some s'plaining to do," Jake said.

"Yeah I know, that's why I called Pete Langdon," Reed said. "He assured me cruisers would stay pretty much clear of this street until we called for them — but we have only a thirty-minute window."

She parked the Urus about thirty feet from Don Coyote's house, which was quiet and unlit. There were no cars parked in the driveway.

Reed and Jake got out of the SUV and methodically prepped themselves. Reed attached her holstered pistol into her black cargo pants, then put several zip cuffs in a big pants pocket. She made sure her phone was on, with its volume turned to mute. Jake clipped his holstered handgun onto the waistline of his black running pants. He slung the Trigger Pouch over his right shoulder. His phone was muted and ready.

Reed insisted on carrying the Enforcer.

"We'll share in the fun," Reed whispered. "You get the flash grenades and I get the battering ram — it's only fair."

The pair walked side by side at a quick pace toward Don Coyote's house.

Neither spoke — there was no need, as they had rehearsed this maneuver so many times, they were driven to distraction.

Curiously, the house's iron gate was unlocked.

Reed and Jake entered carefully.

The front veranda was completely darkened.

They stood at the front door.

Jake nodded at Reed, who returned the nod.

Wham!

Reed slammed the Enforcer into the massive front door with such force, the door split in two.

Jake held the Trigger Pouch and fired a flash grenade into the unlit hallway.

Reed and Jake stepped to each side of the open doorway so as to avoid being incapacitated by the flash grenade's explosion.

There followed a tremendous bang and a grandmaster flash of light that flooded the house's interior.

Reed and Jake entered the hallway with their pistols drawn.

Dimmed recessed lights were on in the living room.

There didn't appear to be anyone in the living room.

"Think everyone's in their bedrooms?" Jake asked.

"Maybe, but let's be careful here, Reed cautioned.

Suddenly, Benecio came out from behind Don Coyote's La-Z-Boy recliner. He aimed an AR-15 rifle at Jake, then turned the rifle on Reed.

Benecio fired two rounds into Reed's chest. The impact from the rounds blew Reed backwards. Her Glock 19 flew out of her hand and skipped across the oak wood floor.

She lay motionless and flat on her back.

Jake calmly aimed his Browning Hi Power pistol at Benecio and fired three rounds at him, striking Benecio in the neck, right shoulder, and right arm. Benecio went down like a punch-drunk boxer. The AR-15 rifle landed in the recliner.

As Benecio no longer posed a threat, Jake rushed over to Reed.

"Baby, talk to me, please talk to me," Jake exclaimed.

He held Reed in his arms.

Reed opened her eyes.

"Well, that hurt like hell," she said.

Jake pulled up Reed's black tee shirt, revealing her Kevlar bullet-proof vest. Indeed, two slugs were buried into the vest's polyacrylamide plastic fabric.

"Talk about an ounce of prevention," Jake said. She started to get her breath back.

Reed sat up gingerly.

"More like six pounds of prevention," she said. "Damn. I'm *savitzing* like crazy in this vest."

"Better to perspire than expire," Jake said.

Reed reached over and pinched Jake.

"It's true, you really can't help yourself," she said.

Suddenly, Andre and Ravel rushed into the living room. Andre held a Desert Eagle fifty-caliber cannon of a pistol. Ravel carried a Smith & Wesson tactical baton.

"Sweet Reed, are you okay?" Ravel said.

Her eyes welled up with tears.

Reed stood up and kissed Ravel on the cheek.

"Yes, Ravel, I'm fine," Reed said. "Gonna have some impressive bruises on my chest, though."

Ravel raised her eyebrows at Reed.

"Forget it, girl," Reed said. "That's Jake's department, thank you very much."

"I'd put on a nurse's outfit for you," Ravel said.

"Tempting, but not tempting enough, I'm afraid," Reed said.

In typical Swiss preparedness, Ravel had replaced her satchel with a well-stocked first-aid bag, which was strapped over her right shoulder.

"As much as I am loathe to do it, should I go check on Benecio?" she said.

"Please," Reed said. "Andre and Jake, search the rest of the house, but something tells me Don Coyote and the twins have skipped out."

"We'll check it out, Reed," Jake said. "And I'll call in police and medical, all right?"

"Yes, please," Reed answered. "While Ravel is tending to Benecio, I think I'll have a chat with that jerk."

She walked over to Benecio and Ravel.

Though incredibly sore, Reed was most thankful to be alive.

Don't know how those stunt doubles do it, she thought.

Ravel was on her knees and tending to Benecio. She wasn't saying a word to him.

"Benecio, next time, always remember to go for the head shot, you dumbass." Reed said.

"Fuck you," Benecio said.

He had lost a fair amount of blood, yet it appeared Jake hadn't hit any of Benecio's vital organs.

"You kiss Don Coyote with that mouth?" Ravel said, as she poked Benecio's shoulder wound.

"Ow, stop it," he exclaimed.

"You're a very lucky man, Benecio," Reed said. "If Jake had wanted to, he could have put three shots right in your forehead — but we wanted to keep you around."

"Why?" he asked.

"Because you're going to tell us where Don Coyote and the twins are," Reed said.

"Fuck I am," he said.

"The fuck you *are* going to talk," Ravel screamed.

She placed the tactical baton across Benecio's throat.

"What is it with you and kidnapping women?" she said. "Talk or I'll crush your larynx."

"Jesus, you crazy bitch, I think you'd really do it," Benecio gurgled. "What do I get if I talk?"

"I'll stop Ravel from removing your junk," Reed said.

"No way, Reed," Ravel said. "Why do you think I packed a scalpel in the medical kit?"

"Man, you bitches play rough," Benecio said. "Okay, okay, Don Coyote left with the girls about two hours ago."

"Where did they go?" Ravel said. She retracted her tactical baton.

"They were driving down to Naples, then they were gonna catch a flight to Tucson. I was *supposed* to join them later on. I even got a first-class ticket and . . . . "

Reed didn't have time for Benecio rambling off point, as the Tampa police and medical teams would arrive in short order.

"Why Tucson?" she said.

"Because that's where we're meeting up with Mateo and Lucia Da Rosa — they're the ones from Mexico who're buying the twins for four million dollars," Benecio said.

Ah, the banality of evil — this little jerk speaks so casually about buying and selling human beings, Reed thought.

"So where in Tucson are they going to complete this disgusting transaction?" Reed said.

"Place called Tanque Verde Ranch, some sort of dude ranch, I guess, you know, where rich snobs pretend to be cowboys and ride horses and shit."

Well, I wouldn't quite put it that way, Reed thought.

Among the premiere guest ranches in the United States, Tanque Verde attracts well-off people from all over the world, including Reed and Jake. They had stayed at the ranch on two occasions.

"Yeah, I think I've heard of the place," Reed said.

Jake and Andre walked into the living room.

"Nobody else here but a few ghosts," Jake said.

Reed quickly apprised Jake and Andre of the situation with Benecio.

Jake approached Benecio, who still was laying on the floor while Ravel attended to his wounds.

"Benecio, I wish I could say it's good to see you again," Jake said. "One question: why did you shoot Reed instead of me?"

"Those were my instructions, asshole," Benecio said. "Don Coyote wanted Reed dead and you alive, so you'd know what it's like to lose the most important person in your life — he wanted you to *suffer*, man."

The sirens outside were getting louder.

"So what's the plan, Reed?" Jake said.

"As Horace Greeley once said, 'Go west, young man.' " Reed said.

"Actually, Greeley borrowed that from John Babsone Lane Soule of the *Terre Haute Express*," Jake said.

Reed, Andre, and Ravel groaned collectively.

"Thus speaketh the French gas bag," Ravel said.

24

Don Coyote was ready for playtime to be over. He had spent two full days at Tanque Verde Ranch, riding horses in the Sonoran Desert with the De Rosas and the twins, playing doubles tennis with the group, eating ribeye steaks and rainbow trout, drinking tequila, and smoking too many American cigars.

At first, he enjoyed sensing his mother's presence at the ranch. In the evening after dinner, when he walked down to the corral to sneak peppermint candies to the horses, he thought he actually saw his mother's handsome figure silhouetted against the afterglow of the desert sunset.

But he became bitter over her passing to the great beyond. He knew he'd never again meet another woman as magnificent as his mother, so Don Coyote fantasized about the crushing pain that Jake Dupree must be experiencing over his dear dead wife.

Only, he hadn't heard anything from Benecio.

Perhaps he's celebrating a bit too much, he thought. *Or* maybe Dupree killed Benecio after Benecio killed Reed O'Hara, *that* would be a most convenient development.

To top it off, the twins were growing increasingly anxious over going to Mexico.

Don Coyote and the twins shared a two-bedroom *casita* at Tanque Verde. Late last night, he overhead them whispering to each other about going home to Tampa, about how they missed their mother and father, and about how creepy Mateo and Lucia were.

When this is all over, going to have to re-program those snot-nosed brats, Don Coyote thought.

It was nine-forty-five a.m. In fifteen minutes, Don Coyote and the twins would meet the Da Rosas in the Tanque Verde parking lot and make the exchange.

Gold for flesh, flesh for gold, can there be a sexier transaction, Don Coyote thought.

Morgan and Cecelia stepped out of their bedroom. They wore matching cowboy hats, Tanque Verde tee shirts, Wrangler jeans, and dark brown cowboy boots. They had put their long blonde hair in ponytails. They were a double vision of the unspoiled American West.

Wonder how many times I could sell these two, Don Coyote thought.

"Ladies, time to go see the Da Rosas," he said. "And I'm afraid I have to insist that you say goodbye to me in a mature fashion, all right? No wailing and gnashing of teeth."

"Yes, dear Father, but it will be sad to say goodbye to you," Morgan said.

Yup, that's Morgan, there's the mole on her neck, Don Coyote thought.

"Let's get a going, little ponies," he said.

The twins giggled nervously as they left the *casita*.

As the three of them walked together toward the parking lot, Don Coyote marveled at the beauty of the Sonoran Desert around him. Everywhere he looked, there were saguaro, prickly pear, and barrel cacti, palo verde and elephant trees, creosote and desert hackberry bushes.

He appreciated that this desert was the home of Gila monsters, Western diamond backs, road runners, scorpions, desert tortoises, and jackrabbits, most of whom came out only at night.

For Don Coyote, the Sonoran Desert was an arid, sun-drenched paradise, the perfect joining of *el sol y la sombra*.

Gonna miss this place, he thought, but afraid I hear San Diego a calling.

As he walked, he quietly sang the lyrics to "That's Alright Mama."

The Da Rosas already were in the parking lot. There were only a handful of cars in the lot. Mateo and Lucia stood by their gold GMC Yukon, a true battleship of an SUV.

"*Buenos dias*, my friends," Don Coyote said.

"Good morning to you and the sisters," Mateo said.

Don Coyote shook hands with both Mateo and Lucia.

"May I see the money, please," Don Coyote said.

"*Por supesto*," Mateo said.

He pressed a button on the SUV's key fob and the Yukon rear hatch lifted.

"And *viola!*" Lucia exclaimed.

Six large storage containers were stacked neatly in the SUV's cargo space.

Don Coyote smiled.

"Let's have a look see," he said.

He pulled out two containers and set them on the asphalt. He then opened each lid just a few inches; each time, he was satisfied that the crate was filled with wrapped stacks of hundred-dollar bills. Don Coyote repeated this process with the four containers still in the Yukon's cargo hold.

"Pop quiz, Mateo and Lucia," Don Coyote said. "How much does a one-hundred-dollar bill weigh?"

"About a gram," Mateo said.

"And how many one-hundred-dollar bills does it take to make a million dollars" Don Coyote asked.

"Ten thousand," Lucia answered.

"Correct," Don Coyote said. "And how much does ten thousand hundred-dollar bills weigh?"

"That's easy, ten kilograms," Mateo said,

"Very good," Don Coyote said. "Therefore, factoring in the weight of the six containers, how much does this four million dollars weigh — in pounds, please."

"I knew you were going to ask us this," Lucia said. "So we had the containers weighed before we left Puerto Vallarta."

"That's very wise of you," Don Coyote said, as he patted the revolver that he had placed in the waistband of his jeans and had concealed with his white *guayabera*. He considered the revolver a loathsome yet necessary evil.

"So what do these containers weigh — again I'd like your answer in pounds, as we're in America after all."

"The six containers weigh almost one hundred *pounds*," Mateo said confidently.

"You are my prize pupils," Don Coyote said. "And now . . . . "

He pulled out a Smith & Wesson snub nose thirty-eight caliber revolver. Its chrome finish gleamed in the bright desert sunshine.

"Just full of surprises, ain't I?" Don Coyote said.

"What the hell are you doing?" Lucia said. She was more angry than frightened.

Mateo, on the other hand, was completely frightened as he cowered behind his wife.

The twins didn't say a word, and simply stood frozen behind Don Coyote.

"What I am doing is rescuing my girls from your perverted clutches," Don Coyote said. "Now, turn around and walk back to your *casita*, and don't come out for one hour."

"Don Coyote, let's work something out here," Lucia said desperately. "How about we take Cecelia and you keep two million dollars?"

Don Coyote struck Lucia across the face with his revolver.

"You whore from hell," he yelled. "How *dare* you try to negotiate with me."

Lucia had a nasty gash on her left cheek and her nose was bleeding.

"I'm so sorry, *senor*," she said. "I was only . . . . "

Just then, three Pima County Sheriff's Department SUVs rushed toward the group in the parking lot. A black Lincoln Town car came up behind the SUVs, which were lit up but not using sirens.

Six sheriff's deputies jumped out of the SUVs. The deputies brandished nine-millimeter Beretta handguns and Colt M4 carbines.

Clearly, the deputies would not brook any foolishness on the part of Don Coyote and the Da Rosas.

"All of you, get down on the ground right now," a deputy shouted.

"What'd I do?" Mateo screamed.

"Get down on the ground — now!" a deputy said. She pointed her Beretta right at Mateo.

But everyone remained standing, as if they were paralyzed by fear.

The front doors to the town car suddenly opened, and Reed and Jake stepped out. They both wore holsters that held their semi-automatic pistols.

Reed and Jake walked up to the deputy in charge.

"Reed, are these the characters you've been looking for?" the deputy said.

"Yes, ma'am," Reed said.

"Well, all right then," the deputy said. "For the last time, all of you get *down* on the ground."

Lucia and Mateo complied.

But Don Coyote grabbed the twins and pushed them in the direction of the deputies.

Morgan and Cecelia screamed.

In this melee, Don Coyote took off running.

He ducked behind the ranch's front office building before the deputies could get a clear shot.

Reed put her hand on the deputy's shoulder.

"Listen, I know where he's going — I'm very familiar with this ranch," she said.

"I can't let a civilian go after a fugitive," the lead deputy said.

"Deputy, I am the most badass civilian you'll ever meet, I know what I'm doing," Reed said. "And we're wasting time — at least let me take point."

The deputy looked at Jake, who just shrugged.

"Fine, you lead the way, but let us apprehend him," the deputy said to Reed.

The deputy knew it was a huge risk in allowing Reed to take point, but she liked her chances that this woman would get the job done.

"Roger that," Reed said.

"Baby, I got your back, okay?" Jake said.

"Always do, Handsome," Reed said.

Reed took off, with three deputies and Jake following behind her.

The remaining deputies handcuffed the Da Rosas, who appeared completely stunned at this turn of events.

Morgan and Cecelia had dropped to their knees. They held each other and cried uncontrollably.

Then Clive and Elin Cutler got out of the back of the town car.

They ran to their daughters, who in turn screamed out to their parents.

The family hugged one another.

"Mom and Dad, can you ever forgive us?" Morgan said.

"You better believe it," Elin said.

She was so emotional, she could barely speak.

"Can we go home?" Cecelia said.

"Absolutely, my dear sweet daughter," Clive said.

Tears streamed down his face.

While this very happy family reunion took place, Don Coyote had managed to get to the stables, jump on a saddled horse that had been readied for a morning ride, and galloped out of the corral and into the Sonoran Desert.

Reed and her posse arrived at the stables not two minutes later. She spotted a chestnut hinny already saddled.

Damn if that isn't Remington, she thought. Best climber in the herd.

Reed jumped on Remington and took off after Don Coyote, who was leaving behind a dust trail.

"Reed, I can't let you do that," the deputy called out, though she knew it was pointless to try and stop that woman.

Of course, Reed ignored the deputy and galloped away.

She was gaining on Don Coyote, as his horse wasn't as sure-footed as Remington was on the winding, narrow trail.

Don Coyote looked back and saw Reed. He knew it was only a short time before she caught up to him.

Out of desperation, Don Coyote veered off the trail and climbed up to a ridgeline. He had his horse trot along a sorry excuse for a trail atop the ridgeline.

Reed saw Don Coyote's gambit and got off the trail as well. Remington easily maneuvered up the ridgeline. Horse and rider cantered toward Don Coyote.

What the hell, you don't live forever, Don Coyote thought. Wonder if I'll meet Mother in heaven or below?

He stopped his horse and turned around in the saddle. Reed was only twenty feet behind him.

Don Coyote pulled out his revolver and started firing at Reed. With each shot, his horse jumped wildly.

With Remington still cantering, Reed calmly unholstered her Glock, took careful aim, and fired one round into Don Coyote's head.

Remington didn't so much as flinch from the gunfire.

Don Coyote did flinch, though. He dropped his revolver and fell dead to the ground.

The Gunfight at Tanque Verde Ranch was over.

25

———

"Jake, this lasagna is marvelous," Judi Ploszek said. "What's your secret?"

Jake smiled at Judi.

"Simple, really," he said. "Reed inspires me to do gooder."

Jake, Reed, Judi, and Jean Mayer sat at the dining room table in Reed and Jake's apartment.

They had gathered to celebrate the Cutler twins' safe arrival home and to discuss Jean becoming commissioner of Reed's nascent co-ed professional basketball league.

"I really like this table, Reed," Jean said.

"Thanks, we put a lot of thought into picking it out," Reed said, who gave a sly wink to Jake.

In fact, Jake chose the Petra dining room table. He was attracted to the table's stone slices cut from fossilized trees from the volcanic central Philippines. The polished brown and black stone slices fit together to form a large rectangle, resembling a kind of abstract picture puzzle.

Jake selected six Chanel black buffalo leather chairs that had low-rise backs and splayed legs, to better showcase the extraordinary tabletop.

"So how are Morgan and Cecelia doing?" Judi asked.

"Last I heard from Clive, the twins are getting settled back at home," Reed said. "They plan on attending the University of Tampa in the fall."

"That's great news," Jean said. "So they won't be straying too far from home?"

"Not any time soon, at least," Jake said. "So who's ready for more lasagna?"

"I'm going to regret this when I get in the pool in the morning, but I'll have a half slice please," Judi said. "Your secret's the sharp cheddar cheese, isn't it?"

"*Dokladnie tak, moj-przyjacielu*," Jake said.

"Polish? That's impressive," Judi said. "Just how many languages do you pretend to speak, Jake Dupree?"

"More than I can count, Judi Ploszek," Jake answered.

Everyone at the table laughed at this frivolity.

"Don't forget, Judi, Jake used to be a spy — it was his job to pretend," Jean said.

"I prefer the term 'operative'," Jake said. "Sorry for asking, Jean, but how did you know I worked for The Company?"

"Oh, Reed told me," Jean said casually.

"Isn't that something," Jake said. He looked over at Reed, who simply shrugged.

"Jake, there's nothing wrong telling responsible people that you worked for the CIA," Reed said. "It's time for you to stop feeling guilty and ashamed — you made terrible personal sacrifices to keep all of us safe, and you need to recognize that *now*, my love."

"Amen," Judi said.

"This is starting to feel like a group intervention," Jake said.

"So, Jake, are you going to dig out that old chestnut about your having to kill me now that I know you were an operative?" Jean said.

"Well, not before we have dessert," he said.

Again, everyone laughed.

"Jean, what are your thoughts about becoming league commissioner?" Reed said.

"It's tempting, Reed, but I don't know if I'm the right person for the job."

"Say what? Jean, you were a strategic planner for twenty years at TGH," Reed said. "And you're a fine athlete — don't you row on the Hillsborough River and play scratch golf practically every day?"

"Sure," Jean said modestly.

"So you know how to talk the talk and walk the walk," Reed said. "And you have that vision thing working for you."

"The vision thing?" Jean asked.

"Yes, you can be in the weeds and still keep the big picture in mind," Reed said.

"Are you considering anyone else for the job?" Jean said.

"I have interviewed other people, but I'm offering the commissioner position only to you," Reed said.

"Is that a formal job offer?" Jean said.

"Yes," Reed said.

"Then I formally accept," Jean said.

Reed, Jake, and Judi applauded Jean's decision.

"That's fantastic, Jean," Reed said. "I'll have Roman Delaney, my office manager and league project manager, go over your salary and benefit package with you."

"You already prepared that package, didn't you?" Jean said, as she was well aware of Reed's thorough preparation before having a meeting.

"Maybe," Reed said evasively.

"Sorry to interrupt, ladies," Judi said. "I'm dying to know what's for dessert, Jake."

"I subscribe to Chef Jamie Oliver's adage of keeping if fresh, healthy, and simple," Jake said.

"Oh no," Reed groaned.

"Tut, tut, tut, my dear," Jake said. "Judi, I'll serve bowls of Florida watermelon wedges with North Carolina blueberries — the fruit will help clear your palate for the cappuccinos."

"Just a lovely man," Judi said to no one in particular.

"Yes, he is," Reed said.

For a long moment, Reed and Jake stared at each other. They silently acknowledged that it was their love for each other that made theirs such a wonderful life.

AUTHOR'S NOTES

Don Coyote was a joy to write.

Truly, the story just flowed out of me.

I never once hit a roadblock.

Bad Habits, my first novel and the premiere installment in the *Tampa Bay Tropics Thriller* series, was an entirely different story, as far as composing the novel.

With *Bad Habits*, I really didn't know what I was doing. Despite reading dozens and dozens of novels, and earning bachelor's and master's degrees in English, I knew I was lost at sea when I wrote the first page of *Bad Habits*.

It didn't help with my confidence that I refused to draft an outline of the novel. I considered outlines a stalling tactic — and I still feel that way.

Writing *Bad Habits* involved so many starts and stops; *talking* about the novel instead of *writing* the novel; and far too many willful distractions such as pressure washing the pool deck or painting the bookshelves in the study.

Admittedly, once the characters sprang to life and the storylines developed, the process of writing *Bad Habits* became easier.

But it remained a challenging experience. Self-doubt, I learned, is a writer's nightmare. At times, I was tempted to give up — after all, my garage really did need some serious re-organization.

Fortunately, I was saved by a beautiful and brilliant woman: Linda Fleming, my wife of forty years, a magnificent health care attorney, my constant muse, and, of course, the inspiration for Ms. Reed O'Hara.

Linda patiently listened to my complaining and excuse making, then simply said, "Enough of this nonsense. You made a commitment to writing this novel — and you are going to keep your promise. And I really don't care that the flower beds need weeding or that you'd like to change the art hanging in the living room."

Message received, my love.

So I soldiered on and eventually finished *Bad Habits*.

But if I were offered it, I might have accepted a literary Purple Heart — though I'm sure Linda would not have approved.

Old Testament novel writing, allow me to introduce you to the good news of New Testament novel writing.

Emboldened by the publishing of *Bad Habits*, I possessed an entirely different mindset when I started *Don Coyote*. I now was a more seasoned novelist. I was brimming with confidence as I sat at the desk in our study and applied pen to paper.

Two interesting sidebars here.

When I write, I *literally* apply pen to paper, using Pilot G-2 gel pens and college-ruled notebook paper. There's something wonderfully tactile about hand writing my stories. I sense it is similar to when a painter applies brushstrokes to a canvas. Besides, if it's good enough for John Le Carre, my literary hero, it's good enough for me.

Also, Linda purchased the desk in our study when she was in law school at the University of Florida. The desk is a mid-century Heywood-Wakefield gem that Linda bought for thirty-five dollars at a yard sale. I believe the desk has a positive energy that motivates me to tell these stories of good triumphing over evil, of love besting hate. Each time I sit at Linda's desk, I am reminded I am a hopeless romantic, and that's okay.

Back to *Don Coyote*.

I was writing every day, so involved with the narrative that I couldn't break away from the story. I simply *had* to answer some very important questions. What was Jake Dupree's dark past that burdened him so? Will Reed O'Hara survive being shot? Does the (I hope) famous shower scene accurately portray the passionate love that Reed and Jake share? And, to paraphrase the real-life Judi Ploszek, why is Jake always making coffee?

In five short months, I finished the first draft of *Don Coyote*. And the revisions went swimmingly.

Even though I am proud of *Bad Habits*, I believe *Don Coyote* is a superior novel.

And why is that?

Because I wrote more confidently and with greater focus.

Because I mapped out in my mind, before I started *Don Coyote*, the overall plot in broad-brush strokes. (I still maintain that an elaborate and detailed written outline only stalls actually composing the story.)

And because I charted the novel's progress in a daily journal, what my granddaughter Mya calls a "man diary."

After I get back from our next cruise, I will begin *Blood Harmony*, the third novel in the *Tampa Bay Tropics Thriller* series. My topic will be the troubling re-emergence of white supremacy in the United States.

Just a few more items to mention.

The vast majority of the names and characters are the result of this writer's imagination. Any resemblance to actual people is entirely coincidental — for the most part.

Regarding these exceptions, I wish to thank Judi Ploszek, Nat Doliner, Jean Mayer, and Chenoa Jenks for allowing me to use their names and to borrow elements of their personalities for their characters in *Don Coyote*.

Also, thanks go out to Tom Murray, my friend of over twenty years who permitted me to use his name and personality in this novel. Yes, Tom is a highly respected marine biologist. But no, he is not a covert operative of any sort. For many years, I suspected he had worked for the DEA or the CIA. I now can state with complete confidence that while Tom Murray is a very nice guy, I doubt he is a spy.

Thanks also to Vibha Dubey, a talented young poet from New Delhi, India, and one of my good Instagram friends. Vibha provided great assistance in making sure I was accurate and respectful in describing Sehar's onstage attire at Namaste. Thank you, Vibha, for being so helpful and such a kind soul.

And thank you, Amy Cianci, the projects manager at St. Petersburg Press. Amy carefully read my manuscript and gave several useful suggestions, especially regarding the Catholic Church. She also patiently helped to refine the cover of *Don Coyote*.

I also extend my gratitude to proofreader April Schlee. She is as much an editor as she is a proofreader. I would pit April against any another proofreader in the country, and would bet on April emerging as the winner.

And Linda, thank you for being my muse, for being my intelligent and kind sounding board, and for being my ever-loving life mate. I remain in awe of your greatness. I echo Jake Dupree's sentiment: Truly, I am the luckiest man in the world.

Until we cross paths again, be well and keep an open mind.

Bread & Roses,

George L. Fleming

COMING SOON

BLOOD HARMONY
A Tampa Bay Tropics Thriller

By
George L. Fleming